Books by Cheyenne McCray

Deadly Intent

Hidden Prey

Hidden Prey

ISBN # 978-1-78686-100-9

©Copyright Cheyenne McCray 2017

Cover Art by Posh Gosh ©Copyright 2017

Interior text design by Claire Siemaszkiewicz

Totally Bound Publishing

Published in 2017 by Totally Bound Publishing, Newland House, The Point, Weaver Road, Lincoln, LN6 3QN, United Kingdom.

Deadly Intent

HIDDEN PREY

To Marie!
Best!
Cheyenne
McCray

CHEYENNE MCCRAY

Dedication

To the great people of Bisbee, Arizona — I may have taken
liberties with our fair town, but I did it with love.

Chapter One

The nightmare had been so damned *real*. Landon Walker sat on the edge of his bed, his eyes bleary and his head aching like a mother. He had to stop trying to find peace at the bottom of a bottle of Jack D, because it only made him feel like hell the next morning. Didn't matter what he did, because he didn't think he'd ever have peace again.

His dream had replayed every last detail of that night when a hit-and-run drunk driver had sideswiped Landon's motorcycle, sending Stacy flying and pinning him beneath the wreckage. A helmet and protective gear hadn't been enough to save her. After he'd managed to get out from beneath the motorcycle, he'd crawled to her, dragging his shattered leg. He could still feel her broken body in his arms.

He ran his hand down his face, the stubble and scar along one cheekbone rough against his callused palm. Fourteen months to the day Stacy had died in the accident, an accident that had been his fault.

Would he ever stop marking time by the date of his fiancée's death?

He turned his head to look at the alarm clock and winced from the pain the sudden movement caused. Damn. He'd be late if he didn't get his ass out of bed. He didn't work some punch-the-clock forty-hour workweek. But Mondays still sucked.

Early Monday mornings he used to play basketball with a bunch of guys who were in law enforcement. On Friday nights, those who weren't working usually played poker. But after the accident, Landon had pulled away from everything but his job. He still worked out—sometimes excessively—in the fitness room in his home. Not only to stay fit but because the strenuous activity burned off excess anger at himself and sometimes at the world.

With his head still aching, he stepped under ice-cold water in the shower in an attempt to wake up. He braced his hand against the smooth white tiles, his head lowered, goosebumps prickling his skin when he let the water flow over him. He kept the water cold as he washed his hair and soaped his body. When he'd finished, he shut off the water and shook his head, droplets flying before he toweled himself off.

The cold shower had done its job and he felt marginally better by the time he pushed open the shower stall's glass door. He might just make it through today after all. Last month had been the first month he hadn't taken flowers to Stacy's grave. For the first year, he'd visited once a month on the date of her death, but after a year, he'd made the decision to move on to save his sanity. Damned if he knew how.

After he'd dressed in jeans and a faded blue T-shirt, he jammed his Colt .45 into its holster on his belt. He slipped on a white overshirt to cover his weapon then stood in his kitchen and wolfed down a breakfast of toast and scrambled eggs. He stuck the dirty dishes in the dishwasher and headed out.

A light morning breeze slid over his skin when he climbed into his charcoal-gray Ford Explorer. He stuffed his key into the ignition and started the vehicle. He headed down the dirt road leaving his ranch and continued onto the paved road that would take him to Douglas.

He had just enough time to make it to the office and take care of a few things prior to heading to Bisbee to meet with his man who'd been working deep undercover. He'd make the twenty-five-mile drive from his ranch in Sulfur Springs Valley to Douglas and to DHS's ICE office in twenty minutes.

Landon had served as a special agent with the Department of Homeland Security's Immigration and Customs Enforcement Agency for eleven years now and had given himself completely to his career since Stacy's death. He'd always been married to the job and he regretted not being there for Stacy more. Now he lived and breathed his work. What the hell else did he have? The job would take his soul one day and he didn't plan to fight it.

At the office, he spent some time going over aspects of the case he'd been working for months. The Jimenez Cartel's tentacles reached far from Mexico, into Arizona. When they chopped off one arm, another grew to replace it. The cartel had to be cut off at its head. No other way would stop or even slow the activities of the organization that dealt in drugs, death, destruction.

They had to get to Diego Montego Jimenez, known as *El Demonio* to everyone around him. The Demon. The nickname for the bastard fit him like a glove.

Landon headed out of the office in the early afternoon. On his way out, he saw Dylan Curtis, another DHS special agent and one of Landon's good friends. At six-three, Dylan stood a good two inches taller than Landon. He wore a Stetson over his dark hair and his ice-blue eyes were appraising as always.

Dylan paused in front of the entrance. Landon stopped too. "When are you going to join the boys for basketball again?" Dylan mimed going up for a shot. "Had some good games this morning. You need to show up and get your ass back in it."

Landon shrugged. He probably should — one more step toward returning to his life as it had been *before*.

"This leg isn't what it used to be." Landon rubbed his leg that had been shattered in the accident.

"Who gives a shit?" Dylan questioned. "Monday mornings, same time, same place as it's always been. Bring the bum leg."

Landon nodded. "I just might be there next Monday."

"You'd better or I'm gonna kick your ass." Dylan hooked his thumbs in his belt loops. "And don't forget poker this Friday night. It's time you rejoined the living and you might as well go all in."

Landon shook his head. "Maybe."

"Maybe, my ass." Dylan switched subjects as he asked, "On your way to meet Miguel?"

"Yep." Landon nodded. "Any news on the delivery?"

"I'm hoping Miguel can give you a concrete time." Dylan frowned. "All I have is what you do — it's tomorrow, but no time or location."

"I'm sure Miguel has it for us." Landon reached for the door handle. "I'll call you as soon as I get intel from him."

Dylan gave a nod. "Tell the bastard hello for me."

"Will do." Landon pushed open the door and walked into the sunny afternoon toward his SUV before heading to Bisbee, a once-booming town nestled in the Mule Mountains.

His thoughts drifted like the occasional puffs of cottony clouds scattered across the brilliant blue summer sky. The grass along Highway 80 waved in the stiff breeze as he drove by. An unusual amount of rain had made everything greener than usual.

Once he reached the east-side town limits, he guided his vehicle around what the locals had called the traffic circle for decades. The roundabout let him out onto the road that took him on to Old Bisbee after he passed the Lavender Pit and the Copper Queen Mine. He headed to St. Patrick's Catholic Church to meet with Miguel.

A replica of a church in Ireland, St. Pat's had perched two hundred feet above the floor of Tombstone Canyon for nearly a century. Stained glass windows and marble filled the towering terracotta building. Beneath the soaring ceilings, Jesus Christ on the cross peered down on the congregation, as did the statues of the Virgin Mary and St. Patrick behind the altar.

The icons seemed to look down on him, judging him for

his absence from the Church and for his abandonment of God. Hell, God had abandoned both him and Stacy when He'd let her die.

The cool, dim interior of the church smelled of incense and candlewax. The heavy double doors closed behind him as he passed the shallow well of holy water. He did not dip his fingers in the water or make the sign of the cross. He slid into the second to last pew in the back on the far right, so he could see the doors by turning his head slightly.

A tiny woman in black, wearing a white lace mantilla, kneeled in one pew, and an older man leaned against the back of the bench seat in another. The old man's head tilted up so he could stare at the effigy of Christ. The man had a broken look about him, as if this church served as the only solace he would find in this world.

Landon mentally shook his head. Raised Catholic, he had pushed away from the Church once he'd gotten to see what a cruel world it could be. How could a good and just God allow evil men to kill or abuse women and children? Or to force them to serve as sex slaves? How had He allowed someone as sweet and good as Stacy to die as she had? Landon would have given his own life for hers.

Clenching his teeth, he took in the padded wood kneeler at his feet. The kneeler, currently in its upright position, would be lowered by parishioners to kneel on during service or while praying when they came into the church to worship.

For one wild moment he thought about getting down on his own knees and praying to a God he didn't think he believed in any longer. He blew out a breath and ran his finger along a hymnal in the wooden rack in front of him. No, his days of praying were long gone.

He pulled himself out of his thoughts and concentrated on the moment. He checked the time on his cell phone and saw he had arrived a few minutes early. He hoped Miguel wouldn't be late. A devout Catholic, Miguel liked to meet at St. Pat's where he felt closer to God.

Sometimes, as Landon left, Miguel would head to the confessionals at the front right. Landon had worked undercover many times and had been forced to commit sins he wished could be absolved by confessing to a priest.

Landon let his gaze drift over the almost empty pews, noting everything. From the moment he'd arrived, he'd been keenly aware of his surroundings and the double doors behind him. He didn't like having his back to the doors, even though he could casually glance in that direction with his side vision. But if he wasn't safe inside St. Pat's, he didn't know where he would be.

The old man got up from his seat and went to the front of the church, to the left of the altar, and lit one candle among rows of little red jarred candles. Some were lit but most were dark. Landon stared at the flickering candlelight for a moment, remembering himself as just a little boy. In the church he'd grown up in, he'd lit a candle and prayed to God with all he had to save his grandfather who'd been dying from cancer. The first disappointment of many to come, by a God who never seemed to answer his prayers.

The old man stood in front of the candles for a long moment before turning and walking beneath an archway between the walls and thick marble columns. Out of the corner of his eye, Landon watched the man leave, a large swathe of sunlight spilling into the church as he pushed one of the doors open. Then the heavy door eased back into place, leaving it dim again.

Landon checked his cell phone. Late. Miguel, normally punctual to the minute, had yet to arrive. Landon didn't let his mind wander beyond his objective. If he did, he'd spend time dwelling on things that couldn't be changed.

Time passed and Landon's gut tightened. Even though Miguel hadn't made it yet, Landon knew he shouldn't be concerned. After all, he'd forged his way deep into the Jimenez Cartel. When *El Demonio* said, "Jump", Miguel didn't ask how high. He did what he had to do to remain embedded in the organization.

Landon's phone vibrated a couple of times and he read the two short text messages then returned his phone to its holster on his belt. His mother, asking if he would be able to make it for Sunday dinner. One of his sisters, telling him not to let their mother down and to show up on Sundays more often.

He blew out his breath. His family had been pushing him for the past year to make it to get-togethers. He'd drawn away once Stacy had died. Maybe he'd grieved long enough. Knowing he should let go of the past and move on didn't mean it would be easy.

Basketball and Sunday dinners would be a start.

Two more parishioners came in and out of the sanctum. The woman in the mantilla hadn't moved since Landon had entered the church. She kept her head bowed in prayer and her white lace mantilla shadowed her face.

More time passed and the two parishioners who had come in thirty minutes prior lit candles before leaving. Landon checked his cell phone yet again and saw he'd been waiting for nearly an hour. The woman in the mantilla and Landon were now the only people left in the church.

Frowning, he got up from his pew and made his way outside, blinking when he walked into the late-afternoon sunlight. He stood at the top of the steps that went down on either side of him.

The fact that Miguel hadn't shown up wasn't anything to be too concerned about. Any number of things could have come up. Miguel wouldn't call or text anyone at DHS, to ensure nothing could be found to tie him to law enforcement.

A hand with a vise-like grip clamped around Landon's left wrist.

He went for his Colt instinctively as he pivoted before stopping abruptly.

It was the tiny veiled woman who had been in the church since he'd arrived.

He released his grip on the butt of his handgun and left it

in its holster. How the hell had she snuck up on him?

The stooped, elderly Hispanic woman pushed the mantilla away from her cheeks and his gaze met small dark eyes nearly lost in a sea of wrinkles. She looked well over a hundred years old, older than his grandmother. Her face reminded him of a withered apple, but her eyes were bright and knowing.

"You will die if you tell her the truth. If you don't tell her, *she* will die." The woman spoke in a low, tremulous voice, in broken English, with a heavy Hispanic accent.

Despite the fact that he didn't believe in crap like premonitions, chills rolled over Landon's skin and he broke out in goosebumps for the second time that morning. He tried to jerk his arm away from the woman's grip but she wouldn't let him go and he didn't want to inadvertently hurt her.

"Remember my words." She released his arm and turned away.

While remaining completely aware of his surroundings, he watched her as she held on to the handrail and slowly walked down the steps. Her words echoed in his head no matter how he tried to force them out.

'You will die if you tell her the truth. If you don't tell her, she will die.'

He shook his head and a natural-born instinct to help the elderly had him realizing he should be helping the old woman down the stairs. But she'd already reached the last step when he came to his senses.

In a town where most houses were built on mountainsides, Landon wondered how someone so old and frail could navigate her way around the steep inclines that could give San Francisco a run for its money.

A black Mercedes pulled up in front of the church, answering his question. A newer model vehicle, it had dark-tinted windows and looked as if the owner had washed and waxed it this morning. A Hispanic man of about thirty, wearing a bright white button-up shirt and dark slacks, climbed out of the driver's side and held the back passenger-side door open. He assisted the elderly woman as she slid into the vehicle and closed the door behind her.

The Mercedes was out of place in the small town of Bisbee, Arizona—Landon had never seen a vehicle matching it any of the times he'd been in town. He wondered who the woman was and if she owned the over-seventy-thousand-dollar car in a place where some houses could be bought for close to the same price.

He mentally noted the license plate number and jogged down the steps, heading to his Explorer. When he reached the vehicle, he climbed in and grabbed the electronic tablet he used for work, pulled up the app he needed, then put the plate number into the database.

The car was registered to a Juanita Salcido at an address farther up Tombstone Canyon. He saved the data. Maybe he didn't need to, but the whole experience had been odd enough that he intended to hold on to the information.

He set down the tablet as he thought about Miguel. Likely he'd been held up, the situation being one where the agent didn't have the ability or freedom to call without compromising himself and his cover.

A gut-deep sensation twisted Landon's insides and he gritted his teeth. Like a blow to the solar plexus, a bad feeling struck him hard.

A real bad feeling.

Chapter Two

Finally, they were just outside Bisbee. Tori tucked strands of chin-length dark hair behind her ear and leaned back in the shuttle van's seat. She looked ahead at the Mule Pass Tunnel that served as the gateway from the west side of town.

Memories slid back of holding her breath from one end of the tunnel to the other. Girls and boys who grew up in Bisbee made it a game any time they headed out of town.

Like other residents, Tori had often referred to it as The Time Tunnel. It was as though they traveled through time, leaving the world of today and visiting an earlier century.

The van entered the dimness of the tunnel and she resisted holding her breath. Seeping water had stained the concrete walls—the project to maintain the integrity of the structure never ended.

When the van reached the other end of the tunnel, she blinked away the bright sunlight and let out her breath. She almost laughed. Without realizing it, she'd been holding her breath after all.

The shuttle continued on and she leaned forward in her seat, her cell phone in her pocket digging into her hip. Her gaze drifted to take in homes perched on the hillsides and the aging narrow road the shuttle traveled.

Waves of memories rolled over her of her years growing up in Bisbee. She hadn't been able to wait to leave when she had graduated from Bisbee High School. She'd wanted to escape the small town and learn what waited out in the great big world. Now, here she was, running back to it.

Her smile faded. She'd never thought one man could

make her whole world crash down around her, chasing her away from her dreams and everything she'd worked so hard for. One man.

Tori ground her teeth. She wouldn't allow this to be more than a temporary blip on her radar. She would go back to her life — only it would be *without* Gregory.

Just the thought of him and what he'd done to her before she'd left him made her feel dirty and her skin crawled.

And now she was running home to Mama.

The backs of her eyes stung. Josie Nuñez Cox had been Tori's safe place, her refuge and, even at thirty-three, she needed her mother more than ever.

Tori put her fingers to her temples. She couldn't believe she'd forgotten not only her laptop, but her six-thousand-dollar clarinet too. She'd left them by the front door of the town house she owned and prayed Gregory wouldn't destroy either in a fit of anger at her leaving. More than likely he wouldn't, because he wasn't prone to physical violence. No, he preferred to sling harmful words when he was angry, beating her down verbally and emotionally.

He'd also expect her to come back for the clarinet, especially. Of the five clarinets she owned, she had paid most dearly for the Buffet Crampon professional. She didn't know how she could survive long without music, but she wasn't going back, not yet. At least her mother still had the old Baldwin upright piano Tori had learned to play on from the age of four and one of Tori's old clarinets might still be around.

If her car hadn't been in the shop, she could have loaded everything most important to her. But she hadn't been able to wait for the car. She'd had to get away from Gregory.

Her gaze drifted out of the window and skimmed over the mountainsides as she fought back tears. The stinging ache behind her eyes slowly dissolved when she turned focus on her surroundings. She could name the homes of old friends and wondered if any of them still lived there or in town.

The shuttle traveled down Tombstone Canyon, past St. Patrick's Church. She'd belonged to the church from childhood until she'd graduated from high school. She had gone through catechism and had received her first Holy Communion and Confirmation at St. Pat's.

Castle Rock loomed before them while the shuttle continued to Main Street in Old Bisbee. Victorian and European-style homes clung to the hillsides.

The shuttle passed Castle Rock then rounded the bend, continuing down the street between rows of old buildings that had been around since around 1910, rebuilt after a fire had ravaged the town. In the early 1900s, the town had been home to over twenty thousand people, the largest city between St. Louis and San Francisco.

Now the town had less than fifty-five hundred people. It had once been reduced to an even lower population.

Bisbee had nearly died in the 1970s when the mines had closed, but hippies had revived it by restoring old buildings and homes, painting them bright colors and turning the old mining town into an artists' community. The history of the place, plus the uniqueness and quaintness of the town, drew tourists from around the world.

The shuttle driver parked in the lot behind the Bisbee Convention Center, which had once been the old Phelps Dodge Mercantile. The driver had told her he wouldn't take the van up the steep winding street to her parents' home, so she would climb up on her own. She didn't mind — she'd been a runner in high school and kept in shape by jogging regularly. It would give her a chance to collect herself before she made it to her mom and dad's. She just hoped her dad wasn't there. She needed some alone time with her mom.

After she tipped the driver, she pushed her cell phone deeper in her pocket then tucked her purse into her bright pink travel bag. She still couldn't believe she'd run off without her clarinet and laptop. She'd been so upset she hadn't been thinking clearly when the shuttle had arrived to pick her up and she hadn't remembered she'd left the bag and clarinet until they had been miles away.

She bent to pick up the bag she *had* remembered and her crop top and low-rise jeans revealed her tan belly and back even more. Gregory had always hated her revealing any flesh, including the tattoo on her lower back, just above her waistband. He hadn't liked the idea of other men looking at her, nor did he approve of tattoos on women. She'd had *Klarinette* tattooed onto her skin in college. She liked the German spelling of her chosen instrument, which had been 'invented' in Germany around the turn of the eighteenth century.

Screw Gregory. She slung the bag over her shoulder. She'd wear whatever she damn well pleased.

The heavy bag's long strap dug into her shoulder as she looked around in the waning daylight. A few cars passed while she walked to the old post office, crossed Main Street, then headed back around an old bank building.

She turned onto Subway Street, a quiet one-way street, and walked up a steep road that took her near what had once been an old YMCA. She continued to climb the paved road on the hillside, past the old Central School.

Her phone vibrated in her pocket and she stopped to pull it out. A number she didn't recognize flashed across the display.

She brought it to her ear and answered, "Hello?"

"Where are you?" Gregory's demanding voice hit her like a punch to the chest. "Why haven't you been answering my calls?"

"I have nothing to say to you." She straightened and set her bag on the ground. "We are through."

"The hell we are." The way he spoke hammered every word. "Get your ass home."

Tori gripped the phone tightly. "I'll come back for my things when I'm ready, but we are done."

Before he could say another word, she disconnected the call and jammed the phone back into her pocket. Her face flushed with anger and her footsteps fell heavy on the asphalt as she trudged up the hill toward the point where Shearer turned into Clawson Avenue. The phone vibrated again, but she ignored it.

Near the north side of the arts center, Tori took a shortcut. Once she was farther up the hill, she rounded a vehicle. To her right was a black SUV close to an old white Toyota parked in an alleyway. The growing shadows obscured the cars, out of sight of anyone but someone walking by, like her, which wasn't often in this area.

Two men—one with white-blond hair and Slavic features, and a dark-haired guy with a pencil-thin mustache who looked to be of Hispanic descent—faced a third man. The third man had his back to the white Toyota. He had a slender physique compared to the other two, but she couldn't see his face.

Tori started to turn her gaze in the direction she'd been headed when the men's voices drew her attention again. A fourth man, this one wearing a tailored charcoal-gray suit, stepped out of the back of the SUV. The man had finely carved features and an athletic build.

Something glinted in the fading sunlight and Tori froze. Her heart thudded when the man in the suit pointed a gun at the lone man who stood with his back to the Toyota.

"Death is more than you deserve, Mateo." The suited man's Hispanic accent was heavy and cultured. "But your death will send a message."

Horror gripped Tori as the speaker aimed his handgun at Mateo's chest. It had a long barrel, like one of those guns with silencers she'd seen on TV.

Mateo didn't flinch and he raised his chin. "Your family's reign of terror will end, *El Puño.*"

The man in the suit gave Mateo an appraising look and a smile curved the corner of his mouth. "A dead man's desperate attempt to make his life end with meaning. Pathetic." The man gestured to the ground. "On your knees."

When Mateo didn't move, the other two men grabbed

him by the arms and forced him to his knees, facing away from the suited man, his hands cuffed behind him.

Tori stared, unable to breathe, much less comprehend the scene.

The suited man moved closer and put the barrel of his gun to the back of Mateo's head.

A spitting sound, and blood and brain matter sprayed over the white car as Mateo dropped. He collapsed on his side and, in her shock, Tori saw his face had been blown off.

Tori screamed. The remaining three men turned and spotted her. The man in the suit raised his gun and pointed it at her.

She dropped her bag and ran.

Terror ripped through her. Adrenaline pumped in her veins, jacking her pulse, and her blood pounded in her ears.

Oh, God, oh, God, oh, God!

The men had the way down blocked off. She had to run higher on the hillside.

"Get her!" the man in the suit shouted. "Kill the bitch!"

A bullet pierced a stop sign as she passed it, the pinging sound saying it tore through metal.

Tori ran faster. Her heart beat harder, out of control, as if it might explode from fear. She couldn't think, she could only react.

Sounds of heavy footfalls grew louder and she doubled her speed. She could outrun these men. She *had* to outrun them.

She glanced over her shoulder and her fear spiked. Maybe two hundred feet away now, the men each held guns, aimed at her.

Another scream tore from her and she increased her speed. Even though she ran every day, the high altitude and the steepness of the streets winded her.

She threw another look over her shoulder. The men closed in on her. One of them stopped and aimed his weapon. She zigged and zagged, hoping that would keep the men from hitting her. She passed a stone wall beneath a house on the hillside and small pieces of rock exploded beside her.

The sting of the rocks striking her face and arms only made her fight harder to keep running. She prayed for someone to help her but then prayed no one would attempt it so they wouldn't be shot.

These men would kill any witnesses, of that she was certain. She had to outlast them by searching for a place to hide. She thought about the old high school. Could she hide there, in the hope that she wouldn't be found?

The metallic taste of blood filled her mouth and she didn't know how much farther she could make it. This time when she looked over her shoulder, she saw she'd gained ground, now farther ahead of the men.

Her heart pounded and her face flushed, sweat coating her body. Her breathing became more labored and her muscles screamed as she ran higher and higher yet.

She rounded another corner, then an SUV. Just as she ran around the vehicle, rough hands grabbed her, jerking her out of the street. She started to scream when a hand clamped over her mouth.

Panic sent more adrenaline surging through her and she tried to struggle and get away from the strong arm wrapped around her. She kicked, her heel connecting with a shin, and heard the man swear.

"I'm trying to help you." The man's voice was low. "Come on."

She stopped fighting and he released her. She whirled to face a big man with a hard look on his scarred features. He grabbed her hand. Instinct told her he was one of the good guys and she ran with him up a short flight of stairs leading to a small house surrounded by tall shrubs. They ducked in a side door and he shut it behind without allowing it to close hard enough to make a sound.

Her chest rose and fell as she tried to catch her breath, her whole body hot, sweat dripping down the small of her back. Her heart might never stop thundering.

Her gaze swiveled to the man.

He gripped a gun in one hand.

She stumbled in the small kitchen, a cry of fear escaping her. She backed away from the man who held the weapon in his right hand as he peered through the slit in the curtains. Her hip hit a kitchen chair and it screeched over the linoleum. She swung her gaze around, trying to find some kind of weapon.

He glanced over his shoulder and must have recognized the terror in her eyes, staring at his gun.

"I'm a federal agent." He pulled his overshirt aside and relief rushed through her when she saw a gold badge on his belt. He turned back to the window. "You can tell me what the hell is going on once I make sure these bastards are long gone."

"Watch your tongue, Landon Michael Walker," came a voice from behind Tori.

Tori gave a startled yelp as she spun to face a woman under five feet tall, who had to be close to a hundred years old. It was easy to see she'd been a little taller before age and gravity had swiped a few inches from her and caused her back and shoulders to stoop.

"Sorry, Grandma Teresa," Landon said and Tori cut her gaze back to him. He was still staring out of the window. And Tori still trembled.

"Who are you?" Grandma Teresa asked, her tone blunt.

The woman had a strong accent. Polish, Tori thought. She'd had a Polish professor during her undergrad years.

"I'm Tori." She swallowed. "Tori Cox."

"You in some kind of trouble?" the elderly woman asked.

"I-I saw something." Tori's entire body continued shaking. "I—" She put her fist in her mouth and bit down, trying to calm herself.

"No sign of the men chasing you." Landon turned away from the window. "I think you're safe."

She blinked and stared at him.

He frowned. "What did you see?"

Tori couldn't think straight, almost couldn't comprehend

the man's question.

"What did you see?" he repeated. "Tell me. Now."

She lowered her hand. Her voice shook when she spoke and she had a hard time getting the words out. "I saw them kill a man."

Landon's expression hardened. "Are you certain that's what you saw?"

"I can't believe it." She brought her shaking hand to her neck. "They shot him. Oh, my God. They shot him."

"I need you to focus." Landon holstered his weapon and grasped her firmly by her shoulders. "Tell me what happened."

"I-I—" Her throat worked. "The alleyway was kind of dark. But I saw them. I wasn't too far from the men. I saw them."

He kept his gaze locked with hers. "Where?"

Her whole body shook harder as all that had happened hit her even more violently. "An alleyway." She tried to focus on her words. "North of the arts center, on the way up School Hill."

He released her and pulled a cell phone out of a holster on his belt. He punched in a single number, likely speed dial. She rubbed her arms with her hands, feeling goosebumps beneath her palms. She bit her lower lip, listening while he reported the possible homicide to the Bisbee Police Department.

When he'd finished talking, his green eyes focused on her. "Tell me everything you saw and heard."

"For heaven's sake, let the girl sit and catch her breath." Teresa shuffled toward a table that barely fit in the postage stamp-sized kitchen as she admonished Landon. "You look like you could use a glass of cold water, young lady." Teresa opened the door of the small older-model fridge.

"Yes, thank you." Tori's mind spun, but she still thought about offering to help the woman.

Landon moved in front of Teresa and took the pitcher out of the fridge. Teresa grabbed a glass out of a dish drainer.

Tori sank into a chair at the table, her body still shaking. Her breathing slowed and her skin cooled some, but her face remained hot.

It was the first chance she'd had to really look at Landon. Her bleary eyes made it difficult to focus, but she forced herself. Anything but think of the man whose face had been blown off.

Landon stood over six feet and wore a blue T-shirt beneath a white overshirt with rolled-up sleeves, which now hid the holstered gun. In spite of the overshirt, she could see his muscular form. He must regularly work out or do something to stay in such great shape. His tough, seasoned look went along with his hard, masculine features and a wicked scar along the right side of his face, from his cheekbone to his jaw. Late thirties, she guessed.

He faced her and her already heated cheeks warmed even more. She couldn't believe that in this situation she'd been taking stock of his assets. She grasped the glass of water he handed her. Her hand hadn't stopped shaking and a little of the water splashed on it.

"Thank you." She drank then set the glass on the table with a light thump. She managed to gather her composure enough to ask, "What agency are you with?"

"Department of Homeland Security." Landon eyed her. "Immigration and Customs Enforcement Agency."

She leaned back in her seat and took another drink of water, hoping it would help settle her nerves. No such luck. "I'm fortunate you were outside."

"I happened to be in the right place at the right time." He pulled out a chair for his grandmother to Tori's right.

"And I was in the wrong place at the wrong time." It surprised her that she was able to do more than stutter.

After the elderly woman had sat, Landon remained standing but leaned over and braced his palms on the table, directly across from Tori.

"Sit, Landon." Teresa spoke in her no-nonsense tone, but the man remained focused on Tori.

"The police are going to need to know what you saw, Tori." It was clear in the way he spoke to her that he wanted to keep her calm, but needed information. "When did it happen?"

"Minutes before you rescued me." She swallowed. "I walked up the hill and took a shortcut. I saw some men talking." She described the two vehicles and the men the best she could with her mind pinging all over the place. "A fourth man got out of the SUV. He pointed a gun at the man standing against the white car." Fear shot through her once again, as if she were still watching the scene unfolding before her. "It happened so fast."

"Did the men say anything?" Landon asked.

"Yes." She struggled to remember what the men had said. Her thoughts jumbled together and she wrinkled her forehead in concentration. "The one with the gun shouted a Hispanic name." She frowned before it came to her. "Mateo. The man he shot was Mateo."

She put the heel of her palm to her forehead. "Mateo said something and called the man with the gun by a strange name...also Hispanic." She struggled to remember, but it lay just out of reach. "Damn. I can't remember what Mateo called him."

As she spoke, Landon straightened, a granite-hard look on his face she couldn't read. "Mateo. You're sure that's the name of the man who was shot?"

She rubbed her palms on her jeans. "Yes."

"Shit." Landon pulled out his cell phone. He appeared both concerned and furious as he punched in a number and turned away.

"Language." Teresa shook her finger at Landon.

Landon didn't seem to have heard or to have seen her shaking her finger at him. He walked through an archway, out of the kitchen, and into another room.

"Where are you from?" Teresa spoke to Tori in a strongly accented voice.

"I'm originally from Bisbee." Tori slumped in her chair,

glad for the reprieve from thinking about what she had witnessed. She reached for her water glass with both hands, sliding her fingers through the condensation. "My parents are Josie and Henry Cox."

Teresa looked thoughtful. "You grew up on Temby Avenue?"

"Yes." It did not surprise Tori that Teresa knew. Tori's family had been lifetime Bisbee residents.

The woman tapped her forehead. "I may be nigh on ninety-six, but the mind's still sharp."

Tori cleared her throat in an effort to speak. "Do you know my parents?"

"I knew little Josie Nuñez since childhood. Back before she married that no-good Cox boy." Teresa met Tori's gaze. "Is he drinking like a fish, same as always?"

Yes, the woman was blunt, but Tori didn't mind the truth. "As far as I know he's still a regular at St. Elmo's."

Teresa shook her head. "A real shame." She eyed Tori. "You don't seem to have come out any worse for it."

"My dad didn't hang around the house much." Tori clenched the glass tighter, trying to focus on Teresa's questions. "Mom mostly raised me."

Teresa frowned. "Josie was a good girl. A real good girl."

Landon walked through the archway, into the kitchen. "I'll be right back." He opened the kitchen door and let himself into the evening.

Moments later, he returned. "I need to get to the scene." He looked at Tori as she held her hand to her throat. "Police are there now, so you'll be safe in my vehicle. Likely the men are long gone. The police will question you and so will I."

"You?" Tori lowered her hand. "Why?"

"I'll explain once we leave." He shrugged out of his white overshirt and handed it to Tori. "Cover up that tattoo and your shirt. If anyone is hanging around and watching from any number of vantage points, we don't want them to recognize you."

Tori stood to take the shirt and slip her arms into it. The shirt hung loosely on her, well past her hips to her upper thighs. She buttoned it up and rolled up the sleeves, concentrating on each task. He pulled a ball cap out of his back pocket and adjusted it for her smaller head.

When he'd guessed the size, he gave it to Tori. "Put your hair up under this."

She took it from him. She wondered if her hands would ever stop shaking. Her chin-length hair took a little extra effort to push under the ball cap. "Can you tell me what's going on? It's something more, isn't it?"

"Questions can wait." Landon turned, bent, and kissed Teresa's cheek before giving her a one-armed hug. "I'll do my best to stop by at the end of the week, Grandma."

"Sooner better than later." Teresa studied him with her watery blue eyes. "I won't be around for long, you know."

"Sure you will." Landon gave her a boyish smile that rubbed away some of the rough edges on his features. "I always knew you'd live forever."

Teresa harrumphed. "Get going, boy."

"Love you, Grandma." Landon opened the door and Tori followed him outside into the near darkness.

Chapter Three

Landon strode to his Explorer with Tori beside him. He'd come out moments before to make sure it was clear with no one in sight who might be after Tori.

His blood thrummed in his ears. Mateo was Miguel's undercover name. The cartel had killed him? God, he hoped not, but considering Miguel hadn't shown up to the meet, there was a strong chance he was the murdered man.

The summer evening had cooled and a light breeze ruffled the hair at Landon's nape. His skin felt hot and tight and he had the feeling he would explode under the right conditions. If someone had murdered Miguel, Landon intended to take down the man responsible for killing him.

With fury burning in his veins, Landon opened the passenger side door of the SUV. He had to pause a moment to toss a pair of his western boots behind the front passenger seat and placed his Stetson on the bench seat in the rear. He'd throw everything in the trunk of the vehicle later.

Helping Tori into the vehicle, he then hurried to the driver's side and swung himself into his seat. He slammed the door at the same time he crammed the keys into the ignition then drove out away from his grandmother's home. He'd backed into parking spaces so he'd be ready to leave at a moment's notice. It was a cop thing.

If it he hadn't gone out to his vehicle earlier, he would never have seen the brunette running up the hill, terror in her expression, and wouldn't have caught glimpses of the two men following her. He hadn't been able to get a good look at the men in the snatch of time he'd had to grab Tori.

After getting Tori to safety, he would have gone after

the men if he hadn't been concerned they would see him leaving his grandmother's home. Putting Grandma Teresa in any kind of danger wasn't an option.

Landon's mouth grew tight as he shot a look at Tori. She had her bottom lip between her white teeth and worried it. The gorgeous woman had big dark eyes, as well as the dark hair she'd tucked under the cap.

"Why were you walking up the hill?" he asked, his tone harder than he'd intended.

She blinked at him, pausing as if she'd been lost in thought. "I just got into town. The shuttle dropped me off by the convention center and I had to walk the rest of the way."

He frowned as he maneuvered his vehicle on the narrow street down toward the location where she'd said she'd seen the shooting. "You don't have any luggage, not even a purse."

Her hand flew to her mouth, her eyes wide. She lowered her hand. "I dropped my bag when the men chased me. I can't believe I forgot. My purse was in the bag. Everything is in it—my driver's license, passport, credit cards, everything."

Beneath his breath he swore. "No question they took it. They know who you are."

"Oh, my God." Her eyes seemed impossibly larger. "Will they come after me?"

"Probably." Landon didn't believe in sugarcoating. "Where were you going? Home?"

"I was headed to my parents' home on Temby." Her voice wavered. "I live in Tucson. I took the shuttle here because my car is in the shop."

"Is your parents' address listed in your belongings?" Landon asked. "Anything that would tie you to them?"

She bit her lower lip then shook her head, saying, "I don't think so."

He glanced at her as she dug in her jeans pocket and pulled out a cell phone. A number scrolled across the lit-up screen, the phone vibrating in her hand. She stared at it and her lips formed a thin line before she sent the call to voicemail and shoved the phone back into her pocket.

When she didn't volunteer the name of the person who had called, he asked, "Will your parents be concerned about you?"

She shook her head. "They didn't know I was coming." Catching him glancing at her, she looked away and added, "I needed to get away from Tucson."

He wondered what she'd run from, but she'd made it clear she didn't want to talk about it. He thought the call she'd received might have had something to do with her running.

The vehicle jolted back and forth over the uneven pavement. Blue and red strobes flashed ahead, the lights from emergency vehicles bouncing off surrounding structures in the growing darkness.

Landon glanced at Tori. "Have you remembered the name of the shooter?"

She hesitated then shook her head, the hat falling down over her forehead. She pushed the brim up, a pinched, worried expression on her face. "Not yet. I'm trying hard to."

After he parked as close as possible to the scene, he looked at her. "Do *not* get out of the Explorer. Understand?"

At her nod, he climbed out and headed to the passenger side. When he reached it, he opened the door.

He put his hand up to make sure she didn't try to leave. "You're going to wait here. It's too dangerous for you to get out of the vehicle."

"But I'm disguised."

"Can't take any chances." He shook his head. "It may not be a good enough disguise."

"Okay." She gave a slow nod. "Can I take off my seatbelt?"

"If you promise to stay in the SUV."

"I promise."

He glanced over his shoulder at the scene and returned

his gaze to hers. "From here you can look to see if you remember anything. Okay?"

"Yes."

"Sit tight." He stepped away, the Explorer door still open, Tori sitting sideways so she could watch from her vantage point.

Lieutenant Liam Marks of the Bisbee Police Department stood a few feet away, talking with another officer. Marks gave a nod to the officer as they finished their conversation and his gaze cut to Landon. The lieutenant approached Landon. Out of professional courtesy, Landon would consult with Marks before jumping into the investigation.

"Agent Walker." Marks inclined his head toward the scene when he reached them. "What's got the DHS interested?"

"Is the victim dead?" Landon asked.

"Sure as hell is." Marks nodded. "Looks like a drug deal gone bad. Found coke in the victim's vehicle and the registration is for a Mateo Torrez."

Landon's gut tightened and anger burned beneath his skin. "If I'm right, the victim is one of ours, an agent who worked deep undercover. Mateo Torrez was his UC name. I need to see the body."

"Sonofabitch." Marks shook his head. "Sonofabitch," he repeated. He glanced at the SUV. "One of your agents?" he asked Landon.

"Tori witnessed the murder," Landon replied.

Marks looked surprised and peered closer at Tori. To Landon's surprise, Marks said, "Tori Cox?"

"Hi, Liam." From Landon's observations, Tori struggled to calm her shaking nerves with difficulty.

"Damn, Tori." The lieutenant frowned. "It's good to see you, but not under these circumstances."

Fear haunted her eyes. "I agree."

Marks glanced from Tori to Landon and back. "I'll need everything from you, Tori."

Tori nodded but flashed Landon a look, almost as if she were scared—not of Marks, but of the men who'd chased her.

Landon settled his hand on Tori's shoulder and gave her a reassuring squeeze. "You'll be fine. I'll be right back."

"Yes." She crossed her arms over her chest as if holding herself tight.

He squeezed her shoulder again before he turned away and strode to where the scene was being processed. He ducked under the yellow crime scene tape.

The body lay beside an older-model, dusty white Toyota. Landon recognized the tag and the make as Miguel's. Landon's heart dropped to the asphalt when he saw the man's build. He faced away, but Landon had a bad feeling in his gut that had grown worse since he'd been at St. Pat's. The inside of the man's wrist had the cartel tattoo, but Miguel had had the symbol tattoed on his wrist as part of his cover.

Landon crouched beside the body and, despite the fact that the man's face was mostly blown off, *knew* it was Miguel.

Anger burned hot and bright inside Landon and he clenched his fists. "Fuck." Then louder, *"Fuck."*

At that moment he wanted to slam his fist into something. Anything. But a broken hand wasn't going to bring back Miguel.

"Recognize him?" asked a young female officer who Landon hadn't seen before.

"Yeah." Landon pushed himself to his feet. "I sure as hell do. He was one of ours, a federal agent."

The female officer shook her head. "Oh, shit."

Landon turned away, drew his cell phone out of his pocket, and punched the speed dial number for Sofia Aguilar, the Resident Agent in Charge.

Sofia answered in her clipped tone. "Aguilar here."

Landon heaved out a breath before answering his RAC. "Miguel is dead."

"Miguel?" Sofia's voice grew harder. "What happened?"

"Appears the cartel executed him in Bisbee." Landon

31

tried to calm himself, to separate himself from what had happened, but it was impossible. "The face is unrecognizable, but I'm sure it's Miguel."

Sofia let out an expletive—she was as good at them as any of her subordinates. "Any witnesses?"

"Yes." Landon looked back at Tori who had remained in the Explorer as he'd instructed. Her face was illuminated by flashing red, white, and blue strobes in the growing darkness. "Her name is Tori Cox. The men responsible went after her, but I got to her first. I have her in my custody."

Sofia had a grim note in her voice. "Do you think the woman will testify when we catch the bastards?"

Landon frowned as he studied Tori, who appeared shaken and lost. He couldn't blame her. "I don't know." He shifted his stance. "But I think there's a good chance she will."

"I'll have a team sent to the crime scene immediately and notify Miguel's wife." Sofia sounded on fire and he could hear the anger in her voice, anger at Miguel's murderers. "In the meantime, we need to get our witness to a safe house. I'll have Johnson meet you at the scene then escort you and the witness to the location."

Landon dragged his hand down his stubbled face. "Yes, ma'am."

When Aguilar disconnected the call, Landon got hold of Dylan.

"Tell me you have something." Dylan sounded as if he'd had a long day. "Did you manage to meet up with Miguel?"

Landon turned away from Tori and studied the scene. "He's dead."

"Jesus." Dylan's voice grew hard and much more intense. "What happened?"

Landon spent the next few minutes running through everything that had happened from the time he'd seen Tori bolting from the two men, her story, and identifying the body.

Dylan cursed. "Miguel was a damned good man. We're not going to let the bastards get away with this."

Landon pushed his fingers through his hair. "The witness left her belongings, including all her ID, at the scene."

"So they know who she is." Dylan growled another curse. "She's not safe."

"I'm going to make sure she is." Landon looked over his shoulder at Tori. While she talked with Marks, she rubbed her arms with her palms as if working to keep herself warm. "I'll call you the moment I learn anything else," Landon said to Dylan.

Landon disconnected the call and headed toward Tori and Lieutenant Marks.

"I'm one hundred percent sure that's our UC," Landon told Marks when he reached the pair. "My RAC is sending out a team now."

"Murder of a federal agent." Marks frowned. "I'm sure you're going to want to take control of the investigation, but we still have jurisdiction, as well."

Landon glanced back at the crime scene before addressing Marks. "We'll share anything we have and I'm certain you will too."

Marks nodded. "We'll make it happen."

The thought that Miguel had been murdered barely computed, even as Landon made arrangements with Marks. "We'll need to search the vehicle, collect Miguel's things, along with the UC registration and whatever else we find."

Landon inclined his head in Tori's direction as he continued. "I'm taking the witness into protective custody. I need to get her out of here."

Marks nodded and turned to Tori. "I'd say good to see you, but I wish it was at a reunion and not a murder investigation."

Tori sagged, her entire body showing how tired she must be. "Same here."

Marks gave her a concerned look. "Don't take any chances."

She shifted on the passenger seat. "I don't plan to. I'm

already scared out of my mind."

"I don't blame you." Marks glanced at Landon. "Anything else I can do for you, Agent Walker?"

Landon shook his head. "I've got it from here."

Marks nodded to Tori. "Take care of yourself."

She raised her hand in a parting wave just before Marks left and walked toward the body.

Landon turned his attention to Tori. "Did you remember anything more than what you told me?"

"I've been racking my brain, trying to remember the name of the man who killed Mateo." She looked in the direction of the body and Landon saw her shudder. "It's as if my brain is frozen. I feel numb. I can't think straight."

"You're suffering from shock." He wanted more from her, but he knew he could push her too far if he wasn't careful. He tried to keep his voice even. "I know I've been asking a lot of you, but you're going to be faced with more."

"I understand." She sounded close to tears.

Landon paused and studied her, then continued, "You witnessed the murder of one of our undercover agents. His real name was Miguel and I considered him a good friend." Landon and Miguel had trained together at the Federal Law Enforcement Training Center, FLETC. They'd gotten drunk together, had even chased women together. Then Miguel had married Jane and had two kids, a couple of years before Landon had met Stacy.

Tori's eyes widened and she seemed to jerk out of the partial numbness she'd said she'd been feeling. "I'm so sorry."

"So am I." Landon blew out his breath, barely able to contain his anger. *So the fuck am I.* "We believe a drug cartel is behind the murder. I'll need you to go through some photographs."

"A drug cartel?" Tori's voice shook. "Does that mean a cartel will be coming after me?"

"We're putting you into protective custody." Landon tried to calm her by keeping his voice even. "We won't let you get into any danger."

She put her palm to her mouth then lowered her shaking hand. "Cartels are ruthless." It sounded as if she knew something about them, something he'd talk about with her later when they had a moment.

He gave a slow nod. "Yes, they are extremely ruthless."

"I'm scared, Landon." She gripped her hands in her lap, her knuckles white. "No, I'm beyond scared. I'm terrified."

"Hey." He rested his hand on her arm and that touch seemed to calm her a bit. "I'm going to make sure you're safe. You have nothing to worry about. We need your help and we'll get this guy."

She swallowed. "What should I do?"

"We'll take you in to look over photos tomorrow." Landon studied Tori. "In the meantime, we will ensure your safety."

"I won't take the chance the men will go after Mom and Dad, so I won't go to their house." Tori shook her head. "I have nowhere to go. My cash, my credit cards, my checkbook—everything is gone."

"We wouldn't allow your parents to be put in any kind of danger." He had her looking at him in surprise when he added, "I'm taking you to a safe house."

"A safe house?"

"It's the safest option. The only option." Landon glanced at her as she started to buckle up. "Did you check with Lieutenant Marks to see if by chance your bag was left behind by the men?"

She fumbled with the seatbelt. "He said nothing was here but the car and the body when he arrived."

Landon helped her with the seatbelt. Just as the metal clicked, his cell phone rang. He checked the screen and recognized the number as Agent Johnson's. "Walker here."

"Hang tight." Johnson never messed around with pleasantries in important situations. That was one thing you could always count on. "O'Donnell and I are en route and we'll meet you in fifteen minutes at the scene to escort you to the safe house."

"Just hurry your asses over here." Landon disconnected the call and looked at Tori. "Now to make sure your parents are safe."

"You think they're in danger?" Tori's eyes grew wide. "Their names and address aren't in my bag and they barely use the computer I gave them, so I don't think they could be found on the Internet. The killers won't even know my parents' names, will they?"

"*Anything* can be found on the Internet if you know where to look." Landon watched Tori's expression as fear for her parents grew. "Property ownership, you name it. Your name could be found as well, and it might list who your parents are."

"You're right." She brushed her palms on her jeans. "Are you going to take them into protective custody too?"

He shook his head. "Right now we're going to put a car with agents outside their home. What's their address?"

She told him and he made another call. When he disconnected, he turned to her. "We'll have a car stationed outside their home."

"I'll let my mom know." The world had gone surreal and Tori felt as if she was watching all that had happened in a dream. She pulled her phone out of her pocket and called her mother.

"Hi, sweetheart," Josie answered, obviously recognizing Tori's number on the caller ID.

"Hi, Mom." Tori took a deep breath and let it out. "I came to Bisbee to see you, but when I arrived—" She swallowed. "I saw someone murder a man. The man who killed him is after me. Also the men who were with him."

"*Dios mio!*" Josie exclaimed. "Where are you? Are you safe?"

"I'm with federal agents." Tori gripped the phone tighter. "They will make sure I'm safe. They're also sending someone to watch out for you and Dad. Those agents will park in front of your house and keep an eye out."

"You think these men will come after your father and

me?" Josie had an edge of panic to her voice.

"It's a precaution." Tori closed her eyes. "These are some very bad men and if they find out where you are, they might hurt you to get to me. I'm so sorry."

"You have nothing to be sorry for, *mija*." Josie spoke in her firm, no-nonsense tone. "We will be careful and the police will keep us safe."

"Sure you'll be okay, Mom?"

"We will be fine." Tori knew her mom. Josie was doing a good job of putting up a brave front for Tori's benefit. "Are you certain *you* are safe?"

"I'm with an agent now and I'll be taken to a safe house." Tori swallowed. "So yes, I will be fine."

"Good." Josie sounded a little relieved but still concerned. "I need to go and get your father now. He's at St. Elmo's."

Tori felt a lump in her throat. "I'll tell the agents and they can go get him. You stay in the house, okay?"

Josie hesitated.

"Please, Mom." Tori closed her eyes. "I need to know you're safe."

"All right. The agents can get him." Josie paused. "But tell them to hurry."

"Thank you." Her throat tightened and she had difficulty swallowing. "I love you, Mom."

"I love you too, *mija*." Josie's voice gentled. "Be careful and call when you can."

"I will." Tori disconnected the call and opened her eyes.

"Where's your father?" Landon asked, obviously having heard her part of the conversation.

She stuffed her phone in her pocket. "Dad is likely having a beer or several at St. Elmo's. Mom agreed to stay in the house."

Landon selected a number from the contacts on his phone and she heard him repeat the information to someone on the other end.

When he'd finished and pressed the End button, he looked at Tori. "They'll be fine. We'll get to them before anyone figures out who they are." He continued, "What about family in Tucson? Do you have a husband? A boyfriend?"

Her skin went cold.

"My — my boyfriend." Her eyes widened. "He lives with me in Tucson. What if these guys from the cartel go to my home because they have the address from my driver's license? What if they've already gone there?"

"Call him. Tell him to leave and stay with a friend."

She used speed dial to call his number and brought the phone to her ear. She heard multiple rings before it went to voicemail.

"Gregory," she spoke urgently. "Something's happened. As soon as you get this message, I need you to go stay with a friend. Get out of the town house immediately. I can't explain over the phone, just do it." She disconnected the call and redialed his number. Once again, it rang several times before she got his voicemail.

"Maybe he's not home." She looked at Landon. "Why didn't I think of him earlier? If something happens to him —"

"You are not to blame," Landon cut in. "You've had a big scare and a lot to process. And we didn't know the cartel was involved, so you had no way of knowing he could be in danger."

Tori bit her lower lip. She'd left Gregory, but she'd never want anything horrible to happen to him. She tried dialing him again, but no answer.

"What should we do?" she asked Landon when she disconnected the call.

"I'll take care of it." He grasped his own cell phone, selected a number from his contacts, and brought the phone to his ear.

He identified himself before being transferred, then spoke with a lieutenant at the Tucson Police Department and explained the situation. Landon asked Tori for Gregory's last name and she told him it was Smith. She gave Landon their home address and he relayed it to the lieutenant on the other end of the line.

"They're sending officers to your house to check on your boyfriend," Landon told Tori. He didn't offer her any false hope by saying something such as, "I'm sure he'll be fine." It didn't seem to be his style to offer hope when there were too many unknowns.

"Thank you." She dug her nails into her palms to try to get a grip on herself.

"In case the cartel does have a problem finding your parents on the Internet, does your boyfriend know where your parents live?" Landon asked.

Cold washed over her and her skin prickled. "Gregory has been there once, but I don't think he knows the address. He's horrible with directions. He didn't get on very well with my mom and dad and they weren't too crazy about him."

Landon gave a single nod. "We need to get out of here."

"Okay." Her voice sounded small, even to herself. She shifted and seated herself fully inside the truck and he closed the passenger-side door.

In moments, a black SUV pulled up beside them. Landon got out and went to the vehicle where he spoke with someone through the lowered window.

Landon returned and climbed into the driver's seat and shut the door behind him. "We're going to get you to a safe house now." He looked at her. "Turn off your cell phone and take out the battery, just in case they have the connections to find a way to track you using it."

She dug the phone out of her pocket and powered it down, then removed the battery.

He eyed her squarely. "Hand them to me."

She hesitated then handed him her phone and the battery and he stuck them in his own pocket.

Everything felt so surreal, as though happening to anyone but her. Even this small action made her feel as if reality had given in to a nightmare.

Landon buzzed down his window and she heard him give the agents on protective detail the signal that they were ready to go. Landon buzzed the window up again before starting the Explorer.

Chapter Four

Diego Montego Jimenez watched his granddaughter studying the chessboard. The girl's forehead furrowed in concentration, her long dark hair spilling over her shoulders and her cheeks while she analyzed the game. Diego knew she planned multiple moves ahead. Angelina's exceptional intelligence kept him on his toes, just as her mother had.

He held back a scowl at the thought of his daughter, Rosanna's, murder. He'd had his son-in-law killed for failing to protect Rosanna. It had been her husband's responsibility to keep her from harm and he had failed. Diego did not tolerate failure.

Diego did not want Angelina to see his anger, so he kept on his mask of the doting grandfather. He *did* dote on the pretty fourteen-year-old girl who would soon celebrate her *quince años* and be a *Quinceañera*, a recognition of her journey from childhood to maturity.

Like all girls her age, Angelina should know only a soon-to-be young woman's hopes and dreams. He sheltered her from the harsh realities of his world. His lovely granddaughter should never know the cruel world she lived in. She would know only love and the joy he could provide her with.

They sat at a small table on one of the sprawling home's expansive balconies, where they enjoyed challenging each other in a game of chess in the evenings after their final meal of the day. The desert of Mexico cooled once the sun went down, leaving it pleasant outside with no breeze.

Waiting for Angelina to make her move, he let his gaze drift over the terracotta flooring interspersed with decorative ceramic tiles. He rested his gaze on the stone rail. He felt like a monarch when he surveyed his own private kingdom.

His crystal-blue swimming pools, extensive gardens, and lush vegetation spread out beneath the balcony. He often stood at the stone balcony rail and looked out across his land, taking in the magnificent view and all that was his, all he had worked so hard for. He deserved to enjoy the fruits of his labor, but he remained ever vigilant, running his business with a firm hand.

When his gaze returned to Angelina, the glimmer of a smile passed over her lips, but she quickly hid it. She schooled her expressions well, though not well enough— yet. She would learn to fully control her expressions, mannerisms, and actions as the granddaughter of the respected and feared Diego Montego Jimenez, *El Demonio*. The nickname pleased him.

Angelina reached with her slender arm, picked up her queen, and moved it across the board. "Check."

She had caught him unawares. Perhaps he had been too lost in thought, not enough concentration. He gave a nod. "Very good."

She beamed then quickly shuttered her expression. "Thank you."

"However, my little angel, it is not good enough." He took her queen with his knight.

Without blinking, she took his knight with a pawn.

After six more moves, a gleam of triumph flashed across her face. She moved her bishop. "Checkmate."

Diego steepled his fingers as he leaned back in his chair. He could not have expressed fully his pride for her. He gave a slow nod while laying down his king. "Excellent."

He met her gaze and her look of deep pleasure slid away and she looked down. "Thank you, Grandfather."

"You are a worthy opponent." He put his hands on the arms of his chair. "Come. Walk with me."

He rose, as did she. When she became a woman, she

would wait for the gentleman to pull out her chair before standing.

The thought of his granddaughter crossing the bridge from childhood to adulthood brought him both pride and a sense of loss. He would miss the little girl she had been, always coming to him for her needs and desires. As a woman she would come into her own, broadening her horizons.

She planned to go to college, but he hadn't made his own decision. He was torn between sending her away to college and keeping her with him. The idea of her going into the world alone did not sit well with him. He had too many enemies and she would be but a woman.

She looped her arm through his and smiled up at him. "Where would you like to walk this evening?"

He swept his arm toward the stairs leading below. "I wish to see my gardens."

"They are so lovely." Her skirt flowed around her calves as they walked. "The blooms are magnificent and the perfume flows through me like the song of life." She played the piano beautifully and he could imagine her fingers dancing over the keys while she breathed in the scents of roses or other flowers from his garden. Daily, Diego's gardener put together an arrangement and the head housekeeper set the vase on top of the grand piano.

Just as they reached the top of the tiled stone staircase, Jaime, Diego's personal assistant, walked through a balcony leading into the ten-thousand-square-foot home. Jaime approached Diego and Angelina.

Diego looked down at his granddaughter and patted her hand. "I must speak with Jaime. Wait here for me."

Used to interruptions, she smiled. "I will be at the balcony." She walked to the balcony, her back to them.

Diego turned to Jaime. "This must be important, as you are well aware I am not to be disturbed when I am with my granddaughter." His tone held a hint of warning.

Jaime did not betray any emotion, as usual, handing Diego

an encrypted cell phone. "You have a call from Alejandro. He claims it is urgent."

Diego frowned as he took the cell phone, wondering why his only son would be calling. Diego did not answer. He never talked business where his granddaughter might hear. He walked into the house, leaving Angelina on the balcony. He worked in his library, across the hall from the archway leading to the balcony.

He entered the library, a place that pleased him greatly. He had a love for reading and books. He had been raised speaking only Spanish, but in college he had flourished in foreign languages and spoke fluent English, Italian, and French. He had lined three walls with walnut bookshelves and filled them with books in all four languages.

When he reached his finely crafted walnut desk, he sat in his leather desk chair and brought the cell phone to his ear. "What is it, Alejandro?"

"The problem you had me take care of has been eliminated, Father." Alejandro paused. "However, there is a complication."

Diego narrowed his eyebrows. He did not like complications, especially in dealing with a U.S. federal agent who needed to be disposed of. "What is this complication?"

Alejandro cleared his throat. "A woman witnessed it. I believe she saw everything, including my face."

Heat rose up around Diego's collar. Alejandro did not normally do the dirty work, but this time Diego's son had wanted to eliminate the agent himself. Mateo had gotten deep into the Jimenez Cartel's family. Diego and Alejandro had trusted the bastard and had taken him in as if he were one of their own.

"You did not take care of this complication?" Diego asked.

"John and Pablo went after her." Alejandro's voice hardened. "They lost her."

Diego surged to his feet, the heat around his collar rising to his face. "They lost her," he repeated slowly. "And she can identify you." Diego could not afford for his son to be identified.

"We do know who she is." Alejandro spoke more quickly now. "She left a bag with her purse that contains her ID, cash, and credit cards. Her name is Tori Cox and she has a Tucson address. We found other information as well that may lead us to her. However, we do not know where she is now."

"Did you search on the Internet for her?" Diego asked. "She may have family there."

"Yes, I did do a search." Alejandro said. "I got multiple Google hits on her. She's a musician, highly regarded, and has performed around the U.S. However, there is no reference to Bisbee or to family. Her Facebook page is private, but lists her relationship with a Gregory Smith. It does not show her hometown. It is as if she has no ties here."

"She must have friends or family there." Diego tried to keep control of his fury. "Send Pablo to Tucson to the address on her driver's license and see if he can find anything that will lead us to her. Perhaps someone will be there who will know where she must have planned to stay."

"I have already sent Pablo, as well as John." Alejandro continued, "It should not take them long to reach and search her home, or to interrogate anyone they might need to."

"Take care of it." Diego disconnected the call and nearly slammed the cell phone on the desktop. He loved his son and would do anything for him. But Diego had a low tolerance for failure from anyone.

Diego breathed in slowly through his nose then parted his lips and blew out his breath. *Inhale. Exhale.*

Alejandro, referred to as *El Puño*, the Fist, would inherit Diego's empire. If anything were to happen to Alejandro, Diego's four brothers would be in line from the oldest to the youngest. Diego had no wish for his brothers to take over the business. It belonged to Alejandro if Diego passed away.

His brothers were fools.

Once Diego regained full control of his emotions, he left the office and returned to the balcony where Angelina waited. She looked out at the pool and gardens lit with strategically placed spotlights.

When he reached her, he rested his hand on her shoulder and kissed the top of her head. "What are you thinking, my angel?" he asked as he straightened.

She smiled up at him. "I have the best grandfather in all the world."

He returned her smile. "As I have the prettiest, most intelligent granddaughter."

She rested her head on his biceps for a moment and he put his arm around her shoulders. He squeezed her to him before they linked arms and walked down the staircase to the grounds below.

Chapter Five

In their agency SUV, the other agents followed Landon's vehicle. The whole time, Tori felt as though she would crawl out of her skin.

At the same time, she was aware a numbness in her mind, as if nothing made sense anymore. She struggled to keep the memory of the murder out of her thoughts, but it refused to leave, always knocking at the back of her brain.

"Why are you driving in circles all around the Bisbee area?" she asked Landon.

He glanced at her. "I intend to make damned sure no one follows us. Even though a tail should be obvious in a small town like Bisbee, it's necessary to take appropriate action. We can't, and I won't, take chances."

It felt as if insects scuttled all over Tori's skin. How could she be both numb and jittery at the same time?

She peered out into the darkness as Landon drove, only his headlights illuminating the paved road in some areas while streetlights lit up the streets in other parts of the sprawling town. As far as stoplights in the whole of Bisbee went, they could be counted on one hand.

They spent a good half hour driving to different parts of Bisbee, including the San Jose, Warren, and Galena areas. When she felt almost dizzy from driving around and around the town, she turned her gaze from the darkness outside.

She looked at Landon who steered the SUV with one hand on the top of the wheel and his other hand lower. The amber glow of the dashboard lights caused his features to seem harsher, the scar a brutal slash across the right side of his face. She wondered where he had gotten it.

Without the overshirt, she saw more of his body's definition beneath his T-shirt. The shirt hugged his biceps and tightened across his chest. Did he have washboard abs? She couldn't tell because of the T-shirt, but the rest of him indicated he probably did.

Despite everything that had happened, she found herself attracted to this almost gruff, virile alpha male. Under other circumstances, she would ask him more questions to figure out what made him tick. She had the feeling Landon had a lot of layers and it wouldn't be easy getting past the surface.

He glanced at her, catching her staring at him, and her face warmed.

She sighed. "I wish I could have stayed with my parents."

He shook his head. "Too dangerous to take chances."

"I know." She bit her lower lip.

He seemed to be watching her for something. "Did you have a laptop or tablet in the stolen bag?"

"When I left, I was so upset about..." She trailed off before continuing. "I left my laptop bag with my clarinet at the front door of my home in Tucson." She rubbed her arms with her palms. "It ended up being a good thing I forgot them since I never could have run away from the men if I'd been carrying them."

She wiped her sweating palms on her jeans again. Landon had saved her life and now he was helping keep her safe when she had nowhere else to turn without putting her family in danger.

She thought again about Gregory and a sick feeling washed through her belly. When would they hear back from the Tucson Police Department?

Gregory had become such a negative in her life. Considering her parents were good people and she trusted her mother's judgment, Tori knew she should have questioned her relationship with Gregory. Even her friends had made comments that, in retrospect, were probably meant to tell her in a roundabout way they didn't approve of him.

Why hadn't she seen it?

She'd been so taken in by what he'd appeared to be. She'd thought he was intelligent, caring, and she'd liked being around him. Gradually that had changed, but she hadn't seen the verbal and emotional abuse for what it had been. How could she have been so blind?

None of that mattered at this moment. His safety did. Gregory could be in trouble.

Her heart thumped hard. Or he could be dead.

She turned to Landon again. "Do you think any of my friends could be in danger? If they somehow got my address off my laptop...although it is password protected."

"How easy is your password to break?" he asked.

She thought about how carefully she'd selected her password. "It's a complicated one using lower and uppercase letters, numbers, and symbols."

"Good." Landon nodded. "They're probably fine."

"Unless Gregory gives them up." She heard the anxious note in her voice.

Landon gritted his teeth and didn't respond. What could he say? For now, he had to concentrate on keeping Tori safe.

In his previous cases, he'd had no problem assuring a witness that she or he would be protected. This time, he had to force himself to tell Tori all would be fine. He didn't like it—he wanted to tell her she needed to get out of town and go far, far away.

People who witnessed crimes by the Jimenez Cartel never lived to testify against them.

Landon's gut twisted. He didn't need to go there mentally. It would only make things harder when it came to reassuring Tori.

He frowned to himself, thinking Tori's parents and her boyfriend, then focused his gaze on the two-lane running through part of the town.

As he drove, he couldn't help but think about Tori's

beauty. He certainly hadn't chosen the appropriate time to find himself attracted to any woman, much less a witness. Not to mention she had a boyfriend.

He attempted to pull his thoughts away from his attraction to Tori while he guided his vehicle onto School Terrace Road.

They passed Bisbee High School and Tori stared at the illuminated school and fields. "It hasn't changed a lot since I went to school there." She glanced at Landon. "Go, Pumas."

He shook his head, a brief smile curving his lips.

They headed up a rise to a shaded street with good entry and exit points and nondescript homes. Landon turned into the driveway of a home mostly hidden behind a line of mature Cyprus trees and pulled up to the detached garage.

Tori looked over the white house with fading forest-green trim and squinted at the low-maintenance landscaping illuminated by his headlights. "Is this the safe house?"

"Yep." He left the engine running. "We'll wait for your guard detail before we go in."

Moments later, the black SUV pulled up next to Landon's vehicle in front of the garage. He kept the engine running and buzzed down his window when Johnson and O'Donnell got out and approached him.

Fair-headed O'Donnell had his game face on, his off-duty mischievousness gone from his light brown eyes. The muscular Irishman's temperament showed up when he needed it. "We'll clear the place." O'Donnell tilted his head in the direction of the house. "Hang tight."

Johnson's shaved head gleamed in the soft glow of a nearby streetlight. The slightly more serious man nodded once to Landon and strode at O'Donnell's side toward the house.

The men kept their weapons concealed but ready as they went inside the single-story ranch-style home and turned on the lights. The agents returned to Landon and Tori a short time later.

O'Donnell walked up to Landon's window. "Clear."

Johnson's dark gaze constantly monitored their surroundings.

Landon buzzed up the window, killed the engine, and looked at Tori. "Wait until I come around to your side and I'll open the door. When you're out, we'll escort you into the house."

Tori gripped her hands in her lap but nodded.

Once Landon had Tori out of the Explorer, the three men surrounded her to walk up to the front door.

Landon's senses remained on full alert as they approached the safe house.

O'Donnell and Johnson had left the door open and the lights on. Landon walked inside, his gaze sweeping the room even though it had been cleared. Tori came in behind him, followed by the agents. Landon locked the door behind them.

The blinds were all closed. Whoever took care of the house furnished it with only the basics. Couch, overstuffed chair, end table, coffee table, a lamp, and a TV. The kitchen would be minimally stocked with canned fruits and vegetables, dried pasta, canned sauce and other easy-to-make food items in the pantry.

Tori took in her surroundings and Landon couldn't read her expression. She glanced at him. "So this is what a safe house looks like."

"It's not much," Landon said. "But no one can get to you here."

She walked around and ran her finger along the dusty TV. "Doesn't look as if it's been used for a while."

"We have several safe houses around the county." Landon walked with Tori toward the kitchen. "I'm not sure when this one was last used."

"I've got TV duty." O'Donnell grinned as he turned on the TV and changed the channel to watch a baseball game. He sat on the couch and put his feet up on the coffee table.

Landon turned to Johnson. "I'll be in the kitchen with

Tori, hunting out something we can fix to eat."

Johnson nodded. "I'll take a look around the house again and make sure everything is locked tight."

When Tori and Landon were in the kitchen, Landon caught her by the shoulders and brought her around to face him. The cop in him wanted to tell her to testify but the man in him wanted to tell her she had the right to refuse.

He paused before telling her, "If you don't want to testify against the cartel, just say the word."

She glanced at him with surprise in her eyes. "Just like that?"

He held her gaze. "Just like that."

She looked away for a long moment, then brought her gaze back to his. "Someone has to pay for killing Miguel and all the other bad things a cartel does. Someone needs to help bring the cartel to justice." She took a deep breath and let it out. "Seems as though that someone is me."

"You're positive?" Landon studied her, drinking in the beautiful woman who faced more danger than she could possibly imagine.

"Yes." She straightened. "It's the right thing to do."

"I'll make dinner." He inclined his head to the kitchen. "You'll probably want to cancel your credit cards and report your driver's license stolen."

"My bank accounts could be cleared out by now." She shook her head, clearly in dismay. "But you won't let me use my phone and I don't have my laptop."

"You can use my tablet to handle anything you need online and use my phone." He rested one hand on the counter. "I'll send one of the other agents to get the tablet out of my vehicle. Will that do?"

"Yes, the tablet should do." She rubbed her palm on her thigh. "Thank you."

Moments later, Johnson had retrieved a case from Landon's SUV and handed it to him. Landon thanked the agent and gave his tablet and phone to Tori to use.

Landon gestured to the table. "Have a seat and take care

of whatever you need to."

She took it from him, sliding into a chair at the kitchen table. "Thank you."

He grabbed bottles of water from the fridge, cracked one open, and handed it to her. "You could probably use one of these."

"I think what I really need is a glass of wine." But she needed the water more than anything. She gave him a small smile before she took a drink. The cool water quenched her thirst. "I should be helping with dinner."

He peeked into the pantry and pulled out a couple of packages of pasta. "You can fix breakfast."

She left the water bottle on the kitchen table. "Deal."

"Spaghetti all right with you? I think there's enough for all four of us." He looked through cabinets as he spoke. He retrieved a stockpot that had seen better days then placed it beside the stovetop.

She slipped out of his shirt and hung it on the back of her chair then took off the ball cap and let it flop on the table beside her. "Spaghetti is more than all right."

As Landon started to make dinner, Tori contacted her bank and credit card companies. She blew out a breath of relief that no unauthorized charges had shown up on her cards and she canceled them. Thank God none of her bank accounts had been emptied. By the time she finished, she'd emptied her bottle of water. She felt drained, the jitteriness gone. It had been a long, horrific day.

She shut off the tablet's screen, set the electronic device aside, and gave Landon his cell phone.

The scene of the man being murdered and the chase played over and over in her mind, no matter how hard she tried to think about other things. Would she ever get over seeing a man shot? She didn't know if she ever would.

While Landon finished up dinner, his phone buzzed. "Agent Walker," he answered.

Tori held her breath, wondering if the call had anything to do with the case.

After a moment, Landon said, "Yes, Officer Berstrom." He listened prior to asking, "No sign of breaking and entering?"

Tori straightened in her seat. Landon could be talking about Gregory.

He listened a little longer before thanking the officer and ending the call.

"You probably guessed the call came from the Tucson Police Department." Landon leaned back against the counter. "No one answered the door at your townhouse when the officers stopped by. They searched around the outside of the premises and found no sign of forced entry."

"That could mean anything." Tori swallowed. "But it's so strange Gregory didn't return my call when I left your number. I am surprised he didn't jump at the chance to talk to me." *And berate me for getting myself into trouble, even though it wasn't my fault,* she thought. For some reason she felt like she should explain. "I left him and he wants me back," she told Landon. "I avoided his calls earlier today, but he did get hold of me once when he called from a number I didn't recognize."

Landon had heated the canned spaghetti sauce while she'd been taking care of her credit cards and bank accounts. A thought slipped through her mind that she'd love to have made homemade pasta and a special sauce for him.

She almost beat her head against the table. She must really be falling over the edge to have thoughts like that at a time such as this. Maybe her mind had grasped onto the thought of something normal in the midst of all the chaos.

He served up four plates of spaghetti and sauce. He gave her one then took plates to the agents in the living room. When he returned, he sat across from her at the table with a plate for himself.

She took a bite and chewed. "It's wonderful." The warm meal was already making her feel better.

He looked at her over his water bottle as she ate. He took a swig then set the bottle down. "It's not gourmet, but it hits the spot."

"Right now it's better than gourmet." She twirled her fork in her spaghetti. "I feel better now."

Landon and Tori ate in silence for a moment. She stared at her plate, seeming lost in her thoughts, while swirling spaghetti around her fork. Even with the worry lines on her forehead and her concerned expression, she had a natural beauty that could never be hidden. Her short black hair shone beneath the kitchen lights. She had looked cute in his shirt, but now that she had it off, he noticed again the full swells of her breasts that would fill his palms. A slice of her flat belly showed beneath her crop top and he thought about the tattoo at the small of her back.

He nearly groaned and reminded himself of all the reasons why thinking about Tori in that way was a bad idea. A really bad idea.

Conversation might get her mind off what had clearly been a traumatic day for her. And it would get his mind off her body.

"Where did you learn to run?" he asked.

She blinked at him as if drawing herself back to reality. "I ran track in high school, mostly distance. I still run regularly, but it's mostly flat, nothing like Bisbee's hills."

Her gaze clouded and he figured she was probably thinking of *why* she'd been running. His might have been an inappropriate question because it had probably brought up the memory. He changed the subject. "What do you do for a living?"

She looked up from her spaghetti. "I teach, compose, play clarinet with the Tucson Symphony, and bass clarinet in a woodwind ensemble. I have the summer off and I'd planned to thoroughly enjoy the break." She raised the fork with the spaghetti wrapped around it. "I sure didn't plan to spend it this way."

"You're a busy lady." He watched her chew then swallow the pasta. "Where did you go to school?"

Before answering, she patted her mouth with a paper towel he'd folded into a square to use as a napkin. "My B.M. in jazz performance and my M.M. in clarinet performance were from Arizona State." She brushed a stray hair away from her face. "Indiana University is where I received my D.M. in woodwind pedagogy with a history minor and a higher education administration minor."

The corner of his mouth tipped. "So I should be calling you Dr. Cox."

She waved him away with a smile. "Don't you dare."

He took a bite of spaghetti, chewed, and swallowed. "I saw your tattoo. Not something I would expect to see on a doctor."

"*Klarinette* is the German spelling." She shrugged. "When I had the tat done in college, it was in vogue to tattoo the name of your instrument with the original spelling from the country that supposedly invented it. I wanted a tattoo, so that's what I did." She set her fork on her plate. "What about you?"

He gave her a little smile. "No tats."

She returned his smile. "I meant your education and your career."

"My B.S. in criminal justice is from the University of Arizona." He twirled his fork in his spaghetti. "I worked for the DEA prior to DHS and ICE."

She studied him. "You must have an exciting job."

He turned over her statement in his thoughts. "You could say there are very few dull moments." He wanted the attention off himself and on her. "Do you have family other than your parents?"

"Cousins, aunts, and uncles." She played with her fork and pasta. "They all live in other states and have big families with lots of children, unlike my parents and me."

"No brothers or sisters, I take it?" Landon asked.

"Only one brother." Tori's face fell. "Brian was addicted to crack. Two years ago, a law enforcement agent killed him during a raid at a house where he bought drugs." She met

Landon's gaze and looked as if she struggled to hold back tears. "Ironically, a DHS agent saved me. He was killed by one."

Landon went still. *No, it can't be.* His thoughts churned over the night he and his team had raided a crack house. Ballistics had matched his gun to the bullet that had killed a drug dealer. One who worked for the Jimenez Cartel.

A small-time drug dealer named Brian Cox.

Shit.

He clenched his jaw. With what she'd been through today, Tori was fragile. He didn't think it would help anything if he told her he'd been the one who had killed her brother.

God damn it.

He'd explain what had happened to her another time. Or maybe they'd part company and he'd never have to tell her at all.

He cleared his throat. "I'm sorry you lost someone close to you."

She touched the corners of her eyes with her napkin. "We were close before he got strung-out on crack. His addiction to the drug and the lifestyle broke my mom's heart, not to mention mine."

She sighed, then continued. "A couple of times he went into rehab and I'd get my brother back. I'm sure you've heard stories like that before." A tear rolled down her cheek and she wiped it away with the napkin. "Then I'd lose him all over again. Now there's no chance of getting him back at all."

Landon said nothing and just let her talk.

"The DHS agents who talked with my parents said he dealt drugs for the Jimenez Cartel. We couldn't believe it." Tori's face looked strained. "I researched that organization on the Internet. I still have a hard time believing Brian would have anything to do with a cartel. Ever." A wash of anger made her features tighten. "Those bastards should pay for destroying people's lives."

Landon knew Brian had dealt drugs for the Jimenez

Cartel. Landon didn't mention the same cartel was likely responsible for Miguel's death. He didn't want to do anything that might influence her when she studied photos tomorrow.

Tori looked as if she attempted to compose herself. "So what about you? Any family around? Other than your grandmother?"

"I don't have a lot of relatives." He was grateful for each of the members of his family he did have. "In my immediate family, I have three sisters who are scattered around the state and my parents still live on the ranch where we grew up."

"Oldest or youngest?" she asked.

He swallowed the last of his water. "I'm the oldest."

Tori had a cute, quirky smile when he could turn her thoughts away from the horror of the day. "So you spent your time championing your sisters."

He thought about all the guys he'd chased off that his sisters hadn't even known about. "It took some work."

Tori rested her elbow on the table, her chin in her hand. It was as though her thoughts had carried her far away. "Brian was two years older than me. While we were growing up, I idolized him. Everything he did, I wanted to do too." She sighed and returned her gaze to Landon's. "It crushed me when he got into drugs and fell in with the wrong people. Watching him self-destruct caused my parents and me a lot of pain. I always had hope he'd come back to us."

She pushed her fingers through her hair. "You grew up in the valley?" she asked. "Did you go to Valley Union High School in Elfrida, or Bisbee High?"

"Valley Union." He leaned back in his chair. "All of thirty kids in my graduating class."

"I didn't realize VUHS had so few students." She seemed surprised. "BHS isn't quite as small, but we only had a hundred-sixty students in my graduating class."

It turned out they were only a year apart in age, but likely would never have run into each other considering the geographical distance between their schools.

As they talked, Landon felt an attraction to Tori so deep it shook him down to his toes. He found himself wanting to run his hands over her soft skin, brush her silky hair away from her cheek, and kiss his way from her ear to the hollow of her throat. He hadn't felt this kind of attraction to a woman since—

A pang of guilt stabbed him in the gut like a hot iron rod. He swallowed and reined in his thoughts. Even though Stacy had been gone for over a year, he'd had no intention of looking at another woman. Not to mention he needed to protect Tori, not think of all the ways he'd enjoy peeling off her clothes.

He rubbed the bridge of his nose with his thumb and forefinger, trying to get his head on straight.

"You're tired." Tori's soft voice brought his attention back to her. "I think it's bedtime for both of us."

"I'll show you to your room." He got up from his chair.

Tori stood. "First, I'll help you clean up."

He almost told her he'd take care of it, but she had a determined expression that told him she wouldn't listen. It didn't take long to put away the leftovers and clean the few dishes and stockpot.

When they were finished, he gestured toward the hall leading to the bedrooms. "There should be new toothbrushes and toothpaste in the bathroom along with clean washcloths and towels."

He gestured to the first door on the right. "This will be your room. You'll need to keep the door open." When she raised her eyebrows, he went on, "It's one of the rules we have when you're in protective custody."

She looked over the room's simple furnishings, including the full bed in the center, before she glanced at him. "Thank you for everything."

"Not a problem." He stepped away as she walked into the room. "I'll be right back."

In a few moments, he returned with a clean extra T-shirt

he'd kept in his Explorer and now gave it to her.

Just as he backed up to leave, she raised herself on her toes and pressed her lips to his cheek, giving him a chaste kiss. "Thank you." She offered a tired smile and pushed the door behind him, leaving it open by a couple of inches.

Landon stood in the hallway for a moment, his thoughts wrapped around Tori.

With a frustrated growl, he turned and headed toward the bedroom he'd be taking in between shifts with O'Donnell and Johnson.

It had been so long since he'd been with a woman. It had to be why he found himself wanting Tori so damned badly.

His mind rejected the thought almost at once. Her spirit and intelligence attracted him even more than her body did.

He heaved out a heavy breath as he reached the master bedroom. He had to be exceptionally tired because he thought of Tori lying and waiting for him on his bed when he looked at it.

Shit. He left the door partially open before going into his bedroom's attached bathroom and stripping off his clothing. He needed a cold shower, for a much different reason than the cold shower he'd taken that morning.

Chapter Six

Gregory Smith tightened his grip on the handle of his briefcase as he strode up the sidewalk past two-story town houses toward the one he shared with Tori. The streetlights illuminated the sidewalk as well as the manicured lawns and landscaping.

What a fucked-up day. He'd been late to work at the law office and had almost missed an important client. Finally getting a free moment, he'd taken his lunch break at home late in the afternoon because he'd had to pick up a client's file he'd forgotten there.

Tori had left him—he'd discovered the note she had placed on the table in the kitchen. He'd gone through their home to find she'd packed up her toiletries and some of her clothes. Her laptop and her favorite clarinet were at the front door, though, so he knew she'd be back. He'd tried calling her cell phone but she hadn't answered.

Once he'd returned to his office, on the opposite side of Tucson from where he and Tori lived, he'd realized in his haste he'd left his damned cell phone at the town house. He'd sent his intern, Sara, to pick it up, but she had never returned to the office. He'd told Sara where he kept the key hidden and she should have been back within an hour. Two hours had passed since then. Maybe she'd had something come up, but she would have called in. Hell, he fucked the twenty-year-old on a regular basis and she had a serious case of hero-worship that didn't hurt his ego one bit.

The tracker he'd put on Tori's phone indicated she had gone to Bisbee. He fisted one hand, thinking of her running home to Mommy and Daddy. While at work, he'd used one of the office phones to call Tori and had reached her, only to have her hang up on him. He'd tried calling back but his calls had gone straight to voicemail.

Gregory ground his teeth as he reached the front door of the town house and his thoughts remained on Tori. Who the hell did she think she was? He'd go get her and drag her ass back to Tucson where she belonged. He'd been to her parents' home once and he could probably find the house again. Tori's worthless drunk of a father and her bitch of a mother had barely talked to him. Josie had just watched him with assessing eyes that made him want to snarl at her. He'd had to fight to maintain control and play the loving boyfriend.

No doubt about it, he did love Tori. He expected her to do as he said and to be where he expected her to be. She belonged to *him*. No one else could touch her.

His love for Tori bordered on obsession. Hell, it *was* obsession. Maybe he shouldn't be fucking his intern, but he had extraordinary needs and Tori couldn't give him *everything* he needed. As long as she knew her place was with him, he had no complaints.

Clenching his teeth, he dug in his pocket for his keys. They jangled as he pulled them out then slipped from his hand and hit the welcome mat on the doorstep. Cursing beneath his breath, he crouched and scooped them up. He hesitated in the crouch for a moment then checked beneath one of the flowerpots near the mat. No key. Sara must have been here, so where the hell had she gone? Maybe they'd passed each other on his drive home. Then why hadn't she put the key back?

With a frown he straightened, got to his feet, and tried the knob without attempting to disengage the bolt or unlock it first. It turned easily in his hand and the door swung open.

What the hell?

Tori always left the light in the foyer on, but now all remained dark. She had a thing about coming home to an entirely dark house. It made her uneasy. He flipped on the light by the door then shut it behind him, setting his briefcase next to her clarinet case and briefcase.

He stuffed his keys back into his pocket and started undoing his tie when he realized a lump was lying at the foot of the stairs.

He dropped his hands to his sides. His stomach churned.

A woman's body, limbs at unnatural angles, white-blonde hair covering her face.

"Sara?" His voice shook as he hurried toward her. Had she fallen down the stairs?

He pushed her hair away from her face. He reeled at the sight of her purple face and her eyes widened with terror. In his horror he noticed her neck and the dark band around it—she'd been strangled.

Murdered. Sara had been murdered.

"Oh, God." His hands shook and he heard his cell phone, the ring coming from the kitchen where he must have left the phone.

He needed to call nine-one-one.

What if the killer hadn't left?

Could he take the chance of going into the kitchen to get to his phone? No, he had to get out of the town house. He'd go to a neighbor's and use their phone.

He pushed himself to his feet and started to turn when he heard a click and felt something cold pressed against the back of his head.

"Where do you think you're going?" came a hard voice with a Hispanic accent.

"You can have everything you want." Gregory spoke in a rush. "I have money in a safe. You can have it. Just let me go."

"A safe. I like the sound of that." The amused voice moved close to his ear. "But we have more important things to discuss."

"What?" Confusion clouded Gregory's mind.

With the barrel of the gun still against Gregory's head, a man stepped into Gregory's line of sight. The man's slender and wiry build made him look as if he could spring into action at any moment. His slim mustache twitched as though he was holding back a smile.

In the background, Gregory's phone rang again.

"Where is Tori Cox?" the man asked.

"Tori?" Gregory couldn't pull his thoughts together. "She's not here. Why do you want her?"

"My reasons are not important to you," the man snarled. "If you want to live, you will tell me where she is."

Gregory realized two things. First, this man would kill him no matter what he'd said. Second, the man planned to kill Tori. Gregory had no idea what kind of trouble she had gotten herself into, but apparently it was bad. Real bad.

Despite any problems they'd had, Gregory loved Tori. He refused to give up anything. Besides, if he did, this man would immediately kill him.

"I'm not sure where Tori is," Gregory's voice shook. "She took off this morning."

"I can tell you she is in Bisbee." The man smirked. "I just need an address."

How did the bastard know? Gregory swallowed. "I don't have an address for anyone in Bisbee."

The man kept the barrel of his gun against Gregory's head. He looked toward the living room and said something in Spanish. Gregory's blood went cold when a second man walked out of the darkened room. The blond man had a brutal sheen to him, his eyes cold and merciless.

"That is John." The first man gestured to the other man. "I am Pablo. You and I are going to become very familiar with each other."

Gregory said nothing. Sweat trickled down his spine, sweat soaking his armpits beneath his suit jacket.

"We must leave this place." Pablo gave a nod in the direction of the kitchen as Gregory's phone rang. "Bring your phone so we can use it to call *Señorita* Tori."

Gregory swallowed, his throat so dry it hurt. If he stalled, maybe the police would come in time.

"Get the phone," Pablo told John.

John said nothing but headed toward the kitchen.

Pablo turned to Gregory. "Give me your keys."

Hands shaking, Gregory reached into his pocket and pulled out his keys then handed them to Pablo.

When John returned, he gave the phone to Pablo who pocketed it.

Pablo looked at Gregory then nodded to Sara's body. "Pick her up. You will carry her to your car and we will put her in the trunk."

Gregory knelt and scooped up Sara's petite form and held her. He dry-heaved when he felt her cold body. Bile rose in his throat. He turned his head to the side and spewed vomit on the floor. He coughed and spit the acidic remnants out of his mouth but could still taste it.

A boot kicked him low in the back and he cried out, almost dropping Sara's body. He wiped his mouth on his upper arm before standing, cradling her to his chest.

Pablo inclined his head in the direction of the door and Gregory started toward it.

John reached the door first and pulled it open. The warm summer night washed over Gregory and he wanted to cry out for help, but he felt the press of the barrel against his spine. Maybe someone would see them and call the police.

They passed no one on the way to the lot where Gregory always parked his Audi. Pablo ordered Gregory to go to his car and he obeyed.

When they reached the Audi, Pablo used the key fob to open the doors and pop the trunk. Gregory's heart and gut were sinking fast as he laid Sara's body inside. Pablo slammed the lid closed.

"Drive." Pablo gave the order to Gregory, who slid behind the wheel on the driver's side. John pointed a handgun at Gregory while Pablo got in on the passenger side. After Pablo slipped in, he handed the keys to Gregory. Pablo pointed his gun at Gregory again while John left and climbed into a dark vehicle Gregory hadn't noticed before.

Gregory's mind raced, trying to think of some way he could get out of this alive and not give these bastards Tori's parents' address. She belonged to him and no one else could touch her. His blood rushed through his veins like wildfire and his heart beat hard enough to explode out of his chest. Maybe having his heart give out would be for the best, because one way or another he would die if he didn't think of something.

Pablo pressed his gun against Gregory's temple. "I said, drive."

Gregory started the car, backed it out of its parking spot, and drove.

Chapter Seven

Fog swirled around Tori as she walked up a steep hill. She couldn't see anything around her, but she knew she had to climb. And climb. And climb.

Someone appeared directly in front of her, causing her to stumble back in surprise and almost fall back down the hill. She regained her balance and tried to catch her breath.

A white light glimmered around a woman wearing a white lace mantilla. Tori couldn't see the woman's face, but she seemed somehow familiar.

Tori blinked. She stood in the depths of a church. A sacred place she had not been to in a very long time.

She looked up at the altar and the statue of the Virgin Mary. Blood-red tears rolled from Mary's eyes and Tori felt her great sadness.

The woman in the mantilla turned, catching Tori's attention again. The woman walked toward the red jarred candles in the front of the church and Tori followed. While she watched, the woman lit a candle…next to the one her mother had lit for Brian when he'd died.

Tori's heart pounded and her mouth grew dry. She recognized the woman in the mantilla. Her mother…lighting a candle for Tori.

Her mother was crying.

The statue of Mary cried.

Tears rolled down Tori's cheeks.

"I'm not dead, Mom." Tori tried to say the words but they wouldn't come out. "I'm not dead!"

Her mother turned and walked toward the church entrance. The huge double doors parted and her mother stepped through *the doorway.*

Tori tried to run after her. She walked as if through hip-deep mud and she couldn't get to the doorway fast enough.

When she finally made it outside, her mother had vanished.

The next thing she knew she stood in total and complete darkness. The church had disappeared.

She looked up into the crushing darkness, seeing the black night shrouded the moon and stars. A box surrounded her, all four sides closing in, squeezing the breath from her. Heart nearly stopping from fear, she held her arms out to either side of her to push walls away, but her hands touched nothing but air.

A man stepped toward her from out of the inky black night, startling a cry from her.

She could see the man, yet she didn't know how with no light, only pure darkness.

Her heart started pounding, hard thumps against her ribs as she stared at him. Shadows obscured his vaguely familiar face. Who was he?

Sweat broke out on her skin as she watched the man slowly raise his arm. A flash of something dark on his wrist and a glimpse of gunmetal gray in the overwhelming darkness.

He pointed a gun at her, ripping terror through her. She screamed.

Dear God, she had to get away.

She tried to turn and run, but her shoes were glued to the asphalt. Her leg muscles ached, straining and struggling to pick up one foot then the other. She couldn't move, couldn't save her own life.

Her entire body trembled as the man stepped closer. Then closer yet. His eyes burned red, his teeth white and pointed when he smiled. Horns sprouted from his head, pushing through his dark hair. Short red horns.

The devil. She would die at the hand of the devil himself.

The gun never wavered. The barrel grew bigger. So big she now could see nothing but the opening. A bullet would be fired through the hole. The bullet would slam into her brain and end her life, just like that man in Bisbee.

I'm going to die.

The devil's image wavered and he began to fade.

"*You will never get away from me.*" The devil's icy voice sent chills through her. *Even as he disappeared, like wisps of smoke through a keyhole, she still heard him clearly.* "*I will find you and you will die.*"

Tori woke and let loose a scream. She clamped one hand over her mouth as she sat up in bed. Perspiration coated her skin while her other fist gripped the damp sheets. Every breath came short and fast as if she'd been running up that hill in Bisbee again.

The sheets were twisted from tossing and turning. Had she dreamed of the devil all night long?

She wrapped her arms around her bent knees and pressed her face against them, her eyes shut. But she couldn't shut out the images of the dream, no matter how she tried.

The truth kept going through her mind, *the truth.*

"The truth," she mumbled. "The truth."

"Tori?" A man's voice came from far away, echoing in her head. She recognized the voice from somewhere and somehow she knew not to be afraid.

The bed dipped beside her. "Are you all right?"

She kept her face hard to her knees and tried to breathe as a strong arm wrapped around her shoulders.

"You had a nightmare," the man's voice soothed her. "You had a nightmare. I'm right here with you."

Slowly she worked to process where she was, what had happened to her and the identity of the man with her now.

It gradually came to her—she sat in bed in a safe house and Special Agent Landon Walker had saved her life. Two other agents were there as well, O'Donnell and Johnson.

Landon had wrapped his arm around her shoulders. He smelled good and somehow his scent, his touch, his presence and his low voice calmed her.

"You're all right, honey." He squeezed her with his arm. "You're all right."

Her skin prickled and she felt sticky from sweat, her hair damp from it. She didn't look at him, raising her head and trying to breathe slowly, in and out. In. Out. In. Out.

When she felt a little more composed, she turned to look at him. "Thank you."

His eyes focused on hers as his thumb stroked her shoulder while he still held her. "You want me to stay a little longer?"

"I'll be fine." She shook her head. "I had a dream. A stupid nightmare."

"It's not stupid." He patted her shoulders. "After the day you had, I'm not surprised you had a nightmare."

"Do you have them?" Why did she even ask him the question?

For a moment he didn't say anything, but then he gave a nod. "I have a recurring nightmare about...something bad that happened."

"I'm sorry." She felt as if she'd touched a spot she shouldn't have, as though she'd asked him something far too personal.

"Don't be." He rubbed her shoulder with his palm. "Are you going to be okay now?"

"Yes." She took another deep breath and slowly let it out. She didn't feel as sweaty but her hair was still damp. "I think I can go back to sleep now."

He moved his arm from around her shoulders. "If you need me, just call."

"Thank you." She watched as he left the bedroom.

He looked over his shoulder one last time before stepping out and leaving the door ajar so a slice of light cut across the floor in the room.

She faced the light as she slid back down and rested her head on her pillow. With the image of the nightmare devil still in her mind, would she ever be able to fall asleep again?

* * * *

Tori wandered out of the bedroom, unable to find Landon. O'Donnell lay on the couch in the living room and Johnson sat at the kitchen table. She said good morning to each of them.

The nightmare hadn't returned, but she still felt remnants of it in the back of her consciousness.

She'd just taken a shower and put on the same clothes she'd worn yesterday since she didn't have anything else with her. She couldn't very well walk around in her panties and the T-shirt Landon had loaned her last night.

A chill traveled through her, goosebumps rising on her skin while her thoughts turned to yesterday and seeing Mateo, or rather Miguel, murdered.

Scenes flashed through her mind. The man against the car — Miguel. Two men with their guns trained on Miguel. A third man shooting him. Miguel's body slumping to the ground, lifeless.

She could almost feel the burn in her lungs and muscles from how she'd run from the men. If she hadn't run regularly to keep in shape and didn't know the area so well, the men would have caught her. Killed her.

Landon had saved her life.

Everything looked different in the light of day, even though the blinds were closed. The kitchen had a window over the sink she hadn't noticed last night.

After seeing someone murdered, it seemed too bright today. But the sun rose and the sun went down, no matter who lived and who died.

Trying to get her mind off the trauma she'd been through, she put her hands on her hips and looked around the neat kitchen. This house needed some serious dusting.

After Johnson had said good morning, he'd gone back to reading on a tablet and she wondered if he was reading an eBook or e-news.

What could she fix for breakfast? She peered inside the pantry and frowned. Nothing she could use to make anything from scratch. She found pancake mix. No flour or baking powder to make homemade pancakes. Someone needed to go shopping.

She settled on the pancake mix. She found a plastic bottle of syrup along with a box of instant mashed potatoes in the pantry. The almost-empty freezer yielded nothing but a bag of crushed ice and a package of peas.

Several minutes later, potato patties sizzled in a frying pan, the syrup heating in a small pot on a burner, and she was pouring pancake batter onto a griddle. Soon she had a rhythm going and she hummed to herself, trying not to think about yesterday and the horrors she faced.

And the dream. The nightmare. She had a hell of a time not thinking about it, the oppressive darkness and the man pointing his gun at her.

The devil.

"I doubt this kitchen has ever smelled this good," came Landon's voice from behind her.

Tori started and looked over her shoulder at him. With his intense expression and the power that radiated from him, he appeared rough and rugged. He was so very sexy in a dark blue T-shirt and faded jeans. She could just about eat him up.

Memories of last night and how he'd held her after her nightmare made her feel warm inside.

"Hi," she managed to get out, realizing she realized she'd been looking him over for far too long.

She turned back to her task and flipped a pancake so that the browned side was up. "You need to do some serious grocery shopping."

He leaned against a counter and folded his arms across his chest, causing his muscular arms to look even more defined. "How did you sleep the rest of the night?"

A shiver trailed her spine as she remembered the nightmare. She shrugged, not wanting him to know just how shaken she still was. "I slept fine." She hadn't dreamed about the devil again, but she'd tossed and turned.

He studied her in his intense way, as if he thought she

72

wasn't being truthful.

"This is the last pancake and then breakfast is ready." She forced a smile.

Landon pushed away from the counter and got out the dishes and silverware and Tori took the food off the heat and put it all onto plates to serve. She and Landon set the plates of potato patties and pancakes on the counter, along with the pot of heated syrup on a hot pad. Landon took O'Donnell a plate after giving one to Johnson.

She was surprised at how hungry she was considering everything that had happened. It had all started with Gregory and her need to flee Tucson. The memory of what he'd done the night before she'd taken off for Bisbee left her skin ice-cold. What he'd done to her had been horrible and inexcusable.

When they'd finished breakfast, Tori and the men went into the living room, preparing to leave for the DHS's ICE office.

All she had to her name at this moment were the clothes she'd been wearing when the whole mess had started. She wished for clean clothes and some toiletries before they left, but wishing didn't make it so. Landon loaned her his overshirt and his ball cap again.

The moment Tori and the men stepped outside the house, wind almost knocked off the hat and a few strands of hair got loose. She pulled the hat down tighter and brushed the strands away with her fingers.

She walked at Landon's side toward the charcoal-gray SUV he'd driven last night. She hadn't been able to see it well in the dark. The newer model Ford Explorer had sleek, modern lines, yet clearly served as a utility vehicle. He opened the passenger side and she stepped up on the running board as he took her hand and helped her up into the vehicle.

Landon's phone vibrated in its holster and he dragged his attention from Tori. He started the vehicle and pulled out his phone to see his mother's number on the screen.

"Just a moment." He held up his finger to Tori before taking the call. "Hi, Mom."

"You haven't called in two weeks." Even as Valerie Walker admonished him, she had a smile in her voice. "Two weeks is too long."

"You're right." Landon sighed. "You know how work is."

"I do know." She spoke softly. "But you still need to take care of you. Are you coming to Sunday dinner?"

He thought about everything happening. "I do want to, Mom. But I've got a case that will probably keep me away this weekend."

She sounded disappointed. "I'll set the table for you, just in case."

"Thanks, Mom." He paused. "I have a favor to ask."

"Of course." Her disappointment seemed to vanish. "Anything for my only son."

He told her he needed women's clothing, preferably functional jeans and tops, as well as toiletries. He couldn't give her any details, except that the agency had no available agents at this time to purchase the needed items. Then he turned and asked Tori for her sizes.

Tori shook her head. "I don't have access to my bank accounts or my credit cards."

"Don't worry about it." Landon spoke firmly. "You can pay me back once you can. For now, let's get you what you need."

She clenched her hands together, clearly hating the fact she had to borrow money, but gave her sizes to him. She also told him what toiletries she needed when he asked.

"I'll head to town now." His mom sounded pleased. "You know how I love to shop."

"Yes, Mom, I know." The corner of Landon's mouth curved. He arranged a time to meet her in the evening. At least asking his mom to do this would give him an excuse to see her while on the job.

It took half an hour to drive to the agency office. Douglas was right on the Mexican border, adjacent to Agua Prieta, located on the Mexico side. Along the way, from Bisbee to Douglas, Tori saw Border Patrol vehicles everywhere she looked.

She'd grown up in Bisbee but hadn't been to Douglas too often. A lot of people didn't feel safe enough to drive across the border due to drug trafficking and the presence of the cartels.

Josie, her mother, had traveled to Arizona from Mexico City as a teen and had eventually become a U.S. citizen. These days she traveled less and less to the country of her birth.

When she'd been young, Tori's parents had taken her across the border several times. She remembered the colorful displays of wares sold by stores and street vendors. Some of the things she'd liked to look at the most had been small statues made of glass and marble, colorful clay pots, rugs, serapes, and sombreros.

Her favorite part of going across the border had been the ice cream carts with *paletas*, Mexican frozen treats. She'd loved the coconut *paletas* more than anything, although the strawberry ice cream bars were good too. Now the same brand was sold in some stores in the States, but standing and eating the *paletas* on a street in Mexico couldn't be beat.

Landon parked in front of a nondescript office building and they climbed out. It surprised her how she'd already come to expect him to open her door and assist her in stepping down from the vehicle. Of course she didn't need the help, but the gentlemanly gesture touched her.

His gaze held hers for a long moment. His eyes were close to the color of peridot, a little darker than the gemstone's natural shade of green. Her lips parted as she realized he hadn't let go of her hand. Warmth traveled between them and she bit the inside of her lip.

He released her and gestured toward the building. "Come on in."

She fell into step beside him. On the front of the building, *Department of Homeland Security* appeared in silver lettering. Under that was *U.S. Immigration and Customs Enforcement.*

Landon held the glass door open for her and she walked into the lobby. He let the door fall shut behind them, touched her elbow, and indicated down a hallway.

She walked beside him but moved to the side when a man approached them.

"You're late." The man jerked his head toward an open door. "The briefing is about to start."

Landon gave a nod toward Tori. "Dylan, this is Tori Cox. She witnessed Miguel's murder last night."

At the words, Tori shuddered. She was a murder witness.

Landon turned to her. "Tori, this is Special Agent Dylan Curtis."

Dylan held out his hand and Tori took it. She liked his grasp, warm and firm. "Thanks for coming forward, Tori."

She gripped his hand in return. "It's nice to meet you, Special Agent Curtis."

"My pleasure." Dylan released her hand and spoke to Landon. "You need to get your ass in here."

Landon dragged his hand down his face. "I'll get Tori settled and be right in."

Dylan nodded to Tori before he went through the doorway. Landon escorted Tori into a room with a desk and three chairs, and mirrored glass in one wall.

She looked at him. "Is this an interrogation room?"

He nodded. "I'll be back in fifteen minutes or so."

"Okay." She sat in the chair across the table from the other two chairs arranged side by side. "I'm not going anywhere."

He put his hand over hers and squeezed prior to turning and leaving the room, closing the door behind him.

Landon paused as he left Tori in the room alone, then headed back down the hallway and entered the large briefing room.

Sofia Aguilar, the Resident Agent in Charge, sat at the head of the room. The RAC almost always had a hard cast to her features, but today she looked fiercer than normal. She'd pulled her dark hair away from her face and twisted it in a knot at the base of her neck. Her dark eyes were sharp as ever.

Landon took a seat when Aguilar began speaking. "As most of you know, someone executed one of our own in Bisbee last night. Miguel Garcia."

The agents in the room erupted with expletives.

Landon clenched his hands into fists as anger burned hot and bright inside him.

Aguilar held up her hand, silencing the agents. "We believe the Jimenez Cartel is responsible. Miguel worked deep undercover within the cartel." She nodded to Landon. "Agent Walker can give more details as he was at the scene last night."

Landon spelled out what happened. "A witness is here now. Knowing it's the Jimenez Cartel will narrow the search considerably when we show her photographs of some of the key players."

Aguilar braced one hand on her hip, which pushed aside her blazer and exposed her shield and her Glock. "Get with her and once she's finished, make sure she's kept in protective custody."

Landon nodded. "We'll return her to the safe house as soon as we're finished."

"How the hell did this go down?" Dylan's forehead wrinkled as he asked the question. "Did he blow his cover, or did he just piss off Jimenez?"

"That's what we need to find out." Aguilar snapped each syllable, expressing without words how angry she was over Miguel's death. She barked out orders before excusing everyone.

Landon's skin heated and he had the feeling he would explode under the right conditions. Yes, he would personally take down the man responsible for killing Miguel.

With renewed fury burning in his veins, Landon headed back to the room where Tori waited.

Chapter Eight

Landon stood in the doorway and looked at Tori. For some reason, he hated putting her through this whole procedure more than he usually did with a witness. Maybe it had something to do with the nightmare last night. Hearing Tori say 'the truth' when she'd woken from her nightmare had sent a chill through him. The thought that it could have something to do with his involvement in her brother's death didn't make sense.

"Come on out here, Tori." He inclined his head in the direction of the hallway. "I'm going to have you study some photos."

She pushed back her chair and followed him to another room. Six monitors covered one wall. She settled into a chair at a conference table in front of the flat-screens.

Landon sat beside her, a tablet in his hands. He set the tablet on the table and turned to her. "Let's start with the blond man you described." Landon used the tablet to bring up six images of men, one on each of the six monitors in front of her.

"That's him." Tori pointed at the bottom middle screen and looked to Landon. "He helped another man force Miguel down onto his knees before the other man murdered him."

Landon's jaw tightened and his body hardened. She'd identified John Graves, a key man in the Jimenez Cartel. No one else in the cartel had white-blond hair that Landon knew of, the reason why he'd included Graves in the lineup.

He stared back down at the tablet and in a moment the images of six other men were on the wall monitors, one image per screen. "Do any of these men look familiar?"

She shook her head. "No."

He scrolled through more images. One after another flashed on the screens and she shook her head as they passed by.

After a while, she blinked rapidly. "All of the pictures are starting to blur. Can you slow down?"

He stopped the images from moving across the screens for a moment. "No problem."

When he started again, she continued to watch as surveillance photos and mug shots went by, one after another.

"Stop." She pointed at one of the surveillance photos. "The man on the left screen. He was the other man who held down Miguel."

Tori had just identified Pablo Perez, another key player. Landon tried to keep his expression neutral. "You're sure?"

"Yes." She nodded. "I'm absolutely positive. He and the blond man chased me." Tori seemed so tightly wound, as if she might spring apart.

"We believe we're dealing with the Jimenez Cartel," Landon began and her eyes widened.

"Jimenez Cartel?" She clenched her hands into fists on the tabletop. "The same cartel my brother had dealings with before the agent killed him in the raid."

A pained feeling shot through Landon. He squeezed her shoulder, hoping to make her feel at least a little safer. "It's going to be all right."

She hesitated then nodded.

Landon narrowed his eyebrows. "What can you tell me about the man who shot Miguel?"

"I remember he wore a suit and had dark hair." She put her hand to her forehead and frowned. "I think he was five ten or five eleven." Her frown deepened. "Miguel called him something, but I can't remember the name."

"Let's go through additional photos." Landon touched his tablet and more faces started to scroll by on the screens.

She shook her head at the images parading before her. "I don't recognize any of them."

Landon studied her. She looked exhausted and like she needed a break.

Tori's head ached as her thoughts churned over and over what she had seen and the knowledge the cartel wanted her dead. The Jimenez Cartel. The same horrible people her brother had somehow been involved with.

Her thoughts turned back to her family and her ex-boyfriend. "My parents. Gregory." She scratched her head. "I don't know what to do. I'm afraid for them."

Landon pulled out his phone and handed it to her. "Why don't you try him at work?"

"Oh. Of course." She thought about it a moment then remembered Gregory's direct line and dialed it. Her call went straight to his voicemail. She tried not to get more freaked out and left as calm a message as she could, telling him to call her, and leaving Landon's number. Then she dialed the main office number and asked for Gregory when Laura, the receptionist, answered.

"He hasn't been in today, Tori." Laura sounded irritated. "He missed his appointments and he was supposed to be in court at ten. His intern hasn't shown up either."

Tori's throat felt crowded. Something desperately wrong had happened. "I'd like to leave a message to call me if he comes in later."

"Yes, of course." When Tori left messages, Laura always came across as sarcastic and put out. She clearly didn't like her job.

Tori thanked her and cut the call. When she handed Landon his phone, she saw concern in his gaze. She repeated what she'd been told.

"What are we going to do?" she asked him.

Landon raised his phone. "I'll call the Tucson Police Department again and file a missing person report. Usually the police wouldn't consider him missing yet. But the cartel's involvement changes that."

She listened to him file the report then end the call.

"There's nothing you can do right now." He appeared to be trying to give her the news in a way that wouldn't upset her. "Our main concern is keeping you safe. We have agents watching your parents' house and the Tucson Police Department is looking for your boyfriend."

For a moment, silence hung heavily between them as he let her come to terms with what he'd said.

"What else do you need from me?" She tried to sound less shaky than she felt.

"This is a witness statement." He pulled up a form on the center screen and started typing. "Let's go over all of it again and see if you can remember anything else."

Feeling as if everything had become surreal, Tori once again began giving her account of what had happened.

When she finished, he glanced across at her, his expression serious. "Is there anything else you can remember?"

She shook her head. "Not that I can recall." She frowned and scrunched her nose as she thought about it. "It seems like there's something, other than the name, that I'm missing. I just can't remember."

"Do you think revisiting the site would help?" Landon asked.

"I don't know." She pictured the scene. "Maybe."

"Let's go." Landon pushed back his chair and Tori did the same. He cleared the monitors before they walked out of the door.

The ride to Bisbee from the DHS's ICE office didn't take long. Landon worked over details in his mind and Tori seemed to be lost in her own thoughts. Tori's guard detail followed in an SUV behind them.

Landon's mind turned to the scene last night. He remembered the unrecognizable face and his blood boiled. *Sonofabitch.* They had to get these bastards.

He thought about Miguel's wife and two kids and

82

gripped the steering wheel tighter. Landon needed to pay his respects to Jane. The memorial service would no doubt be scheduled for the following week.

When they got to the site, the SUV with Tori's guard detail stopped beside them. Landon trusted the two agents assigned to protect Tori, but he couldn't help but feel he needed to be there for her too. He'd never felt that way with any witness and he shouldn't be feeling this way with Tori.

He had difficulty handling even the thought of having her take the witness stand. He didn't like the idea of putting her in even more danger.

He parked the SUV and turned to Tori. "Stay here."

To disguise her appearance, she wore one of his other ball caps and a blue overshirt he kept in his truck. However, he wouldn't take any chances by letting her out of the Explorer.

When Landon climbed out of the vehicle, he slowly surveyed the scene.

Both Johnson and O'Donnell looked around, attempting to secure the area.

Agent O'Donnell glanced at Landon. "It's too open. Too many places a sniper could be hiding."

"We'll make this quick." Landon opened the passenger door and met Tori's gaze. "Stay in the SUV and try to remember everything you can."

She looked from the location of the scene back to him. "I think I'll remember more if I get out."

He shook his head. "Too dangerous. You need to stay right here in your seat."

The play of the muscles in her throat betrayed her tension and discomfort. "Of course."

She stared at the taped-off area and looked as if she might gag at the memory of what she'd seen. Landon wasn't surprised. She'd seen a man's face get blown off. That would be traumatic for anyone who didn't deal with violent death on a regular basis.

"I just remembered. I don't know why I didn't think of it before." Tori shook her head. "The suit the man wore was expensive, probably tailored just for him." Her forehead wrinkled in concentration. "In my career I see a lot of men in pricey suits and his definitely cost a pretty penny."

That could narrow the field a bit, Landon thought. *Only those high up the food chain can afford expensive suits. Very high up.*

"Do you remember anything else?" Landon asked.

She frowned. "Miguel called him by something unusual... like El...and something starting with a P, I think. It's on the tip of my tongue." Her eyes widened. "He called him *El Puño. The Fist.*"

Landon's pulse quickened. Expensive suit and called *El Puño*. It could only mean one person. "I'm going to have you look over more mug shots."

He went around to the driver's side and climbed in before he removed his tablet from inside the center console and set it in his lap. He took a flash drive and inserted it into a USB port on the tablet and opened a file on the drive. The file held photographs of every key member who had been identified in the Jimenez Cartel. He touched the tablet and brought up six images of leading cartel players.

Tori pointed to a man's image from one of the surveillance photos. She looked as if she would scream when she saw it. "That's him. He killed Miguel."

"You're certain?" Landon asked.

"Absolutely." She nodded. "No doubt in my mind."

"Alejandro Jimenez, also known as *El Puño*."

"Yes." She nodded again, vigorously this time. "Yes."

"The son of the Jimenez Cartel drug lord." Landon hadn't intended to say the words out loud. *Shit.*

"The drug lord's son?" A wave of horror crossed Tori's face.

Landon reached out and put his hand over hers. He could feel it shaking. "You're going to be all right, Tori. We'll make sure of it."

She buried her face in her hands. When she looked at Landon again, she appeared worn and drained and he wrapped his arms around her.

"Shhh." He held her securely. "It will be all right."

"Could I possibly have witnessed an execution by anyone more dangerous than him?" Her voice sounded strained as she drew away. "I saw the drug lord's *son* commit murder. I'm a witness against an organization so merciless they won't stop until they hunt me down." Her coughed, trying to swallow. "I don't know if I can do this, Landon."

"You can." He put conviction into his tone. "You're a strong woman."

"I don't feel strong." She bit her lower lip before adding, "Not at all."

He remembered her strength last night when he'd told her she didn't have to testify. Everyone had a breaking point and this might be hers.

Chapter Nine

Gregory's toes barely reached the floor as he dangled by metal handcuffs linked over a hook. The two men who had abducted him had fastened the hook to a chain hanging from a beam high overhead in an abandoned South Tucson warehouse. His body slowly turned like a slab of beef dangling in a meat locker.

Nothing would gel in his brain and he had lost touch with reality. Every bit of him hurt, agony his constant companion. In less than thirty minutes, he'd been beaten, his leg shot so the bone had shattered and most of his fingers had been broken one at a time with pliers.

And the sadistic bastards hadn't even asked him a single question since they'd left the townhouse. No matter how he had begged and pleaded, and promised to tell them whatever they wanted, they hadn't listened.

They'd laughed.

Pablo said they wanted to send a message. Gregory knew they'd enjoyed torturing him and hadn't wanted to ruin their fun.

A phone rang. Through swollen eyes, Gregory watched Pablo answer it and heard his sharp responses.

Pablo tossed the phone onto a nearby table and snarled words at Gregory. "My man hasn't gotten anything from the names you gave us earlier, you piece of shit."

He approached Gregory. "This will end if you give me the address." He sounded as if he would be doing Gregory a favor.

If Pablo killed him now, he *would* be doing Gregory a favor. He didn't know how much more of this he could take.

He tried to get the words out but his throat had become raw.

"Give me the address." Pablo's voice grew menacing again.

Gregory tried to swallow, but his throat felt like sandpaper had scraped it bloody. He ran his tongue over his parched and swollen lips and tasted blood.

He finally pushed out a reply. "I'm sure she's at her parents' home in Bisbee. I don't know the address." Gregory spoke in a voice hoarse from screaming in agony with everything these men had done to him since bringing him to the warehouse. "I told you at my house. Their names are Josie and Henry Cox."

"Those names got us nowhere." Pablo scowled. "You must have made them up."

"They don't have a computer." Gregory swallowed. "Her father doesn't trust the Internet. He's a conspiracy nut and believes everyone is out to get them. He's a drunk too."

A side door creaked open and Gregory could see the darkness outside. The blond man called John walked into the warehouse carrying two cases. Gregory could just make out his own briefcase and Tori's laptop case. Clearly John had gone back to the townhouse and retrieved both.

"Your computers." Pablo sounded satisfied as he took one of the briefcases from John. "Maybe now we'll get somewhere."

Gregory closed his eyes. He didn't have the address on his computer, but Tori no doubt had it on her laptop. He knew Tori's password and these men would get it out of him. She had never known, but he had a software program that tracked keystrokes and he'd learned her password.

He'd spied on her and had gone through her laptop several times, making sure she hadn't been cheating on him. He'd reviewed her email regularly and had even managed to break into her phone sometimes when she'd been in the shower. No text messages, no instant messages, and no emails. He'd made sure he knew her location at all times and had even installed a tracker on her phone —

He went still. The tracker he'd put inside her phone. These men could find Tori with it, even if she turned off the phone and took out the battery.

"Do you have anything else to tell me that will help me find Tori?" Pablo asked.

Gregory avoided Pablo's eyes as he thought about the finder application on his laptop and how easy it would be to tell the man about the device in her phone — it would lead the bastard straight to Tori.

Somehow Gregory managed to hold it in. He'd already given too much. Tori might be as good as dead, thanks to the weakness that had brought him to this point.

She deserved it after all these men had done to him, didn't she?

His whole body went slack. He couldn't bear anymore of the agony that brought him so close to passing out. This could all be over if he gave them what they needed.

No. I can't do that to her.

Why not? This wouldn't be happening if she hadn't done something to piss off these men. It was her fault. *She* had left *him.*

"What is the password?" Pablo asked and Gregory opened his eyes to see the man had set Gregory's and Tori's laptops on a workbench. Pablo had Gregory's laptop open and ready at the password screen.

Before Gregory could respond, John kicked his shattered leg. He shrieked with pain, unable to speak for a moment as tears flushed his cheeks. Spots appeared before his eyes and he nearly passed out.

"Password," Pablo demanded again.

In between sobs, Gregory gave it to him.

Pablo entered the password and Gregory's desktop came up with icons for all the applications he used. The tracker app that would locate Tori's phone was on the right side of the screen. Pablo clicked on the address book icon first.

When the address book popped up, Pablo did a search.

He looked at Gregory and scowled. "I find nothing for a Henry and Josie Cox."

John raised his leg to slam his foot into Gregory's broken leg.

"Wait!" Gregory screamed. "It's probably on her computer." He sobbed. "I don't have their address on mine."

Pablo stared at him for a long moment. "I believe you." He turned to the other laptop. "Is this Tori's?"

"Yes." Gregory could barely get the word out.

"What is her password?" Pablo asked.

John started to bring his foot down on Gregory's thigh again, but he shrieked, "I'll give it to you. I'll give it to you! Just promise you'll stop."

"I don't promise anything." Pablo sat on the edge of the workbench. "Except more pain if you do not talk."

"Anything you want, I'll give to you." Gregory gave out each symbol, letter, and number in her password and Pablo wrote them down. On installing the program, Gregory had been impressed with her complicated password.

When he finished giving the information to Pablo, the man hit Enter and Tori's desktop came up. He clicked on the address book icon and it opened. He immediately went to Cox.

"Ah, here it is." Pablo gave a smile and flashed a glance at Gregory. "If you gave me the correct information."

"I did." Gregory let out his breath. "Josie and Henry are her parents."

Pablo seemed satisfied as he scanned the address book. "She has many friends who we may find interesting to talk to as well."

Gregory thought of Tori's best friend, Paula. He'd never liked her, but he couldn't imagine her being strung up like the men had done to him.

"Look here." John pointed to the screen of Gregory's computer, drawing Pablo's attention. "I recognize this app." He cut his gaze to Gregory then to Pablo. "This is an app for a special tracker for a car or in a phone, independent of the phone as a power source."

Gregory watched, his heart sinking, as John opened the app. John had a satisfied leer on his face. "This shows exactly where she is. She's in Bisbee and she's on a street near the high school."

Pablo smiled at John. "Excellent." Pablo turned his smile on Gregory. "Thank you for making this easy for us."

Gregory hung his head. If he didn't writhe now in so much agony, he would have thought all this to be a horrible nightmare. But the screaming pain in his body told him all too well he hadn't died...yet.

God knew he loved Tori. His obsession with her had started before he had introduced himself, and she belonged to him. But now these men would kill her—unless they planned to torture her first. Gregory closed his eyes again, shutting out the image of Tori being tortured and murdered.

Pablo's voice broke into Gregory's rambling thoughts. "Is there anything else you can tell me?"

Gregory looked at Pablo again. "What did she do? Why do you want her?"

Pablo studied Gregory. "She was in the wrong place at the wrong time. For that she must die."

Chills racked Gregory's body from Pablo's words. "Tori is an innocent. She doesn't deserve to die."

Pablo shrugged. "My boss tells me she does. So we will find her and kill her."

A lone tear rolled down Gregory's cheek and he looked away. Tori belonged to him and had been his to do with as he wanted. She belonged to *him.* But it meant he should protect her and in the end he hadn't. He'd failed her.

Gregory heard a click and knew Pablo had cocked his gun.

He managed to cast his eyes up at the man and saw the barrel pointed at his head. Death would be better than being alive and knowing what Tori would go through because of him. He welcomed death rather than suffering any longer, his body one incredible mass of agony.

Gregory's throat tightened as he stared at the gun. He raised his chin, determined to die with some shred of dignity.

"I am pleased you have been of some use." Pablo gave a slow smile, a smile nothing short of evil. "Goodbye, Mr. Smith."

Pablo pulled the trigger.

Chapter Ten

Back at the safe house, Landon gestured in the direction of the front door. "I'll grab dinner for us and be back after I meet up with my mom."

"Okay." Tori felt numb from everything that had happened.

"Hey." Landon rested one hand on her shoulder. "Two of the best are here with you. Everything's going to be all right."

She nodded, but even though she liked O'Donnell and Johnson, she still felt as if she'd be safer with Landon.

Landon gave her shoulder one last squeeze, along with a reassuring look, before heading out of the kitchen.

Tori's hand shook as she brought it up and put it over her mouth. She felt as though she wanted to cry or scream, maybe both. She'd never been so scared in her life. To have a powerful cartel after her — would any place be safe?

She'd told Landon she would testify and that meant no changing her mind. He wouldn't let the cartel get to her. She needed to be brave.

Be brave…

She wasn't sure she could be — it took everything she had not to lose herself to complete and total fear.

How could her brother ever have sunk so low as to deal with people like the members of the Jimenez Cartel?

Johnson came into the kitchen, carrying a paperback book. "You all right?"

She nodded, moved her hand away from her mouth and straightened her spine. "I'm fine."

Johnson went to the back door and peered through the

blinds prior to moving to the table. He sat where he could easily see both the back door and the entrance from the living room into the kitchen. He'd holstered his gun at his side. It reassured her to see that both agents wore weapons at all times.

He showed her the paperback, a thick one. Stephen King's *The Stand*. She'd read the book at least three times over the years.

He lowered the book. "There's a bookshelf in one of the bedrooms if you like to read."

"Thanks." She wiped her sweaty palms on her jeans. "I'll see what I can find."

She had the first bedroom, but it didn't have a bookcase. A bookcase with three shelves stood against the wall in the second bedroom. It housed a selection of fiction and non-fiction. She usually liked suspense, but right now, she felt as if she lived in a thriller and had no desire to read anything close to that. She picked up a historical romance by Susan Wiggs then went back to her room and lay on the bed with her head on the hard pillow and started to read.

Books were a wonderful way to escape without actually going anywhere. But this time she had a hard time focusing. She kept seeing Alejandro shoot Miguel and she kept going over and over the scene in her mind. Had she missed anything else that could help in the case against the Jimenez Cartel?

Tori woke to a darkened room. She'd drifted off without intending to. The growing darkness made her feel jumpy, as if someone might pop out of the room's shadows at any moment and her heartbeat stepped up. She swung her legs over the side of the bed and fumbled for the switch on the lamp on the lone nightstand then clicked it on. Immediately the light flooded the room with a soft yellow glow and her heart slowed to a more reasonable pace.

The sound of the front door opening and closing had her getting to her feet. Landon, it had to be. The delicious smells of pizza met her when she walked into the living room. The warm smell covered up the musty odor of a house clearly not lived in often.

Landon set the pizza on the coffee table. He looked up and smiled at her. "How are you doing?"

"Fine." She smiled. "And, thanks to the great smell, I'm now hungry."

He opened one of the two large boxes. From out of a bag he brought a stack of paper plates, a bunch of paper napkins, and packets of crushed red chili peppers. On the floor beside the couch were several shopping bags — he must have carried everything all at once.

Moments later, O'Donnell had pepperoni pizza on a paper plate and had kicked back to watch TV again. Landon handed Tori a plate with two slices then put three large pieces onto the third and fourth plates, which he carried into the kitchen. Tori and Landon sat at the kitchen table with Johnson after giving the man his pizza.

Even with the other agent there, Tori got lost in her attraction to Landon. While she ate her pizza, she found herself stealing glances at him as he talked with Johnson. She ached to run her fingers over the coarse stubble along Landon's jaws and trace his firm lips with her tongue.

A stirring in her belly sent tingles of awareness throughout her body. Her hardened nipples pressed against her crop top and she feared that her desire would be noticed by Landon. Maybe even his fellow agent.

Landon glanced at her, catching her watching him. Their gazes met and held for a long moment before he looked at Johnson, who'd just asked him a question.

Tori wiped her mouth with a napkin as she finished her second piece. "It reminds me of when I lived here in town and we used to hang out at the pizza place where you got this." She smiled when Landon glanced at her again. "Bisbee might be a small town in the southwest, but I swear it has the best pizza ever."

He nodded. "They do make a mean pizza."

After he'd finished eating his third piece, he and Tori

took the shopping bags from the living room and into the bedroom assigned to her. She dumped out the bags onto the bed to see his mother had bought her jeans, tops, and socks as well as a large T-shirt and comfy sweatpants to sleep in like Tori had told Landon she preferred.

Her cheeks felt a little warm when she emptied another bag containing panties and bras. It felt intimate having him see what she would be wearing beneath her clothing.

His mother had also purchased a black overnight bag to carry everything in, as well as every kind of toiletry a girl could need, along with a toothbrush, hairbrush, and comb. She put those into a bag she would take with her into the bathroom when she got ready for bed.

"Tell your mom thank you for me." Tori looked at Landon and paused, feeling a moment of awkwardness and embarrassment. "And thank you for everything. You saved my life and you've been looking out for me. I owe you more than I can ever repay."

"You don't owe me anything." Landon's low voice vibrated through her. "I'm just doing my job."

She shook her head. "You've gone above and beyond the call of duty and I can't tell you how much I appreciate it." She stopped talking, suddenly unable to think of another word to say.

For a long moment, they stared at each other. As the silence lingered, the tension grew stronger between them. At that moment she knew his attraction to her matched her desire for him—his eyes and his expression told her he felt the same way. She'd known him for such a short time, yet she knew the attraction went beyond sexual.

The incredible need to have him touch her made her want to slide into his embrace. What would it be like to have his hands caressing her, his lips covering her own? She had to know, every part of her being straining in his direction.

When he moved closer to her, she had to look up to meet his gaze. Without really thinking about her actions, she took a step toward him and stopped with only a couple of inches still separating them. She swallowed as his body heat warmed her through and she caught his scent that made her even crazier for him.

Butterflies stirred in her belly and she could see an even stronger desire reflected in his eyes. She wanted—needed—his hands on her. To kiss him, to taste him.

He didn't move, just looked at her as if he had frozen in place. She raised her hands and slid them up his chest, his muscles flexing beneath her palms.

A low groan rumbled up inside him and he grasped her hips and pulled her closer, her body snug against his. He lowered his head, ever so slowly. She didn't wait for him. She rose up on her toes, moved her mouth to his, and his firm lips pressed to her own.

He kissed her gently, but she felt the tension in his body as if he were fighting to restrain himself. She gave a soft moan as she kissed him harder, slipping her tongue between his lips.

He lost the tight rein on his control. He groaned louder this time and kissed her with a fierceness that set all of her senses on fire. His mouth moved over hers, taking, demanding. He gently bit her lower lip and she gasped at the eroticism of that one little action.

Her nipples tightened and she ached at the juncture of her thighs. She desired Landon with everything she had. She wanted to climb him, wrap her legs around his waist, and hold on for the ride she knew he'd give her.

She clenched his T-shirt in her hands and her mind spun as she became lost in the kiss. He slid his hands along her curves, over the bare skin of her back revealed by her crop top. She loved the feel of his hard body against her softer form. The ridge of his cock pressed into her belly and she gasped into his mouth, the sound lost in the kiss.

When he raised his head, she almost whimpered from the loss of his lips on hers. His pupils were dilated, his chest rising and falling with each harsh breath. Her ragged breathing grew stronger and she could do nothing but be lost in the depths of his gaze. The moment stretched out, the silence between them heavy with their desire.

"I'm sorry." His expression looked pained as he released her hips. He caught her off guard, capturing her wrists and drawing her hands away from his chest. "That shouldn't have happened."

She blinked, the spell binding them vanishing with those few words. Her cheeks heated and she dropped her gaze as she stepped back. With her gaze still averted, she tried to pull her wrists from his grasp but he didn't release her.

"No." She looked back at him. "It was my fault. I shouldn't have—"

"Ah, hell." He lowered his head and captured her mouth with his, still gripping her wrists in his hands. He took her mouth in a demanding kiss, like a man staking his claim.

This time, when he pulled back, she turned her face to him, her moist lips parted, her eyes wide. His expression burned as fiercely as his kiss had done.

"I've never crossed this line before." He kept her wrists clasped in one of his big hands. He brushed the knuckles of his free hand over her cheek and she shivered from the sensual touch. "But I don't know if I can keep my hands off you, Tori. I can't explain it."

"You don't have to explain." She searched his gaze. "I feel it too."

"This isn't a good idea." He blew out his breath and swallowed hard. "It's not good at all."

She opened her mouth to say how good, how right it felt to her and she wouldn't change a thing. She wanted him and opened her mouth to tell him. She lost the words in an instant.

The lights went out.

Chapter Eleven

Landon's senses went on full alert and prickles scrabbled up and down his spine. The blinds blocked what little light might have come from the moon or a streetlight, making the room dark.

"What happened to the lights?" Tori's voice wavered.

"Get behind the door and stay down," he told her. "I'm going to find out."

His eyes adjusting to the darkness, he saw a flash of fear cross her face before she hurried to do what he'd told her to.

He drew his Colt .45 and peered out of the doorway. The darkness made it impossible to see anything down the hall. He eased out of the bedroom and moved toward the living room, holding his weapon with the muzzle pointed up.

The TV no longer blared in the living room, leaving it as silent as the bedroom had been. "O'Donnell." Landon spoke in a low voice as he reached the archway into the living room.

"We've got company." O'Donnell kept his voice down, his response coming from the direction of the front door. "I've called for reinforcements."

His eyes now accustomed to the dark, Landon could make out O'Donnell's outline to the left of the door. He'd be behind the door, waiting, if someone breached it.

Landon eased along the wall toward the kitchen and crouched beside the doorway. "Johnson."

"I've got the back door." Johnson's hushed tone gave Landon a small measure of relief.

No doubt Jimenez's men were outside the safe house.

Landon prayed they did not have night-vision goggles, so the dark would handicap them too.

How the hell had they found the safe house?

Landon gritted his teeth. He'd promised Tori she'd be safe here, and somehow the cartel had tracked them down. There could be only three options. One, Landon hadn't been careful enough and he'd been followed. Two, somehow when they'd gone back to the scene, the cartel had put a tracker on his vehicle or the other agents' SUV. Three, a traitor existed in the DHS, a possibility Landon had a hard time believing but couldn't discount.

None of those options sat well with him or seemed remotely possible.

Then how had the cartel found them?

Gunfire erupted, the rounds of a machine gun tearing through the walls. Drywall and wood splinters exploded with the impact of every round. Landon dove for cover behind the couch. His weapon gripped in both hands, he peered around the couch and saw O'Donnell had flattened himself on the floor. The agent propped himself up on his forearms, still gripping his weapon.

Landon took a few precious moments to move in a crouch to the bedroom. Tori waited in the corner behind the door.

"Are you all right?" he asked her over the gunfire.

"Y-yes." She sounded terrified.

"Stay down," he spoke in a firm but calm tone, trying to keep her from panicking. "Be ready to leave when I come back and get you."

"I will." Her voice trembled as she said the two words.

He moved back to the living room to see the door riddled with holes and a concentration of firepower directed at the doorknob and lock.

The gunfire stopped and, in the next moment, a man slammed the door open with his body. Men charged inside. Light from the lone streetlight spilled into the room through the open doorway and Landon could see the men coming through.

He picked off the first man with a single bullet to the forehead. From behind the door, O'Donnell had rolled onto his side and he shot the next man. A third man had made it through and swung his weapon around to fire at O'Donnell, but Landon put the gunman down.

Landon swung his Colt toward the door again. Reinforcements had better arrive soon.

Shots were fired from the kitchen. More men came from that direction and Landon hoped Johnson would be able to hold them off.

Landon remained on one knee beside the couch. From his vantage point, he could see the doorway to the kitchen as well as the front.

Sirens now sounded in the distance. Landon prayed the men in blue from BPD would arrive in a hurry.

More shots from the kitchen and another man came through the front door, spraying bullets as he charged in.

Landon ducked back behind the couch until the gunfire paused. He rose up from behind the couch and shot at the gunman. The man twisted to the side just as Landon fired and the bullet hit the man in the arm instead of the chest. The gunman dropped his weapon and ducked behind a chair.

At the Federal Law Enforcement Training Center, FLETC, Landon had been one of the best sharpshooters and he rarely missed. Unfortunately, this was one of those rare times. Landon dared a glimpse around the side of the couch, to see the man peeking out. Landon got off several shots but he didn't know if he'd hit the man.

A loud crash, the sound of shattering glass, and Tori's scream came from the bedroom.

Landon turned and bolted down the hallway, peered around the corner, and saw a man had come through Tori's bedroom window. The blinds lay on the floor and broken glass glittered on the carpet. Moonlight now streamed through the window and exposed the gunman.

The man raised his gun and took aim at Tori, who froze in

place near the door.

Landon analyzed the scene in one blink and fired at the gunman in the next blink, hitting him solidly center mass. The man dropped to the floor and Landon kicked away the weapon. The man's body spasmed and blood leaked out of his mouth. Then his eyes simply stared up at the dark ceiling.

Everything went quiet in the house save for approaching sirens.

Landon swung his gaze from the dead man to Tori. "Are you hurt?"

She couldn't seem to take her eyes off the dead man. "I'm okay." Her voice shook. "Do you think they're gone?"

Emergency personnel cut sirens and tires screeched to a stop outside. Landon glanced to the window where flashing blue and red lights could be seen through the blinds. "I don't know if these bastards are all gone or dead, but it sounds like backup has arrived."

Footsteps pounded on the front porch. Shouts of "Police!" came from the front and the back.

O'Donnell called out, "We're federal agents."

"Put down your weapons and raise your hands." Lieutenant Liam Marks' hard voice came from the living room. "We'll check your creds. Until we do, don't make a move."

"They're with me, Marks." Landon held his hands up so he wouldn't get shot as he stood in the hallway and looked into the living room lit only by flashlights.

"Damn, Walker." Marks motioned to his men to stand down and holstered his weapon. "What the hell happened here?"

"Long story." Landon lowered his hands. "This *was* a safe house."

Marks looked over the wreckage and the bodies. His officers were checking pulses and confiscating weapons. "Some safe house."

Landon noticed the Jimenez Cartel tattoo on the exposed

left wrists of a couple of the men's bodies. No doubt most, if not all, of them had it.

Another officer stood on the threshold of the open front door. "Paramedics are pulling up right now."

"Johnson," Landon shouted when he didn't see the agent.

"One of the bastards shot me in the leg." Johnson sounded pissed off more than hurt as he spoke from the direction of the kitchen.

"Shit." Landon growled the word. "I'll be right in." He couldn't leave Tori alone.

"Don't worry about me," Johnson called out. "The BPD boys have it under control."

A police officer stepped from the kitchen into the living room. "An ambulance will be here any moment for Agent Johnson."

More sirens shrieked in the distance.

The power came back on and light flooded the house. Marks tucked his flashlight back into a loop on his utility belt.

Landon nodded behind him, signaling to Tori to come out.

She followed him into the living room and Marks glanced at her in surprise. "I didn't realize you're the protected witness in this place."

Tori nodded but said nothing. The sheen of fear hadn't left her expression.

"It's all right." Landon met her gaze. "The cavalry's here. We'll get you someplace safe."

She visibly shuddered. "I thought I'd be safe in a safe house."

"You should have been." Landon frowned as he turned back to Marks.

"Who the hell is after her?" Marks asked.

Landon moved closer to Marks and Tori followed. "The Jimenez Cartel."

"Jesus." Marks' expression hardened. "How'd they find her?"

"I have an idea." Landon narrowed his gaze. "And I intend to find out if I'm right." He pulled out his cell phone and turned to Marks. "Can you stay with Tori for a few moments while I make this call?" When he turned back to Tori he said, "Don't move from this spot."

"I'll make sure she doesn't." Marks stepped closer to Tori.

Landon gave her a reassuring look. "You're safe now and I'm going to make sure you stay that way."

Tori gave him a slight nod. He turned away and walked out of range of being overheard by anyone. He pressed the speed dial number for the RAC, Sofia Aguilar.

"Sofia, all hell broke loose at the safe house." Landon clenched his phone as Aguilar answered. "Somehow, Jimenez's men found her."

"Is our witness all right?"

"Ms. Cox is fine." Landon thought about how close Tori had come to being shot. "She's scared but safe. For now."

Landon watched as paramedics rushed to wheel a gurney into the kitchen. "The bastards hit Johnson. He has a gunshot wound to the leg."

"God damn it." Aguilar's voice went even harder. "How is he?"

Landon glanced toward the kitchen. "I'll check with the paramedics and report back to you."

"I'll be in contact with his family and get them to the hospital once he's there." By the tone of her voice, Aguilar's temper had shot sky-high. "How did Jimenez's men find her? You're certain they were his men?"

"Yes." Landon's own anger hadn't diminished. "I haven't checked all the bodies, but I saw the cartel's tattoo on two of them."

"Tell me what the hell happened." As Aguilar spoke, paramedics rushed in the front door. A BPD officer directed them to the kitchen to take care of Johnson.

"Not a lot to tell. One minute everything is fine and the next the cartel is coming down on us." Landon shifted the phone to his other ear and told her his theories of how the

103

cartel may have found them. "I need two clean vehicles with agents you trust."

Aguilar paused before responding. "I trust all our agents, but I'll handpick who is sent to you. We'll have the vehicles swept and I'll also send two SUVs to get her to another safe house somewhere in the county. One of the agents will have the address."

"We need to make sure the vehicles are never left unguarded from the outside." Landon still couldn't believe they'd been found so easily. "We'll leave as soon as they arrive."

"It will be taken care of," she said. "Call me if there are any other developments. In the meantime I'll call the ASAC."

"Yes, ma'am." Landon disconnected the call as Aguilar no doubt hung up to dial the Assistant Special Agent in Charge in Phoenix to update him.

Landon glanced at Tori who worried her lower lip with her teeth. "You doing all right?"

She shrugged, but it was not a casual movement. "I'm okay," she said once again.

Landon didn't believe her for a second.

O'Donnell moved close to Tori, Marks, and Landon. The agent had a few minor abrasions on his face and hands, likely from being close to the wall when the bullets had been slamming through wood and drywall.

"Thanks for staying with Tori." Landon turned to Marks. "O'Donnell can take over from here."

"Any time you need help, call." Marks' expression grew even more concerned when he returned his attention to Tori. "Be careful."

She rubbed her arms with both her palms. "I will."

As Marks left, Landon spoke to O'Donnell. "Don't let her out of your sight and don't take her out of the house."

O'Donnell shook his head. "Wouldn't dream of it."

Landon turned and headed for the kitchen. When he moved inside, he saw paramedics lifting Johnson onto a stretcher. Blood soaked his right pant leg. Paramedics had placed an oxygen mask over his nose and mouth and hooked him up to two IVs.

"How is he?" Landon asked one of the paramedics.

"Agent Johnson lost a lot of blood and there's no exit wound so the bullet is still inside," she responded. "But he's stable. We'll get him to the hospital."

A big, powerfully built man, Johnson still managed to appear tough, but he did seem exhausted.

Landon went to him and placed his hand on Johnson's arm. "You're going to be fine."

Johnson gave a thumbs-up before closing his eyes.

Tori thought her heartbeat would never slow, but it finally did. As she looked around her at the devastation, her gut twisted and she felt sick. So many dead bodies with limbs at unnatural angles and wide, sightless eyes. Blood splattered on the walls and in puddles on the floor.

With a small cry, she clapped her hand over her mouth and ran for the bathroom. She dropped to her knees in front of the toilet and her stomach heaved. Everything came up. She vomited and vomited until nothing was left. She vaguely realized someone held her hair back, away from her face.

When she raised her head, Landon stood beside her and let her hair slide from his hand. As he handed her a wet washcloth, she felt a moment's embarrassment that he'd seen her throw up.

She wiped her lips with the cloth as she rose and flushed the toilet. She went to the sink where she washed her hands then tried to rinse the acidic taste out of her mouth. Her eyes were red and watering and her face flushed. She splashed cold water over her face and used a hand towel to dry off.

Landon rested his hand on her shoulder as she composed herself. "Thank you."

He brushed hair away from her cheek. She turned and started to walk into the hall, but he stopped her. "You don't have to go out there."

"I'll be fine. I just got a little sick." She tucked her hair behind both ears. "I don't have anything left to throw up anyway." She still had the awful taste in her mouth. "But I could use a drink of water."

Landon turned to O'Donnell. "Would you mind getting bottled water out of the fridge? I'll take Tori into one of the bedrooms where it will be quiet."

"Sure thing."

Landon escorted Tori to the master bedroom in the back. Thankful no bodies were there, she sat on the edge of the bed. O'Donnell showed up with a bottle of water for her and one for Landon.

Gratefully, she drank the water. The buzz and hum of voices and activity faded away as her thoughts narrowed in on what had happened. Jimenez's men had found her and had come to kill her. For the second time in as many days, she'd come close to losing her life.

She closed her eyes, trying to block everything out. Instead, she heard the shouts of men breaking into the house, cries of men dying, a man coming through her window and aiming his gun at her.

Oh, God. She couldn't believe all of this was happening.

Her eyes popped open and she thought she might be sick again. She swallowed. Her hands shook as she took another drink of water and tried to calm her thoughts.

"We're ready to go." Landon touched her arm and she started and glanced up at him. O'Donnell stood behind him. "We have another safe house to take you to. This won't happen again."

They walked through the living room, dodging crime scene personnel. Tori did her best to not look around her at the bodies or the blood.

The surrealness of the scene made her feel as if she were in a waking nightmare that might never end.

Just as they reached the front door, two black SUVs with dark-tinted windows pulled up in the driveway. Agents climbed out of the vehicles and circled the SUVs while three came to the front door.

In the next moment, agents surrounded her, dwarfing her. They swept her toward the vehicles and before she knew it she sat inside on the bench seat in the back, Landon on one side of her and an agent sitting on her other side. Another agent sat in the front passenger seat as the driver climbed in. The SUV had been kept running.

Once again they drove in circles through Bisbee to make sure they weren't being followed. Instead of staying in Bisbee, they headed toward Sierra Vista. When Tori had first arrived in Bisbee, she wouldn't have believed she'd be traveling back through the Mule Pass Tunnel so soon, this time running from a drug cartel.

For the first time since they'd been attacked tonight, Tori thought of Gregory. She knew deep inside something bad had happened to him and the thought made her ill. If she had thought of him sooner…

Her eyes widened as another thought hit her. She turned to Landon, trying to keep panic out of her voice. "My parents. We need to check on them."

"I already called." Landon put his hand on hers and gave a reassuring squeeze. "The agents on duty said your parents are fine and there has been no sign of anything out of the ordinary."

Tori let out a long, slow breath. "Thank you."

He squeezed her hand one more time. "Everything will be fine. I promise."

She wished she could believe him, she really did. She had a hard time believing anything would ever be fine again.

Chapter Twelve

Diego clenched the cell phone, straightening in his office chair. His voice grew cold as he spoke with one of his underlings in Arizona. The man should have erased the *problem.* "Tell me again how you failed me."

"I am the only one who survived." Carlos' voice wavered. "Everyone else — killed by the American agents."

"Why are you alive?" Diego let ice into his tone. "You ran like a dog."

Carlos sounded as if he might piss himself. "I needed to report to you."

"You needed to eliminate the woman." Diego held back his fury. "I wish to speak with Alejandro."

The tremble in Carlos' voice clearly made it difficult for him to get the words out of his mouth. "Yes, sir."

Alejandro came on the line. "Pablo and John called just now. They know where Tori Cox's mother and father are and they have both the woman's and her boyfriend's computers. If we need any more information then we should be able to find it there."

"Good." Diego leaned back in the padded leather office chair. "Make sure you send men who will not fail this time."

"I will, Father." Alejandro never showed weakness, which pleased Diego greatly. "What do you want me to do with Carlos?"

Diego did not hesitate. "Shoot him."

A moment later he heard Carlos begging for his life, then a single shot.

Alejandro came back on the line. "It is done."

"Good." Diego drew in a long breath then let it out.

"Have his body dealt with and send men to take care of the woman's family. Have the mother and father held hostage until we get the woman."

"It will be taken care of, Father. We still have the tracker on her phone."

Diego disconnected the call and set the cell phone on his desk. He clenched his jaws tight and reined in his emotions. He did not lose control. This temporary problem would be dealt with, with swift finality.

A knock on the doorframe had Diego peering in the direction of the door. His granddaughter stood there and she appeared confused. He mentally cursed himself for not making sure he had locked the door so she would not hear anything she should not.

He put on a smile for her. "How is my angel?"

She smiled back. "Maria brought dresses for me to try on when I am *Quinceañera*. You said you wish to approve of the dress I am to wear."

"Of course." He pushed back his chair and left the encrypted cell phone on the desk. He kept his personal mobile in his pocket. The encrypted cell phone had more security.

Angelina waited for him to reach the doorway, then linked her arm through his. "She has them in my bedroom. You can wait in my sitting room and I will model them for you."

Diego patted his granddaughter's hand. "I am looking forward to seeing you in the dresses."

They walked together to Angelina's bedroom suite in the wing on the opposite side of his home. He preferred her as far as possible from where he held his business dealings. When they reached her sitting room, he sat back in one of the richly upholstered chairs.

Maria waited in the room and she gave Diego a deferential bow. Angelina smiled then whirled and went through the connecting door into her bedroom with Maria following close behind.

Angelina returned fifteen minutes later, smiling and wearing a lavender dress that almost reached the floor and barely showed her ankles. However, it bared most of her back and revealed too much skin for a young woman.

He shook his head. "No."

Her face fell. "I think it's beautiful."

"No," he repeated. "It reveals too much for a young lady of your age."

Holding back a pout, she left the room with Maria. Ten minutes later, she returned wearing a lemon-yellow dress. It had puffy sleeves but bare shoulders and a low neckline like the lavender one.

He frowned. "Who selected these dresses for you?"

"I did, out of the portfolio the dressmaker sent." Angelina grasped her skirt and held it up as she spun around. "Isn't it lovely?"

He narrowed his eyes at Maria, who seemed fearful. "Is there anything more modest?"

"Yes." Maria gave a nod. She turned to Angelina, who now appeared crestfallen. "The pink one. Your grandfather will like it."

Angelina frowned. "But I don't."

"Come." Maria gestured to the connecting door. "When you have it on you will find it beautiful on you."

Angelina didn't look at her grandfather as she left the room. A part of him wanted to give his little angel anything she desired, but he would not allow her to bare herself at such a young age. She would be but fifteen years old. Yes, a young woman, but still too young for such things as dresses that showed too much skin.

This time when Angelina returned, she didn't smile. She wore a pink floor-length dress with many flouncy layers. It had puffy sleeves and suitably covered her back and chest. The perfect dress for a young woman.

"That is the one." Diego nodded and stood. "You are as beautiful as your mother did when she was *Quinceañera*. You resemble her so much."

Angelina still frowned. "Are you sure you don't want to see me in any of the others?"

He beamed at her. "I know beauty and you are the rarest of beauties. This one is perfect for such a treasure as you."

Her frown faded a bit. "I look like a little girl in this dress."

He shook his head. "You look very much like a young woman." He approached her and took both her hands in his. "I am proud of you. Your mother would have been so very proud of you, as well." He squeezed her hands. "I know she is watching from Heaven and singing with the angels as she watches over you."

Angelina's smile returned. Diego knew how much she liked to please him. Her mother had always wanted to make her father happy too. Rosanna had been a daddy's girl and Angelina was her grandfather's girl. He would have it no other way.

He took her by the shoulders and kissed one of Angelina's cheeks then the other. "Do you know how precious you are to me?"

"As precious as you are to me." She smiled. "I love you, Grandfather."

"And you know I love you more than life itself." He gestured toward the door connecting to her bedroom. "It is time for you to get ready for bed."

She gave him a hug then turned and headed into her room, Maria following.

When the door between the rooms closed, Diego put his hands behind his back and rocked on his heels. His granddaughter was truly the most precious thing in his life and he would do anything for her.

He left the sitting room and headed back to his office and the reality of his business. He kept it as separate as he could from his personal life. His granddaughter would never know the realities of his world. She would grow up wanting for nothing and living the life she so richly deserved.

He closed his office door, moved behind his desk, and took his seat. Now to make sure one woman didn't cause his family any problems. No one would be able to protect her from him. He had long arms that stretched from Mexico to the U.S. and no one could escape his grasp.

No one.

Chapter Thirteen

Tori rubbed her arms with her palms as she went to the bedroom window of the new safe house she had slept in last night. She wanted to peek out of the two-story house's blinds to better see the neighborhood she was in, but Landon had given her strict instructions to stay away from the windows.

She felt wrinkled and grubby and she needed to brush her teeth. She still wore the clothes she'd worn yesterday since all of the new clothing and toiletries had been left at the other safe house. They'd had no time to gather anything once the agents had been ready to sweep her away again.

The Sierra Vista safe house was as sparsely furnished as the one in Bisbee, but not as dusty—it looked as if it had been recently lived in. This pantry contained more food than the one at the other house, but not by much.

In truth, she didn't care about any of that. She had trusted Landon when he'd said she'd be safe at the other house, but that hadn't been the case. What if the Jimenez Cartel found her here too?

A knock caused her to jump and turn to the open door to see Landon. His green eyes met hers and he seemed to be drinking her in just as she devoured him with her gaze. No matter everything she'd been through, her potent attraction to this man could not be diluted. It was almost the only constant she had to hold on to.

She wanted to trail her fingers down the strong line of his stubbled jaw to his square chin. She wanted to run her tongue along his firm lower lip and nip at it before kissing her way down the column of his throat.

She had lost her mind. Her cheeks warmed as she stared at him and he met her gaze head on. She remembered the feel of his lips on hers, his body snug to hers, the feel of his hardness pressing through their clothing and against her belly…

She cleared her throat. "Good morning."

The corner of his mouth turned up, a hint of a smile. To her relief he set aside the moment and raised his hands. He held several familiar shopping bags.

"One of the other agents retrieved everything for you." He gestured for her to step aside and she moved back and opened the door for him. He set the bags on the bed and faced her. His eyebrows furrowed. "How are you doing?"

She shrugged. "Do you know how they found us?"

He frowned. "No. We even checked for trackers on the vehicles and nothing."

At her look of concern, he attempted to reassure her. "We have high-tech equipment that detects trackers and the agents have combed every vehicle. We're exhausting all options and we will figure this out."

She rubbed her arms with both hands. "I hope you're right."

He took a step closer to her. "I am."

"What now?"

"You'll stay here." He met her gaze squarely. "I'm going into the office and I'll be back later."

Panic rose up inside her like a flock of birds and she moved her fingers to her throat. "I don't want to be alone."

"You won't be alone." He cupped the side of her face with one hand and rubbed her cheek with his thumb. His touch sent a thrill deep inside her belly. "You'll have three agents protecting you night and day."

"Let me go with you." She hated the tremble in her voice. "I don't want to stay behind."

Landon moved both hands to her upper arms and squeezed. "You'll be perfectly safe here."

She wanted to say, "I feel safer with you," but the words

wouldn't come out. She would just sound like a baby if she did say them. Instead, she said, "I'd like to see my parents."

He shook his head. "It could put you and them in danger. We still have agents outside their home on watch."

She bit her lower lip before opening her mouth to say something.

His cell phone rang. He brought the phone to his ear. "Agent Walker."

He scrunched his brow, listening for a moment. "You're certain?" His face was a mask of concentration as the person on the other end spoke again. Then Landon said, "Thank you, Lieutenant."

He turned to Tori. "That was the lieutenant from the Tucson Police Department." Landon looked grim. "They found Gregory Smith's body early this morning."

Tori stared at Landon and shock speared her body. "Gregory is dead?" The words left her mouth, but she couldn't believe they were true.

Her knees went weak and she would have dropped to the floor if Landon hadn't caught her. He brought her close to him and held her in his arms. Her mind spun with the news.

"What happened to him?" Her words were muffled against his shirt.

Landon hesitated then squeezed her tighter. "Someone tortured then shot him."

Tori's entire body went limp this time. Her mind reeled, unable to fully comprehend what Landon had just told her. Gregory? Tortured and shot?

"I'm sorry, Tori." Landon's lips were close to her hair as he spoke and held her tightly. "A woman's body was found with his, but she hasn't been identified yet. No purse and no ID on her. She was strangled to death."

Tears rolled down Tori's cheeks and her throat was tight. "Gregory's intern didn't show up to work the same day he didn't. The police should start there."

"I'll let them know." Landon's voice was soft but firm.

"It's my fault." Tori tipped her face up to look at him. "They're dead because of me."

He shook his head. "Don't take the blame for what the cartel has done. It's *not* your fault. You just happened on something that you weren't intended to see. You're not to blame."

Tori couldn't stop the tears. Each one felt like a hot trail burning its way down her face. A chest-racking sob left her and she buried her face in Landon's T-shirt. His shirt grew damp from her tears but she couldn't let go. He served as a lifeline she needed to hold on to.

She raised her face to look up at him again. "My parents. Maybe Gregory did find their address and gave it to the cartel."

"We'll get them to a safe house." Landon rubbed her back with his palm. "Now that Gregory's body has been found, it steps things up to a whole new level." He took her face in his palms. "I need to make some calls now. Will you be okay?"

She nodded. "Just get them to safety." Her eyes swam with tears. "I lost my brother. I couldn't bear it if anything happened to my parents."

Something dark flashed in Landon's eyes and he seemed about to say something.

She went on, "I want *you* to be the one to get my parents somewhere safe. It has to be you."

Landon frowned.

"I mean it, Landon." She put determination into her tone. "Make sure they're safe." She paused. "This might sound dumb, but can you get something for me while you're there?"

His brow wrinkled. "What do you need?"

"I have an old clarinet at my parents' home." She felt a wave of embarrassment rising up in her. "I can't stand not playing. It helps me relax and takes me to another place. If it's possible, pick it up when you get my parents. Please."

He hesitated a moment then kissed her on top of her head.

116

"I'll be back."

Her muscles relaxed. "Thank you."

He straightened before he turned and walked out the bedroom door.

Landon clenched and unclenched his hands and his gut felt tightly coiled. He needed to tell Tori he'd been the one to kill her brother.

After the news of her boyfriend's death, he feared she might fall apart if he gave her one more thing to contend with.

The old woman's words came back to him.

'You will die if you tell her the truth. If you don't tell her, she will die.'

What could the old lady have meant by those words? Had she meant the fact he'd killed her brother? Landon couldn't imagine anything happening to Tori. He'd already been through losing someone and he didn't want it to happen again. He didn't want to lose Tori.

His chest hurt and he inhaled deeply then exhaled, trying to calm his thoughts.

He pulled his cell phone from its holster and called one of the two agents watching Josie and Henry Cox's home.

"What's the status?" Landon asked when Agent Bracken answered.

"Not a stir." Bracken sounded bored or tired. Or both.

"Stay sharp." Landon heard the edge in his own voice. "We believe the suspects murdered the witness's boyfriend last night or this morning. He may have given up the parents' address."

Agent Bracken's tone sharpened. "Shit."

"We're getting Josie and Henry Cox to a safe house." Landon looked down the hallway as he spoke to Bracken. He made up his mind—he would go himself, for Tori. "Hang tight. I'll be there in another thirty minutes."

"You've got it."

After talking with Bracken, Landon pressed speed dial

for his RAC. When Aguilar answered, he told her what he needed and she gave the go-ahead.

"Don't take any chances with our star witness," Aguilar said. "We need to nail the sonofabitch for Miguel's death."

"We will get them." Landon said he'd be in touch before he pressed the End button on his phone.

He returned to Tori's room to find her standing where he'd left her.

"I need to help." Her tears had dried, but her eyes were swollen from crying. "I can't just stay here. I need to see my mom and dad."

"You need to stay safe." He hooked his finger under her chin and met her gaze. "I'm going to your parents' home now. I called and all is clear. We'll get them to a safe house and you won't have to worry."

"What if the cartel finds them like they found me?" Her voice wavered as she spoke.

"We're taking extra precautions, Tori." Landon hated the fear he saw in her eyes and wished he could take it all away. God damn but he wanted to wipe those fuckers out so they could never touch an innocent like Tori again.

To do that, they'd need to take down Diego Jimenez, *El Demonio*, himself.

The half-hour drive from Sierra Vista back to Bisbee seemed to take too damned long. He found himself drumming his fingers on the wheel as if that might hurry things along. When Landon and Agent O'Donnell finally reached Temby Avenue in Bisbee, Landon parked behind the agency vehicle stationed in front of the Cox's home. The two agents on duty sat inside the unmarked car.

Landon climbed out of the black agency SUV and walked up to the car. He rapped his knuckles on the driver's-side tinted window, but the agent in the driver's seat didn't respond. Landon knocked again. A bad feeling spiked inside him when the agent still didn't turn. Landon yanked open the door. The smell of gas hit Landon head-on.

Agent Bracken slumped in his seat. Landon coughed from the gas. The other agent's head rested against the window and he appeared to be in the same condition as Braken.

Landon put his fingers to Bracken's neck. His pulse beat strong beneath Landon's fingers. The gas hadn't killed him, just knocked them out.

"Jesus." O'Donnell spoke from over Landon's shoulder.

"Call for backup," Landon said. "They've been gassed." Landon's heart thundered. "We've got to get inside the house. Whoever gassed them might still be here."

O'Donnell called for backup and he and Landon ran toward the house, keeping low. They went to the rear, weapons drawn. One of the panes in the back door window had been shattered, the door slightly ajar.

Adrenaline pumped through Landon. He eased the door open with his foot, keeping his Colt ready in a two-handed grip. He cleared the kitchen with one sweep of his eyes and his weapon. He glanced down briefly to avoid stepping on the broken glass as the sound could possibly alert the intruders. He glanced over his shoulder at O'Donnell who nodded.

From the direction of a hallway Landon could just see from the kitchen a male speaking with a heavy Hispanic accent. "Tell me where your husband is and I might kill you quickly rather than slicing you up into one small piece at a time."

"I will never tell you." The woman's voice trembled. "Go ahead and kill me because you'll never find him or Tori."

The woman shrieked and Landon had to fight the urge to charge straight toward the voices. He had to keep his cool, but he hurried through the small kitchen and dining area. He cleared the living room before easing down the hall and heard the woman's sobs.

"Tell me or I'll cut you again." The man spoke slowly, deliberately. "Now."

O'Donnell followed Landon, who peeked around the corner of the doorway into a bedroom just enough to see two thirty-something men with a woman of roughly fifty who was kneeling on the floor. Blood flowed down her cheek from where she'd been cut with a knife and her eyes were red from crying. Due to the strong resemblance to Tori, the woman had to be Josie Cox.

One of the men, about five-six with a thin mustache, wore a tanktop and jeans. He stood behind Josie and clenched her hair in his fist. He gripped a knife laced with blood in his opposite hand, the knife close to her throat.

The bald man who stood nearby topped the first man by three inches. He held a gun loosely at his side, clearly not threatened.

Landon leaned back and indicated to O'Donnell that two armed men were in the room with the victim.

Landon signaled the count then swung himself into the doorway, his gun pointed at the man with the knife. O'Donnell moved beside him with his weapon trained on the taller man.

"Police!" Landon shouted the universal word for law enforcement used during a raid, startling both men.

The bald man swung his weapon up to fire at them. O'Donnell shot the man in the chest before he got a shot off. The bald man fell backward, his gun clattering to the floor. He gasped and wheezed as blood bubbled from his mouth.

O'Donnell immediately kicked the gun out into the hallway, away from the dying man. He moved back to the doorway and positioned himself so he could see into the hall to cover their backs. He kept an eye on the activities in the room.

The man with the knife jerked Josie's head back. He forced her down on her haunches as he gripped her hair. He kept his knife to her throat. "I'll kill her." He spoke the words with bravado, but Landon could see his nervousness.

"If you do, I put a bullet into your brain." Landon moved into the room, his training keeping his head clear and calm. "Slide your knife to me on the floor and let her go and I just might let you live."

The man hesitated, his knife dangerously close to Josie's throat. One quick movement and she'd be dead.

Landon didn't plan to give the man the chance. He squeezed his Colt's trigger.

A hole appeared in the man's forehead, spattering blood and matter on the wall behind him.

The knife tumbled onto Josie's lap. The man collapsed onto the floor, a single drop of blood rolling down his forehead from the hole.

Sirens could be heard in the distance. Landon looked to O'Donnell. "Clear the rest of the house." The agent gave a nod and Landon holstered his weapon before he went to the woman. "I'm Special Agent Walker with the Department of Homeland Security. Are you Josie Cox?" He took her hand and helped her to her feet.

Her eyes were wide and frightened. "Who were those men?"

"Some of the men who are after your daughter." Landon rested his hand on her shoulder. "Other than the cut, did they hurt you?"

Josie shook her head. "No. I think they would have killed me if you hadn't been here." Her voice trembled. "Is Tori okay?"

"She's fine and we have her in a safe place." Landon tried to reassure the woman as O'Donnell checked the man he'd shot for a pulse. He shook his head, indicating that the man was dead.

Landon turned his attention back to Josie. "Where is your husband?"

"Probably at St. Elmo's bar in Brewery Gulch." Josie touched her hand to her cheek, winced, then brought her fingers down to see they were coated with blood. "At least I hope he's there and other men haven't found him."

Landon grabbed a plain white T-shirt from off a chair. "Hold this to your cheek to stop the bleeding until we can get the cut attended to." She took the T-shirt from his hand and pressed it over the wound. "How did your husband get out of the house without the agents noticing him?" Landon asked.

Josie gave a nod in the direction of the bedroom. "I'm guessing he went through our bedroom window and made his way through the neighbors' yards then took a back route to the gulch. The man has to have his booze and I won't allow any around here. I empty the bottles in the sink if I find them."

At the sound of vehicles coming to a stop outside, O'Donnell turned and headed out of the bedroom.

Landon gestured to the doorway. "Are you steady enough to walk?"

"Yes." Josie wobbled for a moment and Landon prepared to catch her if she fell. But she didn't and he walked beside her to the front door. She kept the T-shirt pressed to her cheek.

"Can you do me a favor?" Landon asked.

Josie, still clearly shaken, managed a nod. "Anything."

"Does Tori have a clarinet here?" He looked down at the petite woman. "She wanted it if you were okay."

"Of course. I'll get it." Josie seemed glad to have something to do. "Hmmm…I think she left a box of reeds here the last time she visited too. That girl is always practicing. I don't think she can live without playing her clarinet."

Landon accompanied her to a pretty back room with lots of pink that must have belonged to a much younger Tori.

Josie picked up a small black case resting on the white nightstand next to the bed. "This isn't nearly as nice as her professional one, but at the time we couldn't afford anything that cost more." She glanced at the mirrored dresser. "Ah, here's the box of reeds." She picked up the small box and paused long enough to put it inside the clarinet case.

"I'm sure she'll appreciate it," Landon said, walking with her through the house and to the living room where a pair of agents now waited. "Stay with Mrs. Cox," Landon instructed before he left the woman and went outside.

The mountainside streets of Bisbee were so narrow cars

could only park on one side of the street. The emergency vehicles had parked in a line with barely enough room left for any car to pass.

Police, DHS agency vehicles, an ambulance, and a fire truck helped crowd the place. O'Donnell spoke with police officers. Paramedics treated the two agents who'd been gassed.

Fortunately, no vehicles had blocked in Landon's Explorer. On his way out of the yard, Landon met up with Lieutenant Marks.

"I think we've been seeing too much of each other lately." Marks grinned. "Way too much."

"Agreed."

Marks frowned. "Josie and Henry Cox live here. Are they all right?"

"Mrs. Cox is just shaken up and has a slight injury." Landon stared down in the direction of Brewery Gulch. "We need to find Henry Cox. Mrs. Cox said he must be at St. Elmo's. We need to get both of them into protective custody."

"Why don't I come with you?" Marks walked beside Landon as he headed toward his SUV. "I know what Henry Cox looks like and he knows me." Marks shook his head. "Even though I've known the man for years, he's not what you'd call an agreeable person. Getting him to a safe house isn't going to be easy." He looked at Landon and gave him a wry smile. "Unless you have a fully stocked bar."

They reached Landon's agency SUV. "I don't think it's in the taxpayers' budget."

Landon took a moment to tell O'Donnell where he intended to go. O'Donnell would stay to work with police and DHS until Landon returned.

Landon maneuvered the SUV through the glut of vehicles so he could go down the narrow street. Only one vehicle could travel down at a time, so oncoming traffic had to pull to the side to allow him to pass. He turned on the red and blue grill lights so he didn't have to worry about anyone not giving him the right of way.

Once they were in Brewery Gulch, Landon put a police placard on the dash as they parked illegally, as close to the bar as they were able to. They walked the rest of the way down the gulch.

They reached the bar and Marks gestured to the neon *St. Elmo* sign. "Even though there are live bands and dancing, locals and tourists come to St. Elmo's for one reason."

Landon's lips twisted with humor. "To drink excessively."

Marks gave a quick grin. "Exactly."

Landon pushed open the door and they walked into the dimly lit interior. Above them swung neon signs for numerous brands of beer, along with a neon sign of a crawling man beneath the words: *Drunken People Crossing. Beware.* Over the bar, behind countless bottles of liquor, hung a backlit stained glass sign — *St. Elmo, Since 1902.*

It took a few moments for Landon's eyes to become accustomed to the darkened bar. He took in the few people inside, including two men sitting at the bar and a couple in the corner who were sitting on stools at a high top.

"There he is, good ol' Henry Cox, safe and sound." Marks went straight toward a man at the end of the bar who lifted a draft beer with a full head of foam. Henry had the flushed features some alcoholics had and a beer gut to go along with it. His wrinkled light-colored button-up shirt as well as his tan slacks clung loosely to his frame.

Marks leaned on the bar beside the man. "How's it going, Henry?"

Henry turned dull red eyes on Marks, eyeing the police lieutenant's uniform. "What the hell do you want? I ain't done nothin' wrong."

Landon watched the exchange, on guard for any belligerent behavior from the drunk.

"No, you haven't done anything wrong." Marks shifted to stand closer to Henry. "Not that I know of."

Henry gripped his beer mug, raised it to his lips then hesitated. "What the hell do you want?"

Marks kept his gaze on Henry. "A man attacked Josie."

"My Josie?" Henry's mug thunked so hard on the bar top that beer sloshed over the rim. He came out of his drunkenness, his eyes wide, and said with clarity, "Is she okay? I'll kill the sonofabitch who hurt her."

Marks put his hand on Henry's shoulder. "She's shaken up and has a small injury, but otherwise she'll be fine."

"Holy shit." Henry slid off his barstool and would have fallen if Marks hadn't grabbed him by one arm. "I gotta get home to Josie."

Marks gripped Henry's arm. "We'll take you."

The bartender noticed Henry leaving. "Pay your tab, Henry."

Landon pulled out his cred wallet. "Will twenty cover it?"

The bartender gave a nod, a flicker of concern in his eyes when he saw the badge. Landon slid free a twenty with a five for a tip and dropped them on the bar before turning away and following Marks.

When they got the drunk man into the back of the agency SUV, Landon drove back up the mountainside to Temby. Marks returned to his duties after Henry Cox had settled in.

O'Donnell walked Josie over to the SUV. Paramedics had bandaged Josie's cheek and she likely needed stitches. They'd have to get a doctor to the house where she would be staying. It wouldn't be safe to take her to a hospital.

Josie climbed into the back with Henry, who started asking her what the hell had happened. Josie set Tori's clarinet between the front seats.

O'Donnell and Landon left Josie and Henry to their discussion and spent the next ten minutes sweeping the SUV, using a special piece of equipment that could detect tracking devices. When they had checked out the Explorer, they climbed in, and Landon had to once again navigate the narrow street and hill.

"Where are you taking us?" Henry demanded.

Landon glanced at Josie and Henry in his rearview mirror. "The men who attacked Josie are only two of many who will attempt to kidnap you or take your lives. We're getting you someplace safe."

"I'll be safe in my own damned home." The belligerent drunk stepped hard on Landon's nerves.

Landon glimpsed back at the road. "Your wife might agree with me." He glanced in the rearview mirror and saw Josie nod.

"They almost killed me, Henry." Josie's voice trembled. "I don't want to go back. These agents can protect us."

The bleary-eyed drunk swayed. "I can protect you."

"Like you did today?" Josie pushed her untidy hair out of her eyes. "When you were at St. Elmo's instead of home like you were supposed to be?"

Landon glanced again at Henry in the rearview mirror.

The man looked as if he might argue but wisely clamped his mouth shut.

Maybe he isn't so stupid after all, Landon thought then immediately dismissed the notion. He had the keen ability to judge people and he figured he'd pretty much nailed Henry's type.

Landon's thoughts turned to Tori. He had the impossibly strong urge to be with her again, to watch her, to protect her. He needed to drop off Josie and Henry then get back to Tori.

Chapter Fourteen

The day dragged so slowly Tori thought she'd lose her mind. With a paperback in her lap, she sat on the edge of the bed and stared at the window in the bedroom she'd been given. Again she wanted to raise the blinds, this time to view the sunset, but she stayed away from the windows as the agents had insisted.

She wondered where in the Sierra Vista area they were. She'd heard it had grown unbelievably large for the area since she had last been here and it had been dark when they'd driven to the town. They could be anywhere. Close to the desert, close to the Huachuca Mountains, or in the middle of town. She had no idea.

Earlier, one of the agents guarding her had given her the news her parents had been transported to a safe house and were no longer in any danger. Despite the fact she thought the agents were keeping something from her, much of the tension in her body had dissipated when she'd learned her mother and father were safe. Landon had taken care of them just like she'd asked.

It terrified her to think about the cartel finding her parents like they'd found Gregory.

And hurting her parents the way they'd hurt Gregory…

Her eyes ached and her fingers hurt from clenching them so tightly on the book.

She wondered when Landon would return, or if he intended to leave her protection to the three agents with her now. She should probably feel safe with these agents, but for some reason she only felt truly safe with Landon. He'd saved her when the cartel had attacked the house last night.

The fact she wanted him didn't have anything to do with the fact she'd been ready to jump him before the lights had gone out.

No.

Well maybe.

"That's lust talking," she mumbled to herself.

"What about lust?" came a deep male voice from behind her.

She started and jumped to her feet, the paperback hitting the floor with a thump. Her face flamed as she spun to face Landon, seeing the corner of his mouth tipped into a sexy grin.

Her mind raced to change the subject. "How are my mom and dad?"

He set down her clarinet case. "They're fine. Your mother got it out of your bedroom."

"So she's all right." Tori smiled with relief. "Thank you."

"You apparently like pink," he said with humor in his voice.

She couldn't help a grin. "You saw my bedroom."

He grinned back. "Couldn't miss it."

She blinked as it occurred to her he hadn't said anything about her father. "My dad?"

Landon's expression turned serious. "We got there in time to save your parents. Two of our agents were attacked, but they're alive."

"Two of your agents were attacked?" Tori's eyes widened. "Because of me?"

"Like I told you before, it isn't your fault." Landon stepped closer and clasped her hands in his. "They were gassed, but they'll be fine."

She sagged with relief. "Thank God."

He looked grim. "We'll take Diego and his organization down and they will pay for what they've done."

It occurred to her that he'd said they'd gotten to her mom and dad in time to save them, but nothing about their well-being. "My parents—were they harmed at all?"

"The men roughed up your mom a little and she sustained a wound to her cheek." Landon's voice hardened. "Your father was at St. Elmo's when it all went down."

"They hurt Mom?" She heard the near panic in her voice. "I want to see her."

"It's safer to keep you apart." Landon moved his palms up and down her arms in a gentle caress clearly meant to calm her. After a few moments, some of the tension keyed up in her dissipated. Some.

She blew out a long breath. "As long as they're safe wherever they are."

"It's getting late." He studied her. "You look as if you can use some rest."

"Are you going to leave me?" She spoke the words before she could stop herself and her face warmed again.

"If you want me to stay, I will." His features didn't look as harsh in the dim light of the lamp on the nightstand.

Without thinking, she raised her hand and ran her finger along the thick scar on his cheek. Her voice softened. "What happened?"

He froze and pain flashed in his gaze. "A motorcycle accident." His words came out terse, almost angry.

She jerked her hand away. "I'm sorry. I didn't mean to pry."

His features relaxed. "Don't be sorry. It happened a year ago. My fiancée, Stacy, died in the accident."

She could feel the strength of his grief but also his acceptance. She touched his arm, trying to comfort him in what small way she could. "That's awful."

"Yeah, it is." He looked away before meeting Tori's gaze again. "It took me a long time to get past it, but I've finally come to terms with what happened."

Tori gave a slow nod. "I can't imagine what you've been through."

"To Hell and back." He reached up and toyed with a strand of her hair. "What about you? Your boyfriend is dead."

"He verbally and emotionally abused me. I finally got smart and left after—" She shook her head. "He as good as raped me the night before I left. He thought I cheated on him and he forced himself on me."

Landon's expression grew dark. "Sonofabitch."

"That's how I ended up here. I fled the next day." She dropped her gaze. "But for him to die in such a horrible way. I feel responsible."

She didn't know that she'd ever stop feeling responsible.

"Hey." Landon drew Tori into his arms. At first she resisted, but then she relaxed and burrowed into his embrace, her cheek pressed into his T-shirt, her body so soft against his. He looked down and saw tears squeeze from beneath her closed eyelids as she stifled a sob. "It's natural to want to blame yourself. I blamed myself for my fiancée's death when the blame should have been squarely on the hit-and-run driver."

He never expected those words to come out. He'd felt responsible for her death for so long. Was it true he didn't feel that way any longer? Or had he said it only to make Tori feel better?

If he hadn't been at fault, he couldn't use that excuse any longer to push people away.

He'd probably have no problem coming up with something else to keep others at a distance.

"Did they find the driver?" Tori's question drew him back to her. Her face pressed into his shirt, her body warm in his arms.

"Yes." He stroked Tori's hair. "The driver wrapped his car around a telephone pole and managed to live through it. The drunk bastard is in prison for what he did."

"Even though it doesn't make up for what happened, I'm glad you had at least some resolution." Tori shifted against him, as if she wanted to get even closer.

Almost absently, he rubbed his thumb along Tori's delicate jawline while they both remained quiet. He liked the way she fit in his arms. It felt...right.

He should tell her about what happened with Brian. Now.

Every good intention vanished as she tipped her face up to look at him. Her eyelashes glittered from the remainder of her tears and her brown eyes seemed even darker than normal. Their gazes met and held and he didn't think he'd ever be able to look away from her again. She drew him to her in so many ways and he couldn't stop himself from wanting to get closer to her.

The other agents remained downstairs while he had come upstairs, alone. With Tori.

This isn't smart.

Hell, he was nowhere near being smart.

He held his breath then let out a slow exhalation, lowering lowered his mouth to hers.

The moment their lips met, she gave a sigh, surrendering herself to his kiss. That sense of surrender fueled him, making him desire her even more than he already did.

He moved his lips over hers, hungry for the taste of her, the feel of her. Her scent filled him as if a part of her slid beneath his skin. Her soft lips tasted exquisite on his tongue. God, he knew he could never get enough of her.

She leaned into him, letting their body heat meld, fusing them together in a way that defied explanation. Her sighs turned into a soft moan as he moved his hands over her shoulders, down her arms, and to her waist. She wore one of her new T-shirts and he pushed the hem up just enough to feel her soft skin along the waistband. He gripped her slender waist in his hands, his fingers brushing the base of her spine and her tattoo.

Her hunger and his grew in matching intensity. She moved her palms up his chest to his shoulders and gripped them as if afraid she would slip away if she didn't hold on tightly.

He slipped his palms from her waist to her ass, feeling the perfection of it as he squeezed her closer to him. His cock, impossibly hard, pressed to her, straining to get free from behind the tough denim of his jeans.

Their clothes — far too many. He wanted to feel her warm silky skin against his, nothing keeping them apart. He wanted only to nestle between her thighs and drive his cock deep inside her heat.

The rumble rising in his chest was like a lion staking a claim on his territory and she made an answering purr, giving herself completely to him. Not just surrendering, but offering herself for his pleasure. She asked for nothing, just gave him everything she had.

She sighed again as he slid his lips along her jawline to her ear. She gasped when he nipped at her earlobe and shivered in a delicate way, telling him he'd just found one of her erogenous zones. He sucked the soft flesh into his mouth and nipped at it again. Another shiver ran through her body.

He moved his lips down the column of her neck to the hollow at the base of her throat. The soft purring sounds she made caused his cock to grow even harder and he rubbed himself against her in a slow, deliberate movement.

A gasp escaped her when he cupped her breasts and flicked his thumbs over her taut nipples through the fabric of her T-shirt. She speared her fingers into his hair and encouraged him to lower his head so his mouth lowered to her breasts. His body shook from the power of his need for her when he circled her nipple with his tongue, wetting the T-shirt and causing her to suck in her breath. She gave a small cry and gripped his hair tighter, encouraging him to move his mouth to her other nipple.

He had to taste the salt on her skin, feel its softness in his mouth. He pushed her T-shirt over her perfectly sized breasts and licked each of her nipples through her satin bra. She caught her breath when he pulled her bra beneath her breasts so they were bared for him.

She pushed his head down again, guiding him so his mouth hovered directly over her nipple. He skimmed his lips over the hard nub and she moaned as he sucked it and flicked it with his tongue. Her nipples were hard peaks for him to nip at each one. God, but he loved the way she tasted. He loved that she didn't hesitate to show him what she wanted. He loved everything about her.

"Landon." His name sounded like music coming from her lips.

"Landon." A different voice cut through Landon's haze. A male voice.

Tori jerked away, frantically tugging at her clothes. Landon stayed in front of her so she couldn't be seen. She looked mortified and Landon gave her a reassuring expression.

Keeping Tori behind him, he slowly turned to see Dylan standing in the doorway. He had his arms folded across his chest, his shoulder hitched against the doorframe. A hint of amusement played across his features.

"What do you want?" Landon's voice came out rougher than he'd intended.

"Better me than one of the other agents." Dylan flashed a grin. "I have business to talk with you about when you're ready."

Landon glanced back at Tori who appeared to have collected herself. She still looked embarrassed but gave a nod. He squeezed her hand before turning and following Dylan out of the room.

Dylan shook his head as Landon joined him in the hallway. "You picked a hell of a time, not to mention she's a witness. Are you out of your god damned mind?"

Landon's jaw hurt from clenching his teeth so tightly. He couldn't blame Dylan for walking in on them. Hell, nothing should have happened between him and Tori. Like Dylan said, Tori was a witness.

She'd been so damned sweet to his taste, to his touch. He didn't know if he could keep his hands off her.

Landon dragged his hand down his face, his stubble catching on his palm. "What do you need to discuss?"

"Once you told Aguilar that Tori ID'd Alejandro Jimenez,

John Graves, and Pablo Perez, I worked up the affidavit for the arrest warrants and pitched it to the U.S. Attorney's Office." Dylan hooked his thumbs in his jeans' pockets. "Thought you'd be happy to know we have warrants for the arrests of all three bastards."

"Good." Landon felt a hint of triumph. "Fucking great."

Dylan started toward the stairs. "We've had teams of agents scouring the area to locate and arrest these guys."

Landon walked down the stairs with Dylan. "Now we just have to find and serve the sonsofbitches and take them in."

Tori's face burned when she picked up the paperback she'd dropped on the floor. What had she been thinking? A house full of agents surrounded her and she'd just made out with one of them. How far would it have gone if Agent Curtis hadn't walked in?

She barely knew Landon and she'd let him practically take off her shirt. No, more like she had encouraged him to go further and further. She'd wanted him. She still wanted him—more than she could remember wanting any man.

Her thoughts turned to her parents. Landon had said they were both all right and she trusted him to tell her the truth. She knew she could rely on Landon being honest with her, whatever might happen.

When her nerves tried to get the best of her, or she needed a distraction, she always liked to pick up an instrument and play, especially her clarinet. During this traumatic time, she hadn't had anything until now and it had been driving her crazy.

She opened the case holding the clarinet her parents had purchased for her when she'd earned first chair as a freshman in high school. They had spent more money on the clarinet than they'd been able to afford, but they'd pulled it together.

Memories washed through her as she assembled the instrument and she thought of her best friend. Tori and

Paula often practiced as a duo as well as doing a lot of the fun things women liked to do. Tori missed shopping with her friend, talking for hours, going to movies, meeting up for coffee or dinner. Ordinary things Tori couldn't do anymore.

Thank goodness she'd left the box of reeds at her parents' home the last time she'd visited them, and her mother had thought to grab them for her. Otherwise, she would have had to wait until someone bought a box for her—if she could find someone who had the time to do so.

She wet a reed then absently let her fingers dance over the keys, her eyes closed.

At their first concert of the season in September, the Tucson Symphony Orchestra would be performing Gustav Holst's *The Planets*. One of her favorite parts in the suite for clarinet was in 'Jupiter, the Bringer of Jollity', and she let the tune fill the air.

Her fingers moved, music flowing through her. Music completed her heart and soul in a way nothing else could and carried her far from the here and now.

Music had helped her escape from reality as a small child when her father had been a belligerent drunk. It had allowed her emotional freedom the times she'd been bullied in school. It had set her free for a while from Gregory's verbal and emotional abuse.

And now, once again, it took her away.

Escape, she just needed the escape.

The last note faded and she sighed, her eyes still closed for her to hold on to the moment.

The bed dipped and the bedsprings creaked. Her eyelids flew open and she set the clarinet on her lap. Even before she'd opened her eyes, she'd known it was Landon beside her. His magnetic scent and his electrifying presence sent tingles along her skin.

She met his gaze and felt warm all over again as she let herself be caught in the spell of the unusual green shade of his eyes.

"You are incredible," he stated. "Your music is magic."

"Thank you." She smiled. "Usually, not a day goes by that I don't do something music-related, especially practicing." She shifted on the bed to face him better. "I wanted to ask you if I could have a notebook along with pencils and pens."

"Sure." He gave a nod. "Do you journal?"

"Not really." She shook her head. "I compose. It's something I do because I love it, but it's also good therapy."

"Not a problem." He gave her a smile. "Just tell me what you need and I'll get it for you."

"Thank you." She returned his smile, but it faded when she remembered what they'd been doing just a short time earlier. "I'm sorry about what happened. I shouldn't have—"

He put his fingers over her lips. "Hey. You don't have anything to apologize for. If anyone should apologize, it should be me."

Studying his roughly carved features, she didn't want him to have to feel as if he should apologize. She wanted him to tell her it hadn't been a mistake and the kiss had meant everything to him that it had to her. She wanted him to say how he'd wanted to kiss her since they'd met, just as she had.

For a long moment neither of them said anything. "I loved it," almost spilled out of her mouth but the words stayed in her head where they belonged.

He gave her a long, searching stare. "Are you tired?"

She blinked at the change in topic. "Yes."

"Then I'll let you get some sleep." He put his hand on her shoulder and squeezed it before he stood.

She got to her feet too. "Are you leaving?"

He hesitated and looked as if he wanted to touch her again. "I'll be in the living room."

"Thank you." She crossed her arms over her chest, holding herself tightly, feeling she might fall apart if she didn't.

He hesitated then leaned down and brushed his lips over her cheek. "Get some rest, honey."

Her eyes widened a bit at the endearment, but he turned away and walked to the bedroom door. He glanced once over his shoulder, his gaze meeting hers.

And he left.

For a long moment, she gripped her clarinet as she stared at the place where he'd been standing. Landon attracted her more than she wanted to admit, even to herself. She didn't just feel a physical attraction, but something deeper, on a level she probably wouldn't recognize even if her best friend pointed it out to her.

She and Agent Landon Walker were *not* meant to be. She'd better keep that fact in mind before she ended up losing her heart.

Chapter Fifteen

Smoke filled the air as Diego crushed the stub of his Cuban cigar in the ashtray on the corner of his desk. Fury heated him, crawled up his spine, and sent tension through every part of his body. The woman had escaped the first attack and now her parents had as well.

But Alejandro had said his plans for tonight would work. The bitch had to die.

If she didn't, American agents could arrest Alejandro, as well as the two men assigned to protect him and to clean up any messes that might arise. And this was one big fucking mess.

Diego would never allow his son to be tried for any crime, much less imprisoned. Once his men had eliminated Tori Cox, Diego would make sure he had every last person involved killed. The dead couldn't speak.

He sensed a presence and he cut his gaze from the ashtray to the doorway to see Alicia. At nineteen, the youngest of his housekeepers, she had an inviting smile and even more enticing body.

Right now, he wanted to relieve some of his anger.

"You called for me?" she asked in a small voice, somehow still sounding sexy.

"Come in and close the door." He snarled the command. "And lock it."

She gave him a frightened look, obeying. Her eyes widened and her hand shook when she turned the lock.

He motioned for her to come to him. She hesitated and he narrowed his gaze. The look in her dark eyes became one of true fear and that made him hard.

When she reached him, he raised his hand and backhanded her. She cried out as her head snapped to the side. In his mind, she became the woman who had put his son in danger, the woman who needed to be killed.

He restrained from snapping Alicia's neck. Instead, he gripped the front of her blouse and ripped it open. She gave another cry and he backhanded her again. He still had a grip on her blouse with one hand, holding her so she didn't stumble backward.

He raised his hand to strike her again. "Shut up, bitch."

Tears formed in her eyes and she clamped her mouth shut. Diego moved his gaze to her breasts. He loved the size of them. He'd wanted to fuck her since Esmeralda had hired her, but he hadn't touched her. He only hired beautiful young women and most of them were willing and pleased to serve him in every way possible.

At this moment he didn't want a willing woman. He wanted a powerless woman...just like the woman in Arizona would be when he smuggled her into Mexico and used her before handing her off to others. He had now decided he did not want to kill her. No. He wanted to make her pay in other ways.

Diego's gaze roved over Alicia's beautiful body. He still loved his wife who had passed away years ago. But a man had his needs and right now Diego needed to take out his anger and frustration on someone. Alicia was that someone.

She bit her lower lip to keep from crying out again as he took her large nipples and pinched them hard. He twisted them and her eyes watered, tears rolling down her cheeks. He released her nipples long enough to spin her around and force her face and torso against the desk. Her whole body shook.

He shoved her skirt over her ass, pleased to see she wore nothing beneath her clothing. She had a beautiful ass. He forced her legs apart with his knees before he unfastened his belt and pants.

In one thrust, he buried himself inside her and she made

a muffled sound. Her dryness excited him—he liked the friction. She wasn't a virgin, an unfortunate thing, as he would have liked to be the first to take her.

He fucked the bitch hard, taking out all his fury on her. The slut deserved to be on the receiving end of his anger. She should have kept herself pure. No doubt she'd worn nothing beneath her uniform so she could fuck his driver or his gardener, or any one of the many men on his staff. Maybe all of them.

His anger magnified and her body rocked against his desk as he slammed into her. His tension and wrath balled up in his groin.

He all but exploded when he came. He thrust until he'd completely shot his semen inside her and spent himself, becoming almost too exhausted to pull out.

When he did, he tucked himself back inside his slacks and fastened his belt. She didn't move from where she lay on his desk, but her body continued to tremble.

He pulled her long hair, jerking her to her feet. Glimpsing her face, he saw a drop of blood had formed on her lip where she'd bitten it. Black mascara streaked her face and her eyes were red, her cheeks wet with tears. She had marks on her face from where he'd backhanded her.

"Straighten up." He gestured to her clothing. She tugged down the skirt and he handed her a handkerchief. "Take care of your face."

She took the handkerchief and wiped away the black marks from her cheeks. He looked at her exposed breasts and started to harden again. She grabbed her blouse, now free of buttons, and pulled the sides together, covering her breasts.

"Get out of here and go clean yourself up." He pointed toward the door. "Before you leave, make sure no one will see you."

She didn't hesitate this time. She hurried toward the door. Just as she grabbed the handle, he spoke, "I expect you to remain with us." She didn't turn away from the door as he added, "I know your family and I will kill them if you speak of this. Do you understand?"

A visible shudder rippled through her body and she nodded before unlocking and opening the door and peering out.

She fled.

Diego felt more relaxed but in complete control of himself and those around him. He didn't like this feeling of being out of control when it came to the woman in the U.S. who had witnessed his son murdering the scum who had wormed himself into the heart of his organization. It would be only a matter of time before they murdered the woman called Tori Cox.

Chapter Sixteen

Landon and Dylan eased up to the door of the house on the outskirts of Douglas, where they hoped to find John Graves and Pablo Perez. If they were lucky, Alejandro Jimenez would be there too.

Peeling white paint on the outside of the house and the weed-choked yard with junk strewn everywhere gave the house a neglected look. Considering the state of the place, Landon would bet Alejandro would have nothing to do with a crap hole like this.

The bright sun shined through gaps in spotty clouds, heating the air. Landon's heavy body armor made him feel even hotter. Sweat dripped down the side of his face and rolled onto his neck.

Dylan leaned against the house and held his weapon down in a two-handed grip. "Your informant better be right."

"Carl's reliable." Landon watched other DHS agents move into position. "Usually."

Dylan grimaced at Landon. "It's the 'usually' part I don't like."

Gripping his Colt .45, Landon silently moved to the opposite side of the door to stand on one side while Dylan took the other. Dylan, like the other agents, wore body armor. Dylan and Landon each had a tactical holster strapped to their thighs.

Four other agents waited with Landon and Dylan by the door. With each agent in place, Landon peeked through the window and saw John Graves. Landon's lips tightened into a thin line and he nodded at Dylan.

Landon reared back and jammed his foot against the door. The locking mechanisms were inferior and the door broke free and swung open, hitting the wall with a crash.

"Police!" Landon shouted.

In the same instant, he swept his gaze over the scene and saw three men in the front room, all holding weapons. The men whirled to face the door as it crashed open. Landon got off two shots then ducked back behind the doorframe.

One of the men gave a grunt of pain right before the shooting started.

Dylan swung around the doorframe just long enough to get in a few shots prior to moving aside. A man came close to a window and one of the snipers picked him off. Dylan and Landon took care of the other two and cleared the room before more DHS agents swarmed in. Shouts of "Police!" filled the air.

Two of the men were dead. They'd injured one man, John Graves. Blood seeped from a wound in his abdomen and he lay sprawled on the floor but tried to get up. He'd dropped his weapon a few feet away. When Landon stood over the son of a bitch, he aimed his Colt at Graves' head and the man went still. Landon kicked Graves' gun aside.

Landon recognized the two dead as wanted men from the Jimenez Cartel. Agents went to each body and checked for a pulse and shook their heads when they found none.

With O'Donnell standing over Graves, his gun trained on the man, Landon and Dylan moved down the hallway to a closed door. Incredibly loud music pounded from inside, a heavy throb and the deep bass causing the walls to vibrate.

Landon and Dylan moved to either side of the door. With a nod to Landon, Dylan kicked the door in with a loud crash. He and Landon immediately pointed their weapons at a man and woman in bed.

The woman screamed.

"Police!" Landon shouted. "Freeze. Hands in the air."

Pablo slowly raised his hands, but the naked woman wrapped herself in a sheet and shrank away from Dylan and

Landon. Dylan cleared the room and checked the bathroom while Landon kept his Colt trained on Pablo Perez, who scrambled to sit up.

Dylan ordered the woman to drop the sheet and raise her hands. She clearly read the danger in his eyes and she hurried to obey as he continued to point his weapon at her.

Landon moved toward the bed and Perez sneered at him. Landon took the handgun resting on the nightstand, put on the safety, and tucked it in his jeans. He knelt and scooped up a pair of pants from the floor, checked the pockets for any kind of weapon then tossed the pants onto the bed.

"Get dressed." Landon backed a few feet away as he spoke to Perez. "Slowly."

Perez slid off the bed and pulled on his pants, never taking his eyes off Landon.

After checking the woman's clothing and tossing it to her, Dylan ordered her to get dressed as well, keeping his own weapon aimed at her.

Landon tossed Perez a button-up shirt from the foot of the bed. Perez slid it on and buttoned it. After Perez had put on his shoes, Landon handcuffed him. "We have a warrant for your arrest."

Perez spit on the floor.

"Out." Landon pushed Perez toward the door. "Move it."

Dylan cuffed the now dressed woman and they left the room first.

Perez, his head held high, walked down the hall to the living room, Landon gripping his upper arm. John Graves still lay on the floor, pale from loss of blood as emergency medical technicians worked on him. Agent O'Donnell remained close by.

"How bad is it?" Landon asked the EMTs as he brought Perez to a halt.

One of the technicians leaned back on his haunches. "Bullet went clean through."

Graves bared his teeth in a pained scowl but remained still as EMTs wheeled in a stretcher. O'Donnell never left

Graves' side, even when they loaded him onto the stretcher. O'Donnell handcuffed him to it and helped take him out to the waiting ambulance.

For the sake of officer safety, in case more men with guns were hiding, the agents searched the house. While they checked it out, they found no sign of Alejandro Jimenez. However, they did find a shitload of cash and drugs lying out, plain to see, in the kitchen and in a back room.

Landon and Dylan marched Perez outside and Landon shoved him into the backseat of one of the agency cars and shut the door hard behind him. The men watched the ambulance and agency vehicle leave, their drivers speeding them away.

"We got two of the sonsofbitches." Landon looked at Dylan. "You ready?"

"Hell, yes." Dylan started toward his SUV. "Let's get this party rolling."

It didn't take long to travel the distance from the house in Douglas to the DHS office. They ushered Perez into one of the interrogation rooms. Dylan and Landon went in the room a short time later, where they'd handcuffed the man to a chair. Dylan leaned up against the doorframe as Landon stood in front of Perez.

"We have an eyewitness putting you at the scene of a homicide three nights ago." Landon kept his tone and his expression controlled. "The murder of a DHS agent."

Perez's expression grew cocky, as if he feared nothing. "I want a call and I want my lawyer."

"You've already been identified." Landon gave Perez a hard look. "Now's the time to start talking if you want to save your ass."

Perez shrugged. "I want my lawyer."

Landon's temper flared even though he'd known going into the interrogation Perez would not give up anything easily. "We know Alejandro Jimenez pulled the trigger while you and John Graves held down the agent. You will get prison time."

Perez smirked. "Give me my call."

"Did I mention the crack we found lying around the house you were in?" Landon managed to rein in his temper. "Found your stash with one hell of a lot of cash." He gave Perez a look of disgust. "Think your cartel is going to stand by you when you lose close to a million dollars in cash and crack?"

For the first time, Perez appeared unnerved. "Just get me my damn lawyer."

Landon shook his head. "Even if we didn't have anything to hold you and cut you free, you'd probably be gunned down the moment you set foot outside this place."

Perez licked his lips.

"If you give us everything we want on Diego and Alejandro Jimenez and help us put them away, we can put you under our protection and offer you a deal." Landon stared unflinchingly at Perez. "If you don't, you know you're as good as dead as far as the cartel is concerned."

Perez said nothing but Landon thought he saw a hint of fear before the cocky expression replaced it. "Go to Hell, motherfucker."

"If Graves gives us what we need then our offer to you is off the table and you go to prison for a long time. And you'll be a dead man as far as the cartel is concerned." Landon gave the man another look before walking to where Dylan stood. He glanced over his shoulder at Perez who glared at them. Landon added loud enough for Perez to hear, "We'll give Perez time to consider everything."

Dylan opened the door and they walked out of the room. "Let's go see what Graves has to say."

When they reached the Douglas hospital, Landon and Dylan went to the information desk and were given the location and room number for Graves.

As they walked through the hospital, flashbacks nearly caused Landon to stumble and halt. The smells and the very atmosphere of the place reminded him too much of Stacy and the night she'd died. He'd been carted away to the hospital. Stacy's body had been taken to the hospital too, for the official declaration of her death. For more than a year he'd told himself he should have died, not her.

A thought occurred to him. Tori had changed that. Somehow, after meeting her, he didn't have a death wish any longer.

What the fuck was with him? He barely knew the woman.

It didn't take long for Dylan and Landon to reach the room where they held Graves. Two agents were stationed on either side of the doorway.

Landon spoke with the junior agents. "Has anyone outside of hospital staff stopped by?"

The agent to the left of the doorway shook his head. "No one."

"Only nurses and a doctor have entered the room, all of whom had been cleared." The other agent spoke up. "A nurse and the doctor are with Graves now."

The nurse opened the door and came out into the hallway. Landon introduced himself and Dylan to the nurse before asking about Graves' condition.

The woman, appearing to be in her late forties, held a chart to her chest. "The doctor is with him now. You can ask him when he comes out."

A moment later, a man in a white hospital coat and green scrubs stepped out of Graves' room.

"Dr. Harrison?" Landon asked.

"Yes?" The doctor adjusted his stethoscope around his neck as he looked from Landon to Dylan. "How can I help you, gentlemen?"

"I'm Special Agent Walker and this is Special Agent Curtis." Landon inclined his head in the direction of Graves' room. "How is the patient?"

"Mr. Graves is in a stable condition." Dr. Harrison didn't appear to be concerned. "The bullet went through his side cleanly and no organs were damaged. He's been treated and should be discharged to DHS by tomorrow."

"Too bad," Dylan muttered under his breath, low enough

that hopefully only Landon could hear him.

"Thank you, Doctor." Landon nodded to Graves' room. "We'd like to ask him a few questions."

Dr. Harrison gestured to the doorway. "Go right on in."

Landon and Dylan entered the room. One of John Graves' wrists hung from a cuff fastened to the bedrail. The blond man aeemed a little worse for the wear, his face pale and drawn. He scowled when he saw the agents but he didn't speak.

"We're going to have a little talk, Graves." Dylan stood near the bed. "And you'd better listen closely."

The conversation went much like the one with Perez had. The excessively angry and stubborn Graves also kept asking for a lawyer.

"You know you won't walk out of this alive." Landon eyed Graves squarely. "Diego Jimenez doesn't like loose ends. You assisted his son in executing a federal agent and your testimony would help get him convicted. He's not going to let you live."

Landon knew they were starting to get to him as Graves' blinked rapidly and passed a hand over his face. "Fuck you."

"I think you're the one who's going to be thoroughly fucked when this is all over with." Landon rested his hand on the bar agents had handcuffed Graves to. "Think fast because you don't have much time."

Like Perez, Graves remained mute. Landon and Dylan left the room.

"One of them will come around." Dylan jangled his keys in his hand as they headed through the hospital's automatic glass doors. "I'm betting on Perez."

Landon squinted at the bright sunshine and pulled a pair of sunglasses out of the pocket of his overshirt to slip on. "I'm betting you're right."

* * * *

Tori sat on the couch in the living room downstairs and O'Donnell reclined in the overstuffed chair. The ugly furnishings with goldish-brown upholstery and scuffed wood coffee and end tables had clearly seen plenty of use.

She'd spent some time with her clarinet, which had soothed her, but she felt caged now. She glanced at O'Donnell, who still had small cuts on his face from the night at the first safe house when they'd been attacked.

One of the popular reality singing shows played on the TV and she thought her brain would explode. To her trained ear, it physically hurt to listen to the bad singing, guitar, and piano playing. Granted, some contestants sang and played their instruments beautifully, but the bad ones gave her a headache.

"You okay?" O'Donnell asked, drawing her out of her thoughts as the commercials came on.

"I'll be fine." She tried to smile. "Just going a little stir crazy. I could really use a glass of wine right now."

"I don't blame you for being stir crazy. I'll get you some water." He looked apologetic. "Sorry we don't have anything stronger."

He stood and headed in the direction of the kitchen then paused in the archway between the rooms. "Hey, Danson. Toss me a couple bottles of water." He stayed in the doorway where he could keep an eye on the front door and Tori while he waited for Agent Danson to hand him the bottles.

Where could Landon be? He'd been gone since early this morning and now the sun had gone down. Would he return today? A new ache in her chest surprised her. Why did she need to see him so badly?

Need or *want*?

Both.

She leaned her head back against the couch and looked up at the ceiling. She didn't know how on earth she would manage living in protective custody. It made her claustrophobic. Having one of her clarinets helped, but she would love a notebook to compose in. She couldn't find paper or a pen anywhere in this damned house. Composing and playing her instrument soothed her whenever something upset her. She'd been through it plenty of times with Gregory.

Her throat constricted as she thought of him. He'd been a bastard but he hadn't deserved to die the way he had. His intern hadn't deserved to be murdered, either. Even though Landon had told her not to blame herself, she couldn't help feeling the deaths were her fault.

When O'Donnell returned, he handed her an icy-cold water bottle that chilled her fingertips.

"Thanks." She took a drink. The cool and refreshing water assuaged her thirst, but she really did want something stronger.

O'Donnell's phone buzzed. He pulled it out of his pocket and answered it. "About time." O'Donnell got up and went to the door.

A moment later he let Landon in. Tori's belly flip-flopped and she couldn't believe how fast her body reacted to seeing him. Just thinking about his kisses and the way he had caressed her body made her nipples taut beneath her T-shirt.

He met her gaze and raised a bag. "Hope you like Chinese."

"Love it." She got to her feet, the warm smells of the food he carried making her stomach growl.

She followed him into the kitchen that had a small dining area off to the side. He set all of the white containers at the center of the long table and she helped him open everything while Agent Claire Danson grabbed plates out of the cabinets.

After Landon took a plate of food into the living room for Agent O'Donnell, he returned with a slim bag she hadn't noticed before. The bag had the name of a music store scrawled across it. He handed Tori the bag then sat next to her at the table.

Her lips curved into a broad smile as she opened the package and pulled out a beautiful notebook called The Musician's Notebook, with staves for writing music, tablatures for recording chords, and space for writing lyrics. The black notebook had quotes from legendary musicians about the creative process and the thrill of performance.

She almost teared up from the fact he'd taken the time to get her the notebook. "You don't know how much this means to me."

"No problem at all." He returned her smile before spooning white rice onto his plate and following it with broccoli beef. "Pencils are at the bottom of the bag, along with a pen."

"Thank you." She slipped the notebook back into the bag and set it on the chair beside her prior to reaching for the carton of kung pao chicken.

"If you end up going into the Witness Security Program" — Agent Danson tilted her head to the side — "you will never be allowed to perform in public again or even teach music." She gave Tori an apologetic smile. "You won't be allowed to do anything relating to your current career. The cartel could find you if you did."

Tori paused in mid-motion, her hand on the Chinese food container. She looked from Danson to Landon. "What?" Had she heard right? She *prayed* she hadn't.

A hard expression crossed Landon's expression and he glared at Danson. "If — no, *when* — we take down Diego and Alejandro Jimenez, it won't be an issue."

Tori's appetite vanished. "What you're saying is if you don't get them, I'll have to go into hiding and never perform again? I wouldn't be able to teach music?"

"It's one of the rules of WITSEC." Danson drew Tori's attention back to her. "You have to take on a new career, change your name, move to a different part of the U.S. and can never be in contact with your family or friends from your old life."

Tori's mind reeled and she placed her palms flat on the

table to steady herself. Never perform again? Never teach again? Never see her family again? Never see her friends from school, or the symphony, or anyone else she knew?

Dear God.

She pushed back her chair. "Excuse me. I'm tired and I'm going to bed." She scooted her chair back up to the table and didn't so much as glance at Danson or Landon as she left the room and headed up the stairs to her bedroom.

Tears burned in her eyes. She wanted to slam the door shut behind her so it vibrated through the house. She wanted to scream and beat on the walls with her fists. The cartel could take everything from her. *Everything.*

She sat on the edge of the bed and covered her mouth with her hand to hold back a sob.

A knock came at the door. "Tori?" Landon's voice.

She didn't speak and he pushed open the door. He held the bag with the musician's notebook. He set it on the nightstand, next to the paperback book she'd been reading.

He sat beside her on the bed and tears began rolling down her cheeks. Landon put his arm around her shoulders. At first she resisted but then she allowed him to draw her close to him and rested her head on his chest. A hard lump rose in her throat and the floodgates opened. Her entire body shook with the force of her sobs.

"We'll get them." Landon stroked her hair. "We'll take down the bastards and you won't ever have to run ever again."

More tears squeezed from her eyes. "I can't give up my life, my family. I can't give up everything I love."

Landon said nothing for a moment and his silence said everything he didn't.

She trembled. She didn't know if she could ever stop crying. He held her for a long time, comforting her.

"Shhhh." He held her close. "We'll get them. You need to believe we will."

She gave one last shuddering sob. When she drew back, she stared up at him. "Please. Please get them."

Without thinking about it, she moved her face closer to his and brushed his lips with hers.

He sucked in a breath, as if she'd caught him by surprise. She drew back but he slid his fingers into her hair and cupped the back of her head before bringing his lips down on hers. He kissed her in return, slowly exploring her mouth. He traced her lower lip with his tongue then gently nipped at her lip and tugged on it.

"You smell so damn good," he murmured. "I love the feel of you in my arms."

"I like it too." She looked into his eyes. "I don't want to stop. I want you."

"You don't know how much I want you, honey." He held her close, her head burrowed into his chest. "Unfortunately, we have chaperones."

She sighed. "It was a dumb idea."

"It was a wonderful idea." He nuzzled her hair. "You are amazing." He leaned back and wiped away her tears with his thumbs. "Why don't you come out and get something for dinner?"

"I'm going to go to bed." She brushed her hand over the front of her blouse and he glanced down. Her nipples were hard, poking against her T-shirt. "It's only too obvious what I want. I need time to think about all of this and I might as well get some sleep." She put her hand on the bag containing The Musician's Notebook. "Thank you for this."

He gave her another soft kiss. "Goodnight, honey."

She drank in his green eyes, wishing she could look into them as he slid inside her. "Goodnight."

He pressed his lips to her hair before getting up and going to the bedroom door. He gave her one last lingering look then walked out of the room. He drew the door almost closed behind him, leaving it open a couple of inches.

After he left, she sat on the edge of the bed, staring at her hands. Musician's hands. Other than her family, she loved music more than anything. It meant everything to her.

Tori closed her eyes tightly and let out her breath. She

needed to listen to Landon. She had to believe in him and believe the agents would take down the members of the cartel who were after her. She'd get her life back then.

All would go back to normal. As normal as it could after everything that had happened and everything that was to come.

Chapter Seventeen

Something soft and firm brushed Tori's lips and she stirred. A mouth moved over hers in a long, languorous kiss that stole her breath.

She dreamed about kissing Landon, the most beautiful thing she could imagine at this moment. God, how she wanted to trace his abs with her tongue and her fingers before she kissed him even more deeply.

If he were real right now, she would see the length and girth of his erection then take it in her hand. She would feel the softness and the steel of it then lick a path from the tip to the balls and back. She would love to go down on him, take him to the back of her mouth. The feeling would be a powerful one, knowing she had control of his pleasure.

So real. The kiss felt so real. He sucked her tongue, took her bottom lip into his mouth to lightly bite it and lick the soft flesh, something that drove her crazy.

Their mouths and lips became more frenzied, more urgent, her answering him with incredible passion. A warm hand cupped her cheek, a thumb stroking up and down while holding her still so he could kiss her hard and deep.

It grew harder to breathe as her body revved up. She needed him. God, how she needed him.

She let out a soft sigh when the kiss ended. Her lips felt moist and they tingled. Her eyelids fluttered and in the near darkness she found herself looking into Landon's gaze.

Her eyes widened and she parted her lips to say something, but he put his hand over her mouth. Was something wrong? No, nothing could be wrong. Everything was right, so right. His hand smelled like soap and she breathed in his scent.

Even in the dim light, she could make out the desire, want, and desperate need in his gaze. Knowing he desired, wanted, and needed her created a potent feeling of power within her. She could see it in the way he looked at her, the way he'd kissed her.

"Shhh." He skimmed her cheek with his knuckles and threaded his fingers into her silky hair, only stopping to hold her tight. "I'm sorry." Need, deeper than usual and almost strained, filled his voice. "I stopped to check on you, and you looked so beautiful I wanted to kiss you. Now I don't know if I can keep my hands off you."

Earlier he'd said he would protect her and he wouldn't let her go. A strong sensation of him claiming her as his own nearly made her mind spin with its headiness. At this moment she wanted him to claim her, wanted to be his.

"I'm glad you did check in." Breathless and shameless, she didn't care if she sounded needy. "And just maybe I don't want you to keep your hands off me."

Bedsprings creaked as he shifted his weight and he leaned over her and braced his hands on either side of her body. Light seeped in from beneath the closed door and a little more came through slanted, not fully closed blinds.

The heady, intense feeling she had at the thought of the other agents in the house ramped up her excitement. Could they be caught again? Only this time it would be far more than kissing.

She wanted to rock his world while making sure the other agents didn't know.

In the faint light, she saw the intensity of his expression. She wanted to trace the wicked scar along his cheek with her fingers and lips. He looked so good, so large and powerful. He made her feel safe and at the same time he made her want him.

His scent...it permeated every pore of her body, fueling her desire for him. She drank him in, filling her lungs with Landon's wonderful, clean scent. It had her squirming and aching between her thighs even more.

Her nipples had tightened beneath her sleep shirt as she grew wetter. Her nipples were so sensitive, especially when they were hard. She wanted him to lick them, suck them with his hot mouth. To drive her crazy with need.

She raised her arms, weaved her hands around his neck, and pulled him toward her until his mouth hovered over hers.

"I think you need to climb onto this bed with me." She played with the short hairs at his nape, her body moving as if he had already slid inside her. God, how she wanted him inside her. "Just to make sure I'm safe, of course."

He breathed even harsher than she did. "Probably not a good idea." He pressed his lips to hers then brushed his mouth a fraction above. She had no doubt he hovered so close to the edge it wouldn't take much to push him over into the temptation of taking her. "On second thought, it's the best idea I've ever heard."

She smiled and speared her hands into his hair and sifted the strands between her fingers. She held his head tight, like she never wanted to let him go. "That's because it is the best idea ever." She kissed him and nipped at his lower lip before drawing his tongue into her mouth. Her need for him became more urgent and she kissed him with even more passion.

He kissed her hard, letting all his desire pour through her where their lips met. He showed how much he wanted to possess her, mark his territory, and claim her as his woman.

He broke the kiss and traced his lips along her jawline to her ear. "Damn. You're too much of a temptation."

The temptation to touch her clearly overpowered him as he moved his hands over her body. He started to edge up her shirt until it slipped under her breasts. He slipped his fingers under the cloth, cupping her breast and tweaking her nipple.

Wanting to keep him close to her, she grasped the short hair at his nape and moaned into his mouth, arching her back to get even closer to him. His cock felt so hard against her belly. She wanted to strip off his T-shirt and jeans and any other clothing he might be wearing. She wanted to climb on top of him, wanted to feel their naked bodies sliding together, and she wanted to ride him, hard. His cock would hit her cervix, in her so deep he'd be rubbing her G-spot and feeling so good inside her.

When their mouths parted, she had to drag air into her lungs with effort, a result of all the erotic sensations rampaging through her. By the roughness of his breathing, she knew it affected him too.

"Do you think Danson and O'Donnell will know we're together?" The thought might cool her ardor a bit, but she didn't care. How could it be so hot to have them close while she did everything in her power to rock Landon's world?

"We'll be fine." He rubbed his thumb along her lower lip and she caught his finger in her mouth. His breath hitched as she sucked it, like she wanted to suck his cock. "It's my turn to sleep upstairs while they monitor the front and back doors downstairs." He sounded strained, as if he tried to focus on his words. "They're not going anywhere."

With the other agents out of the way, she had more of a chance to explore Landon. She smiled and pushed the blanket to her waist.

He captured her T-shirt-covered breasts in his big hands. Her breasts felt heavy from her desire, her nipples growing tighter beneath his touch. He circled each nipple with his thumbs, causing her to clench her teeth to hold back moans of pleasure. Her nipples were so sensitive it made her crazy.

Her reaction seemed to get him even more worked up and he tugged at her sleep shirt and slid it up and over her breasts.

"We need to be quiet." Landon gave a low groan, pushing her sleep shirt up higher. "But damned if I know how I'm going to manage it with you beneath me."

His words fueled her and she arched her back as she helped him pull the shirt over her head. The new sensation of cool air on her nipples had her bucking and squirming beneath him. She couldn't help her body wanting him inside her.

"So beautiful." He dropped the shirt on the floor before lowering his head, his mouth hovering above her breasts, his breath hot against them. She thrust her breasts up to get them closer to his mouth. "You're so damned beautiful."

He ghosted his lips over her nipple and she gasped when he enveloped the hard nub in the soft, wet warmth of his mouth and she had to bite her lip to keep from crying out. His licking and sucking drove her out of her mind. She inched her hands over his body, the hardness of his muscles making her want even more. In her haze, she wanted everything he could give her.

"Landon." She gasped and writhed in his arms, begging him with her body to take more of her. She clenched her fingers in his hair when he ran his tongue around her nipple. "I want you inside me." The need burned inside her like an inferno. "I need you like five minutes ago."

"God. I will. Soon." He sucked her nipple hard before taking her other one into his mouth. She gasped and squirmed as he raised his head and gave her a look filled with fire. "I'm going to fuck you, honey. I'm going to stretch you, be deep inside you. I'm going to show you who you belong to. But first I need to make you come."

His words made her shudder with desire. "Don't make me wait." She moved her hands to his upper arms then his shoulders and gripped them. She loved the feel of his muscles flexing beneath her palms. "I want you inside me. Now."

"Patience," he murmured, but she could tell his attempt at slowing down cost him and he wanted her just as badly.

She fought for breath, slipping her hands down his chest to his belt buckle. He sucked in his breath as the touch of her fingers between his jeans and his belly. When she insinuated her hand down until she brushed the soft head of his cock, he groaned.

Turnabout was fair play. He had teased her and now she

would return the favor.

"Get those clothes off, Landon." She found it hard to even speak the words. The anticipation drove her out of her mind, just knowing he would be long and thick. She couldn't wait to feel all his heat in her hand, her mouth, her body.

He stood, hunger burning in his gaze. He looked reluctant to part from her for even a moment. She sat up in bed, bracing her hands on the mattress as he stepped back and she watched every movement he made. She brought her hands to her breasts, her eyes focused on his while he unbuckled his belt then unfastened his jeans.

He had a pained expression, watched her fondling her breasts. She stared at the bulge in his jeans, waiting to get her first look at his cock.

His hands seemed to tremble a bit when he pushed his jeans and boxer briefs down to his knees. He widened his stance, completely freeing his cock and balls.

She caught her breath, wanting to touch and taste his long, thick cock and lick his balls. She could almost feel him stretching her, a welcome invasion.

The need to have him inside her made her wild for him. She let the sheet fall completely away, reaching for him. He sucked in his breath as she wrapped her fingers around his erection and used her other hand to cup his balls. She ran her thumb over the pre-cum on the top. Using it as a tether, she drew him closer to her.

Tension coiled in Landon's groin, an intense sensation that made him afraid he would explode just from her touch.

Still holding his cock, Tori sat up then got to her knees on the bed. Her breasts were generous, her areolas a deep wine color, her nipples large and hard. She'd been made for his hands and mouth to explore — her smooth skin, lovely curves, and her soft lips.

The look in her eyes mesmerized him. She gripped him and slowly stroked her hand up and down his erection. She cupped his balls with her other hand where they were tight against his body.

His eyes almost rolled back into his head as she moved her finger slowly over the skin just behind his balls. The sexy and erotic sensation nearly drove him to his knees. But God help him, he couldn't have moved if he'd tried.

She shifted on the bed and he looked at her silky black panties. At that moment, nothing could be sexier than seeing her in only those little panties. Her womanly scent washed over him, the sweet smell of orange blossoms from the bottle of lotion she'd asked for mixed with the scent of her desire.

"I want to taste you." She met his gaze as she gripped his cock and balls. "I want to feel you inside my mouth."

He groaned at the incredibly erotic words she spoke and the primal look in her gaze.

She didn't give him time to think about what she would do next. She lowered her head and circled his cock with her tongue before sliding his erection inside the wet warmth of her mouth until it bumped the back of her throat. She gave a satisfied hum, a low sensual sound that vibrated throughout him.

He didn't know how she did it, but she opened up the back of her throat and took him in deep without having a gag reflex. She also didn't seem to need to come up for air, as if she had an expanded lung capacity. And the way she used her tongue... He wondered if it had anything to do with her being a musician. Whatever it was, she had the amazing ability to turn his world upside down.

He clenched his teeth as he watched his cock disappearing into her mouth between her swollen lips. Lips swollen from their frenzied kisses.

A groan of pleasure almost escaped him, but he held it back. He had no intention of letting the other agents know he had his cock down Tori's throat.

He hadn't planned on her going down on him, but now he couldn't think past the feel of her lips on him and the sight of her head bobbing up and down when her dark eyes met his. It was so fucking hot to see her watching him with his cock sliding in and out of her mouth.

"Damn, Tori. *Damn*." The tension building in his groin became so intense he almost exploded into her mouth.

She gave a hum of pleasure, a hungry sound that vibrated through his cock and straight to his groin. He hung on the precipice of an orgasm to beat all other orgasms. He'd never felt anything like this in his life.

"Stop, honey." He had to grasp her head in his hands and hold her still. "I want to be inside you so damned bad."

She stopped slowly, keeping her lips tight as she pulled him out of her mouth, still fondling him. He nearly went crazy, feeling her trace the area just behind the balls at the base and back to the front where the sac attached to his body. She ran her tongue down the length of his cock to his balls, slipped one into her mouth, and sucked.

Holy shit. He longed to fuck her until she couldn't see straight, much less *walk* straight. He needed to push inside her and feel that first giving of her body to take him. He loved the pounding and going deep as he tipped her ass with his hands. He'd seen how sensitive her nipples were and he ached to pinch them as he took her.

Fuck almost seemed like too coarse a word to use with Tori, but he wanted to do exactly that. A part of him recognized he wanted more than that, a primal urge to claim her even though he had no right to.

She let his erection slide out of her mouth, his cock aching and jutting out at her as if begging for more. Hell, he could barely stand after what she'd just done. The way she'd licked him, sucked him, deep-throated him. *Damn.*

When she reached for him and started to tug down on his pants, her hands skimming his thighs, he stopped her. He had to fight not to claim her this very second. He needed a moment to take off his clothing and his weapon.

After he'd removed his Colt from its holster and set it on the nightstand, he dug a condom packet out of his wallet and placed it close to the gun. He knew he shouldn't be doing this, shouldn't even be in her room, but he had to be with Tori more than he needed anything else in this life.

He toed off his shoes before letting his jeans drop to the floor while pulling his T-shirt over his head, all in record time. As she lay back on her pillow, he grasped her panties and slid the silky scrap of cloth down her legs and over her feet. He dropped them beside his jeans.

She had trimmed the soft hair between her thighs and he ran his finger over it. She moaned softly, a shiver traveling over her skin. She arched up off the bed and cupped her breasts, clearly missing his attention.

Her eyes never left his as he eased onto the bed and straddled her thighs then braced his hands to either side of her shoulders. His cock and balls brushed her skin and he gritted his teeth, holding back a groan.

"You're so damned special." He loved how she squirmed beneath him at his words. He looked down at her, taking in everything about her. He wanted to send more shivers throughout her entire body before he finished. He lowered his head and pressed soft kisses from her mouth to her ear. "You are an amazing woman."

She reached between them and gripped his cock. Her hand felt hot as she ran her thumb over the head, her other hand grasping his balls. He barely kept from coming, spilling every drop of semen on her belly.

"I'm too close to coming." He caught her hand in his and forced her to stop. "But hold on to that thought." She gave him a smile and he was lost. She belonged to him and he would never let anything happen to her and he would never let her go.

Tori squirmed beneath Landon, needing him so badly she could almost scream from it. She still had hold of his cock and guided it to her entrance. "Inside me. Now."

He ignored her demands and grasped her hand, drawing it away from his erection. He pressed soft kisses down the curve of her slender neck to the hollow of her throat.

She made an involuntary sound, halfway between a cry and a moan, and he put his hand over her mouth. "Not so loud, honey."

When he stopped her from speaking, it ratcheted her excitement. The sensual curve of his lips sent a crazy sensation to her belly, like butterflies gone wild, and she grew wetter between her thighs.

Despite the fact she wanted him inside her now, he took his time sliding his hands over her and kissing her in ways and places she'd never been kissed before. He managed to press hot buttons she hadn't even known existed. But he noticed and exploited them mercilessly. His callused hands made her feel alive, his every touch setting her on fire.

He eased down her and she tensed when he moved his shoulders between her thighs. The anticipation of him going down on her sent tremors through her and she had to hold back moans trying to spill from her lips. He pressed her thighs farther apart with the width of his shoulders.

A strangled gasp escaped her and she bit her lower lip as he stroked her folds, finding her clit. He lowered his head and she almost cried out from the exquisite pleasure of his mouth on her, licking and sucking. He gave a groan that sounded of sheer pleasure as he tasted her.

He moved his mouth over her, licking her, sucking her. Doing everything he could to drive her wild. She gripped the sheet in her fists, trying to still her body. His tongue teased her folds, drawing from her feelings she'd never experienced before. He slid two fingers inside her, reaching for her G-spot and causing her eyes to widen with pleasure and a sheen of perspiration to coat her skin. It felt like heaven.

Her thoughts spun as every part of her seemed to coil almost too tightly and she felt as though she might come undone, her mind and her body.

What he did to her made her writhe with pleasure. Her legs trembled and she clamped her thighs around him. Her nipples ached to be pinched, caressed, sucked. She gripped his hair, holding him to her, yet she couldn't handle much more of the way he took control of her body.

Even as she had the thought, it felt as if an explosion rocked her body. Her vision grew blurry and she barely registered the fact that he'd reached up and clamped his hand over her mouth again before fondling her clit with his fingers. He drew out her pleasure and she shook almost violently from the force of her orgasm.

As she came down, he placed soft kisses on the insides of her thighs. He pressed his lips to her mound before brushing his mouth over her belly. A shiver of renewed desire traveled through her when he dipped his tongue into her navel. A delicious sensation shot through her from her bellybutton to her clit. She'd never had multiple orgasms but she felt as if she could come again with a mere touch.

When he had eased up her body, he studied her with a gaze full of emotions she didn't recognize. He looked like a fierce, powerful, and proud warrior claiming his prize from a war. His mouth came down hard on hers as if he had untamed pent-up passion and it flowed into her. Her own desire built up again in a hot wave threatening to sweep her away.

He broke the kiss, rose, and looked down at her and she held out her arms to him, wanting him to come back to her. Instead, he leaned to her side and grasped the condom packet. In moments he had covered his cock and shifted his body over hers. She hoped she could be with him again and be the one to roll the condom down his cock.

"Take me inside you." His request sent a thrill through her.

She grasped his erection in her hand and placed it at the entrance to her core and her channel flooded with more moisture. He groaned, sucking in his breath, and the muscles in his arms and neck grew tight. She knew he held back the urge to thrust inside her hard.

In an effort to urge him on, she wrapped her thighs around

him. She raised her hips and dug her heels into his muscled ass and he drove his cock deep inside her. She tipped her head back, gasping as he filled her, stretched her, reached deep inside her, bumping her cervix. Her muscles clamped around him as if they never wanted him to leave.

"That feels so good, so damned good." Landon gave a low growl. "I've wanted to be inside you since I met you. I've wanted to take you and make you mine."

More thrills shot through her with the thrust his cock in and out. Just the right size for her, he easily reached her G-spot. The incredible sensation of his cock sliding against that one special place made her feel complete. She wondered if she'd be able to come with him inside her, something she'd never been able to do before.

They strained together, their movements in time with each other as if they were of one mind, one body. His hands stroked her skin and she dug her fingernails into his back as she lost herself in the sensations.

The soft scrape of his springy chest hair grazed her sensitive nipples, brushing them with every twitch of their bodies. The sensation heightened her pleasure and it lanced straight through her to the depths of her core. She bucked in tandem with him, loving the deep penetration.

Sweat coated his skin and she felt a droplet of perspiration roll down the side of her face. He kept his movements slow and steady, but firm and hard too. She prayed the bedsprings wouldn't creak so the other agents wouldn't hear then almost didn't care if they did.

He drove in deep then held himself still for a moment and studied her. Her body continued to clench around him. She was so keyed up, unable to stop on a dime. She wanted him to move, but his gaze captured hers.

With his eyes focused on her, he linked his fingers with hers. He stretched her arms above her head, their hands still clasped, and he began moving in and out again with long firm strokes.

Tension drew her body tight, from her head to her toes.

She perched so close to the edge, so very close. Her body felt like one sensitized mass of nerves. All the passion she felt, all the lust she had for Landon, became stronger as her mind spun with pleasure, her body more alive than it had ever been.

The feelings were so powerful that in moments she found herself shooting toward an orgasm she knew would send her straight to the stars.

Her eyes widened and her lips parted when she reached the peak. He drove her over it with his continued thrusting. She gladly jumped the cliff, losing all control over her mind and body.

An involuntary cry tried to escape her lips, but Landon sealed his mouth over hers and drew her cry inside himself. He took it all as her body trembled and shook with the force of her climax.

She closed her eyes when he kissed her and the orgasm took her to another universe. Her body tingled from head to toe and from behind her eyes she felt as if starlight rained down on her.

"Open your eyes." His rough voice and his demand filled her with pure desire. "I want to watch you as I come inside you."

She obeyed and looked into his eyes. The connection sent renewed thrills through her body, and to her surprise, all sensation began to wind up inside her again. She closed in on climaxing a third time.

He kept thrusting and she wished he didn't have to wear a condom so they could feel each other skin to skin. She would be able to feel his cock pulsing, pumping his cum inside her.

She knew the moment when he joined her. She watched his features tense as he stared into her eyes and saw when he shot over the precipice.

He threw his head back and bared his teeth, coming hard. All of his muscles on his forearms, neck, biceps, and chest stood out. He looked as if he fought a battle, trying not to yell out his climax.

His cock pulsed in her throbbing channel as he continued to thrust. Her eyes fluttered as more stars appeared, dragging her once again to a place she'd already visited twice.

He kissed her again, taking from her a cry that almost escaped this time. Her body shook. Would she be able to take one more tremor of her core? She'd never experienced anything like this in her life. She'd barely had one orgasm before. How many times had she come? Three? Four?

It didn't matter. Not when she gradually fluttered down from the stars.

He rolled onto his side, taking her with him so she lay in the crook of his arm. He held her close as they both breathed hard and her heart pounded like crazy. She willed her heart to slow and her body to relax.

Gradually she felt completely limp, beyond relaxed, and as if she'd never be able to move again. It was impossible. She sighed, too sated to do anything more than move closer to his big, warm, muscular body. The scent of their sex filled the air and made her smile.

He placed his forehead against hers, his sweat mingling with hers. "Do you know how incredibly beautiful you are right now?"

She gave a soft laugh. "All sweaty and with my hair a mess?"

"You look amazing." He kissed her. "I've never seen anyone more gorgeous than you at this moment. With your face flushed, your lips swollen, and how messy your hair is after I've thoroughly taken you... Damn, you're hot."

"Yes, I'm very hot. And sweaty." She smiled, totally satisfied. "You look pretty darn good yourself."

A smile curved the corner of his mouth. "I can stay a little longer." He brushed her cheek with his fingertips. "Danson and O'Donnell won't leave their posts until I relieve one of them. But I think I'd better take a shower first." He brought her hand to his lips and kissed the back of it. "I smell like sex."

She snuggled closer to him. "It's a good scent for you."

"I like it." He rubbed his thumb over the back of her hand in a slow, sensual circle. "Just not sure it's the wisest perfume to wear in a case like this."

"You may be right." She smiled. "And this might not have been the wisest thing we've done."

It had been crazy, letting him take her in a house with other agents during a time when she feared for her life. It was perhaps the craziest thing she'd ever done, but it had been worth every precious minute. Being with Landon made her feel safe and alive and ready to face anything that might come their way —

The loud retort of a gunshot tore through the quiet night.

Chapter Eighteen

Landon bolted upright in bed, his heart slamming.

"Gunshot!" Terror crowded Tori's voice as she sat up too.

"Get dressed and don't make a sound." He rolled out of bed, grabbed his jeans from off the floor and shoved his legs into them. "Hurry."

Thank God he'd left his belt in the belt loops with his phone and his gun holster. He buckled the belt and didn't bother to put on any more clothes. He grabbed his service weapon off the nightstand and gripped it in one hand. What the fuck had he been thinking, climbing into bed with Tori?

He hurried to the bureau and shoved it across the carpet to brace it against the bedroom door. He'd locked the door earlier, but it wouldn't hold. The piece of furniture wouldn't be heavy enough to keep anyone out for long, so they couldn't count on it.

From his side vision, he saw Tori snatch her jeans and T-shirt from a chair and jerk both on.

The sound of gunfire and shouts continued downstairs then Landon heard the sound of feet pounding up the stairs.

He ran to the window and pulled up the blinds before unlatching the window and shoving it open. He peered outside, narrowing his eyes.

"Come here." He gestured to Tori to follow him. "I don't see anything below. I think your best bet is to go out this way."

The doorknob rattled hard. Someone was trying to open the bedroom door and Landon's heart slammed.

"There's a trellis you can climb to the ground." He helped her into the window as men shouted and tried to get in the room. "I don't know how well it will hold or for how long, so jump when you can."

"You're coming with me, right?" Her gaze filled with horror.

"Hurry. Go." He glanced over his shoulder and saw that the door had opened a few inches and the bureau was moving. He turned to Tori. "We're at the foot of the Huachuca Mountains. Get into the forest. I'll find you."

She hesitated only a moment before slipping over the windowsill. Her voice shook. "Oh, God, I hate heights."

He held on until she had a good foothold. "At least you won't be dead."

"I will if I fall." But she still made it out of the window even as her arms shook with obvious fear.

The men rammed the door hard and the bureau moved several more inches.

As soon as Tori started down, Landon held his weapon with one hand and swung his leg out of the window. He eased over the sill at the same moment the men forced the door all the way open.

Landon got one shot off at the first man who came through. The man dropped. A second man stepped over the body and saw Landon, who had climbed out of the window, now trying to gain purchase on the trellis with his bare feet.

The man aimed his gun and fired. Landon bit back a shout at the pain slamming into his left shoulder, instantly weakening him.

He almost fell off the trellis. He barely managed to grab it with his right hand, but lost his grip on his weapon and the Colt tumbled to the ground below. Somehow, he managed to hang on to the trellis with one hand.

Another shot hit the sill and fragments of wood exploded near Landon's face. He knew he wouldn't be able to hold on for long with one hand. He looked down and saw Tori waiting for him at the bottom of the trellis.

"Run!" He gritted his teeth against her hesitation. "Go, damn it!"

A man leaned over the sill and Landon had no choice but to drop to the ground. More pain erupted through his shoulder as he hit the dirt and his vision grayed. A bullet whizzed by his ear.

He felt the hard imprint of his Colt beneath him. He rolled off the gun, grabbed it, and aimed at the face in the window he could just make out in the darkness.

The man trained his weapon on Landon, who lunged to the side. He ignored the explosive pain in his shoulder the best he could and got off several rounds at the man now leaning out of the window.

A cry came from the man before his body tumbled over the windowsill and landed with a loud thump. He lay still just feet from Landon, who didn't have time to think when a larger man's form filled the window above.

Bullets slammed into the ground a few inches from Landon. He pressed deeper in the shadows against the wall and knew he couldn't be seen.

Men shouted in Spanish. Landon was fluent in the language, but he couldn't hear clearly. His mind spun from the pain in his shoulder, his hearing buzzed, and his adrenaline had climbed sky-high.

He saw no sign of Tori. Hopefully she'd listened to him and run into the mountains as far away as she could.

Keeping low, he ran from the house and through a back gate left wide open.

The house exploded.

The power of the blast flung Landon forward. He hit the ground with such force it jarred his teeth and the excruciating pain in his shoulder speared his body.

Something slammed into the back of his skull. Pain burst in his head. His vision dimmed and he struggled to maintain consciousness.

Then everything went black.

A tremendous explosion and Tori screamed, seeing the house go up in a fireball. "Landon!" Fear for him tore through her body. Her heart pounded even harder, a hard rock of a lump forming in her throat.

Stones and twigs jabbed the soles of her bare feet as she ran back toward the house even though she knew no one could have survived the explosion. Her mind rejected the thought Landon might be dead. No, she wouldn't believe that. He'd gotten out. She *knew* it.

She prayed for it.

Smoke roiled to the sky above towering flames. No one could have survived it. Were some of the cartel's men still around? Or had they all been inside?

In spite of the danger, she had to find Landon. She had almost reached the back gate when she saw a large form on the ground. A man, a big man, and he lay on his side.

Her heart thrummed harder. Landon? She couldn't tell. She raced to the still form and dropped to her knees. The man was naked from the waist up and wore no shoes.

"Landon!" The cry came out as a sob. He didn't move. She touched his shoulder and her hand came away covered in blood.

Horror filled her and she thought she might stop breathing. He'd been shot. Was he dead?

He groaned and moved.

A measure of relief went through her as she frantically tried to think what to do. She glanced up and saw nothing but the fire. No men coming after them with guns. No one anywhere.

She had to bind Landon's wound. She wore only the long T-shirt she slept in and the jeans she'd managed to get on before climbing down the trellis. She hadn't even had time to put on her panties. She tore at the bottom half of her shirt and managed to rip apart one seam.

Panicked, she searched for something to help her, then spotted a knife on his belt, next to his phone holster. She jerked the knife out and cut the shirt enough to get it started and tore off as much of the material as she could.

Heat from the fire ravaging what was left of the house

warmed her skin. She coughed from the smoke and ashes floated around her.

Sirens blared in the distance.

She had to shift Landon's body to wrap the T-shirt under his armpit and up around his shoulder where one of the cartel bastards had shot him. Who else could have attacked the safe house but the cartel?

Landon groaned with obvious pain. She tied the cloth as tightly as she could and it grew wet with blood almost at once.

"Come on." She grasped his good arm. "You've got to get up. They might find us."

He held his hand to his forehead as his eyes opened and she tugged at his arm. He sat up and shook his head as if trying to rattle his thoughts back in place.

"What are you doing here, damn it?" His words were a little slurred and she thought he probably had a concussion. "I told you to run."

"I had to come back for you."

"How the fuck did they find us?" He tried to stand. "It shouldn't have been possible."

Somehow she managed to tug him to his feet. He stumbled. He weighed so much more than her that he almost took her down to the ground with him. "I hear sirens, Landon." She glanced over her shoulder at the burning house. "We can go to the police."

"No." He steadied himself. "We don't know who's been compromised or if we've been set up and the cartel managed to get their hands on law enforcement vehicles." He spotted something and she looked to see his weapon. She scooped it up before he could attempt to, and managed to slide it into the holster on his belt.

"If we can't trust anyone, let's get out of here." She grasped his hand and started toward the darkness of the tree line, the gateway to the forest.

He seemed to gain his bearings then moved faster, keeping up with her. They entered the forest just as red and blue lights flashed in the street behind them. The blare of a fire truck's horn and sirens came on the heels of the police.

Landon dropped to one knee. The light from the fire blazed high enough to illuminate him and she saw so much blood coating his side. Her pulse thumped in her throat. It had to be bad.

"I'm going to see if I can find something to cover your wound." She started to get up. "Maybe at a neighbor's house. I'll be right back."

He grabbed her hand using his good arm. "We stay together."

"But you're hurt." She hesitated. "Shouldn't you be still?"

"Just stay with me." He took her hand and they ran within the tree line. More houses were along the street. "There." He pointed to one of the houses. "An old truck in the driveway."

This time he pulled her. She didn't know where he got his strength from, but he looked like a fierce warrior as they hurried.

A porch light illuminated the front door of the home, but the light didn't reach the truck. The windows were dark and she hoped they would stay that way. Although with the loud explosion, she didn't know how anyone could still be asleep.

When they reached the older-model truck, Tori tried to open the door. Locked. She whirled around, searching for something heavy but not too heavy. After a moment she spied a brick paver along a walkway. She snatched it up and smashed the driver's-side window with a loud crash and knocked out the glass.

Down the street came shouts and yells as firefighters fought the blaze and the police cordoned off the area.

Landon reached into the truck, unlocked the door, and jerked it open before taking the paver from Tori and busting the steering column with it. He brushed some of the safety glass off the seat, climbed in, and hotwired the old truck. With his injured arm he struggled and it probably took him longer than it would have if he hadn't been shot.

In moments the engine revved and he scooted over to the passenger side. "I hope you can drive stick."

"I hope so too." She gave him a concerned look. "It's been quite a few years."

"Like getting on a horse." His strained smile seemed more like a grimace. "Just don't kill the engine."

"Easier said than done."

He gave her a few quick directions, including releasing the parking brake first. Her blood still rushed in her ears as she did what he told her. She stepped on the clutch, released the parking brake, and eased the clutch out, praying the whole time the truck wouldn't stall. Fortunately, the truck faced the street, so she didn't have to back out.

Just as she drove out of the driveway, the lights came on in the house. She didn't turn back as she stomped on the gas and tore out onto the street, tires squealing.

Behind them the fire reached for the sky, the light flickering and illuminating everything around it.

She looked at Landon who had found a dirty rag on the floorboard and held it to his shoulder. Thank God part of her T-shirt covered the wound or the rag would likely cause an infection. Still, he would require antibiotics.

"I need to get you to a hospital." She swallowed as she glanced at the road. "It's been so long since I've been to Sierra Vista I don't know where one is."

"We can't go to a hospital." He sounded as if he tried to talk through gritted teeth. "I have a friend who's a doctor."

"Okay." Tori let out her breath. "Then that's where we're going."

Chapter Nineteen

Tori followed Landon's directions to a neighborhood across town from where the safe house had been. "How did the cartel find me?"

"I'm not sure." Landon's expression remained grim as he pressed the cloth to his shoulder. "Damn, I hate to think any DHS agent could be working for the cartel."

When Tori glanced at Landon, he appeared even paler and sweat beaded his forehead. He didn't seem as though he would be able to hold up much longer.

"Turn here." He gestured to a street on their left. "Last house on the right."

She sped down the street and came to a hard stop in front of a large house. At first glance, it appeared to be a beautiful home in a very nice neighborhood.

The truck jerked and the engine died as she forgot to put in the clutch.

Tori scrambled out of the truck and barely made it to the passenger side before Landon started to tumble onto the sidewalk. She helped him balance then climb out and they hobbled up to the house. He had to lean on her. With his size and height, she worried she wouldn't be able to keep him from falling without going down with him.

He came to a stop. "Wait."

"Landon, we have to hurry."

He shook his head and dug in his jeans pocket. He pulled out Tori's cell phone and the battery. His hands were surprisingly steady as he examined the phone in the glow of a streetlight.

"Shit." Landon growled the word.

"What?" Tori felt utterly confused.

"Damn." He indicated something small and metallic that glinted in the light near where the battery would normally be. "Considering you'd had nothing to do with the cartel prior to witnessing the murder, I would never have guessed."

Perplexed, she watched him drop the phone and the battery on the ground. "Guessed what?"

"Grab that rock." He pointed to a good-sized rock serving as a part of the desert landscaping. When she returned with it, he said, "Now smash the hell out of that phone, especially what I just showed you, then pick up the pieces."

She frowned but did as he'd told her and smashed and smashed the phone and battery until he approved and said nothing could have survived what she'd just done to it. Every bit of fear, pain, and frustration had gone into each swing she'd made.

When she had decimated it, she scooped up the tiny pieces like he'd instructed and pushed them into her pocket. "Why did we just murder my phone?"

"I showed you a small, sophisticated tracking device." Landon looked both weak and grim. "Someone planted it there. It doesn't make sense, but it could have been someone close to you, like your ex-boyfriend."

She stared at Landon. "Gregory. He used to show up at places I went and I'd always wonder how he found me."

Landon's features tightened. "He must have given the information to the cartel."

She felt lightheaded from thoughts of Gregory, what he'd done, and his death. She shook it off. "We've got to get you inside."

Thankfully, he didn't argue. With his good arm over her shoulders, they made it up to the door and she pressed the doorbell. A frantic feeling caused her skin to prickle and she pressed the doorbell again and again until she heard the bolt lock being disengaged and the door opened.

An alert-looking woman wearing a white bathrobe

opened the door. The tall woman managed to appear beautiful even though she wore no make-up and had sleep-tousled hair.

She must be the doctor's wife, Tori thought.

"Hi, Beth." Landon looked exhausted and pained and it sounded as though he could barely speak. "Dr. Fallon, this is Tori. Tori, meet Dr. Bethany Fallon."

How did he even have the presence of mind to introduce them in his condition?

"We need your help." The frantic feeling inside Tori ramped up. "He's not doing well."

"I can see that." Dr. Fallon turned to Landon. Concern laced the woman's voice as she looked him over. "This way." Dr. Fallon turned and hurried into the house.

Supporting Landon, Tori ignored everything but the woman she followed.

Tori helped Landon into the house and closed the door behind them before heading after the doctor.

They followed the doctor at a slower pace, Landon grimacing with every step. When they reached the hallway, Dr. Fallon stood beside the first door on the left. "Gunshot wound?"

Tori nodded. "Yes."

"Come on in."

Tori helped Landon hobble into what appeared to be a game room. A billiards table took up the center, a built-in wet bar to the side.

"Help me get him up," Dr. Fallon spoke to Tori in a no-nonsense tone.

Even though blood covered him, the woman didn't flinch at having him on what looked like a very expensive billiards table. When he lay flat on his back, Beth told Tori where to find clean bar towels behind the wet bar.

Once Tori left to do as instructed, Dr. Fallon hurried from the room. Tori grabbed a stack of towels, went to Landon, and pressed a bar towel against the wound. Moments later the doctor returned with a medical bag. She pulled on surgical gloves and started attending to Landon.

"It doesn't look good." She narrowed her gaze, examining his shoulder. "No exit wound. It's going to require surgery and we need to get you to a hospital. I'm not fully equipped here."

"Can't." Landon set his jaw and spoke in short staccato sentences. "Tori's a protected witness. Security breached. Can't go to a hospital. Might be found."

Dr. Fallon's gaze flicked from Landon to Tori and back. She frowned. "I suppose we'll just have to make do. But I'm afraid you've lost a lot of blood."

"Not as bad as it looks." He grimaced. "I trust you to patch me up just fine."

The doctor shook her head. "What's your blood type?"

Landon shifted and winced. "AB positive."

"What's yours?" she asked Tori.

"A positive." Tori couldn't remember if A could give to AB or if AB could only take AB.

"Thank God George is type O positive. It's why I married him." Dr. Fallon started cleaning and sterilizing the wound. She spoke to Tori. "Go upstairs to the last room on the right and wake my husband. Tell him I need him in the billiards room now."

Tori hurried, her bare feet pounding on the carpeted wood staircase. She went to the room she'd been instructed to go to and knocked. Moments later, a man of about sixty, wearing pajamas, opened the door. Tori gave a very brief explanation and the man grabbed his bathrobe and tugged it on while they hurried down the stairs.

As Mr. Fallon pulled up a stool to sit on next to the billiards table, the doctor set up an IV between the two men and gave Tori instructions on how she could help.

Dr. Fallon told Landon she would give him an anesthetic strong enough to knock him out but he refused. "I need to be fully alert. I've got to protect Tori."

"You're in no condition to do anything right now." The doctor searched through her medical bag. "She's safe here."

"We can't stay long." Landon bared his teeth as if more pain slammed into him. "We have a stolen truck in front of your house that clearly does not belong in this neighborhood."

Dr. Fallon looked down at Landon. "I'll use a local anesthetic then, but it won't relieve all the pain. It's going to hurt like hell."

Landon's mouth tightened. "Do it."

She gave him the local and prepped him for her impromptu surgery, including administering heavy antibiotics. When she had fully prepared for the procedure, she started working on his shoulder. Landon clenched his jaw and his face screwed up as he tried to hold back a cry. His now pale skin glistened with sweat and droplets rolled down his forehead. His face morphed into a mask of agony, but he refused to make more than a grunt.

Tori used one of the cloths to mop the sweat from Landon's brow. She gripped his biceps with her other hand, trying to give him some comfort.

As the doctor continued to work to dig out the bullet, Landon's body suddenly went limp and his eyelids fluttered and closed. Tori caught her breath and her eyes widened.

Dr. Fallon noticed Tori's reaction and paused. Her gloves were bloody so she asked Tori to raise Landon's eyelid and also to check his pulse, which beat sure and strong beneath her fingers.

When Tori relayed the information, Dr. Fallon nodded. "He passed out, which is the best thing for the stubborn ass. He should be fine."

The entire time the doctor worked on Landon, Tori's whole body buzzed. Landon's blood covered her gloved hands. Dr. Fallon focused intently on her task.

It seemed to take forever before Dr. Fallon finally removed the slug. "Here's the little bastard."

When she raised the slug with the tweezers, Tori flinched. The small piece of lead had come so close to Landon's heart.

By the time Dr. Fallon had patched up Landon, pale

sunlight lit the game room. Mr. Fallon relaxed in a stuffed chair after the doctor disconnected the IV between him and Landon. Still out cold, Landon lay on the billiards table, but the doctor had given Tori a pillow to put beneath his head.

"He'll be fine." The doctor seemed to notice Tori's apprehension. "He likely has a concussion too, so you'll need to keep an eye on him."

Tori scrubbed away blood from her skin in the stainless steel sink in the kitchen, then washed out the sink. When she finished, she found crackers, cheese, and a glass of juice for the doctor's husband like she'd been asked to.

Dr. Fallon went upstairs. When she left, Tori gave Landon a sponge bath, wiping away blood from his torso until none remained. He did have a six-pack, she thought idly as she moved the sponge over the expanse of his muscular chest.

He'd saved her life again. God, how she wanted them to survive and she hoped maybe they could have a chance at something.

She mentally shook her head. It was no place for her mind to be going now.

Her thoughts turned to the tracker on her phone. All this time, Gregory had been spying on her. She couldn't say it surprised her. He'd always been so jealous of her that even when she'd gone out with her girlfriends, he would show up.

The doctor returned a short while later with her hair damp, smelling of soap with a light flowery scent. She had changed out of her bloodstained robe and wore a T-shirt and capris.

Landon hadn't woken during the time the doctor had been gone. She touched his uninjured shoulder. "He looks as though he can use the sleep."

She directed her attention at Tori who still wore bloody jeans and a T-shirt. The shirt now resembled a crop top thanks to her having torn off most of the cloth to make a bandage for Landon. The doctor cocked her head to the side. "Does he have any clothes? Do you?"

Tori shook her head. "Everything was blown up. We have nothing with us."

"Blown up?" Dr. Fallon glanced at her husband and back to Tori. "Maybe you should explain what happened now that things have settled."

"I'll check the news." Mr. Fallon pointed a remote at a large flat-screen TV in the corner of the game room. He muted the TV as a commercial came on. "Anything newsworthy will show up on this channel."

Tori had no doubt the adrenaline high she'd been on had kept her from going into shock. That and the fact that so much had happened made her almost numb from it all. When would it stop?

Her gut clenched and she felt queasy. In truth, it might never end.

Another thought came to her she hadn't had time to think about.

Were O'Donnell and Danson dead? They'd been in the house with Landon and Tori.

Oh my God.

Dr. Fallon returned her attention from the muted TV to Tori. "I'd really like to know what happened."

"We owe you that much." Tori swallowed and launched into a brief explanation but avoided mentioning why they both happened to be barefoot and why Landon didn't have a shirt on.

"I don't think I can tell you everything, but it comes down to the fact I witnessed something I shouldn't have and now the cartel is after me. They've managed to track me down twice. Landon saved my life both times."

The doctor gave a slow nod. "Sounds like you could use a break."

"A really long break." Tori rubbed her temples. "With all of the terrible things that have happened, there are no words to convey how truly awful it all is."

"It's horrendous." Dr. Fallon looked at Landon who still slept on the billiards table. "As far as something to wear,

Landon's a big man and my husband's clothes would be too small for him."

The woman glanced at Tori as she continued, "I'm a lot taller than you and I have a larger bone structure, so you'd drown in anything I have. The best bet is the twenty-four hour Walmart. Ted can go while it's still early and pick up a few things for Landon and you to wear for now."

"You said Landon hotwired a truck. I'll pull it into the garage too." Mr. Fallon raised a cracker. "Just as soon as I finish these crackers and cheese and the juice."

The doctor gave her husband a fond look. "Thank you, dear."

"I don't have any money to buy clothes or other things." Tori hated this feeling of not having anything. She'd always been so independent and proud to pay her own way. "All my ID and bank cards were stolen."

"Landon and I go way back." Dr. Fallon brushed away Tori's words with a wave of her hand. "We can work it out later. There's a notepad and a pen on the bar you can use to make a list of everything you need."

"Thank you." Tori gave Dr. Fallon a grateful look. Tori scooted off the stool she'd been sitting on, grabbed the notepad and pen, and jotted down the bare necessities. She refused to have Mr. Fallon go on a complete shopping trip for her. They could make do with the minimum for now. The doctor told Tori to add dressings for Landon's wound so Tori could change it frequently.

"Here's the report." Mr. Fallon drew Tori's attention to the TV as he turned up the volume.

Tori stared at the TV, which was showing the replay of firefighters dousing flames last night, followed by this morning's devastation, nothing but the smoldering remains of the former two-story house left.

A female reporter stood near the scene, in front of the mass of law enforcement and emergency vehicles. "Police are not saying what caused the explosion or if the house was occupied at the time."

So no one knew if the other two who had been helping protect her were dead. Not yet.

Were they? She thought about the two agents, her chest squeezing with fear for them and sadness for their families if they had died.

The station flashed back to the news anchor and Mr. Fallon muted the TV once again. "I'll get your things." He pushed himself up and out of his chair. "In the meantime, you can shower. You'll probably feel a lot better once you do."

"Most definitely." Tori gave him a tired smile. "Thank you."

"You're welcome, young lady." He took the list Tori had written then approached his wife and put his hand on her shoulder before giving her a quick but firm kiss on the lips. "I'm off on my quest."

Dr. Fallon reached up and squeezed her husband's hand still resting on her shoulder. "Why don't you bring home breakfast?"

He nodded. "How about something from that fancy French bakery you love so much?"

"Thank you, dear." She patted his hand. "See you when you return."

When Mr. Fallon left, Tori turned to Dr. Fallon. "Thank you both so very much. Landon could have died if you hadn't saved him."

The doctor smiled. "It wouldn't be easy to bring down a man like Landon Walker. Stubborn and determined as hell."

Tori's mouth curved into a smile too. "How do you know each other?"

For the first time, Dr. Fallon's cool appeared shaken, but she straightened and masked it almost at once. "My little sister was his fiancée."

"Stacy." Tori hadn't meant to say it aloud, it just came out.

The doctor looked surprised, likely because she hadn't

expected a witness to know something so personal. Still, she continued, "Stacy was almost thirty when she died."

"Landon mentioned her." Tori thought about what Landon had told her. "He's blamed himself for her death."

"I know." Dr. Fallon glanced at where he still lay sleeping. "And I've told him countless times he's not at fault."

Tori shook her head. "I'm so sorry about your sister."

"Yes." The woman continued to study Landon. "So am I."

Landon stirred and groaned.

"He's waking." Tori hurried to the billiards table and gripped the side as she leaned over and stared at Landon who blinked at the bright sunlight coming through the window. She smiled at him as he turned his head and looked at her. "Welcome back."

He reached out his hand and grasped hers. For a moment their gazes locked and he said nothing. He finally spoke in a hoarse voice. "Thanks to you we made it."

"I just busted your butt to get you out of there with me." She gripped his hand in both of hers. "How are you feeling?"

"Like hell." He moved his shoulder and grimaced. "But the pain means I'm still alive, so that's what counts."

She lowered her head and kissed him without thinking twice about it. When she raised her head, her cheeks burned and she glanced over her shoulder at Dr. Fallon.

"I—" Tori started but fell silent.

"So you've finally found someone." Dr. Fallon's smile seemed genuine as she moved to the opposite side of the table. "It's about time."

Tori shook her head. "We're not—"

This time, Landon cut her off. "It took the right woman to come along."

Tori opened her mouth and closed it. She couldn't think of anything to say, so she chose to say nothing.

"Why don't you go take a shower while I examine Landon?" Dr. Fallon gestured to the stairs. "There's a clean robe hanging on a hook inside the guest bathroom. It will be big on you, but it'll be fine until George gets back with your clothes."

"Thanks." Tori smiled, grateful for the reprieve as Landon gave her hand one last squeeze.

She turned and left the room, Landon's words echoing in her mind. *"It took the right woman to come along."*

Had he meant what he'd said?

She shook her head. In her exhausted state, she had no business analyzing what feelings might be developing between her and Landon. It was definitely not the right time.

Chapter Twenty

Such a fine day. Diego leaned back in his lounge chair beside the swimming pool, the sun warm and pleasant on his bare skin as his granddaughter swam with his great-nephews and nieces, his brothers' grandchildren. The crystal clear water shimmered in the sunlight while ripples splashed lazily against the edge of the pool.

Yes, it was indeed a fine day. His men had eliminated Tori Cox and he had ensured Alejandro's safety. A smile creased Diego's face. Thanks to the man who had installed a tracking chip in the woman's phone, Alejandro's men had found her.

Diego had wanted to smuggle the woman into Mexico and teach her a lesson, but eliminating her had a certain satisfaction to it as well.

He scowled. The American agents had arrested Pablo and John, who remained behind bars. The federal agents no longer had a witness to Alejandro murdering the federal agent—except for Pablo and John. However, they wouldn't be released due to the large amount of illegal substances found in the home they had been occupying at the time the warrants had been served.

Pablo and John were loose ends and he didn't tolerate loose ends.

But for now, Diego allowed himself to relax in the heat beating down on him. He had not relaxed for days. Today he could celebrate. Life was good.

Angelina climbed out of the pool, water rolling down her slender form. She grabbed a towel and wrapped it around her shoulders to walk toward him then sit on the edge of a nearby lounge chair. Her hair hung in long wet ropes around her pretty face, tiny water droplets clinging to her dark lashes. His little girl was growing into a fine young lady, yet he still found it difficult to believe her party approached so quickly.

She smiled at him. "You are in a very good mood today, Grandfather."

He raised his sunglasses. "Who could not be on such a beautiful day?"

"It is beautiful." She tilted her head to the side. "Something has happened to make you so happy. What is it?"

"I have the greatest granddaughter in the world." He tucked a small outdoor pillow behind his neck. "How could I not be happy?"

"As I have the greatest grandfather." She looked at the long tables set up on the lawn not far from the pool. The staff had placed one table apart from the rest and covered it with a cloth and serving pieces. "Josephina said everything is ready. It is time to eat."

Diego breathed in the pleasing smells of their dinner. "Let us not disappoint her."

He eased his legs over the side of the lounge chair and got to his feet. He clasped his hands behind his back as Angelina accompanied him to the tables.

When they reached the table with the food, Josephina, his cook, gave him a deferential bow. "I hope you find everything to your liking."

He let his gaze drift over the spread before he glanced at her again. "It looks and smells fabulous, my dear Josephina."

She bowed again. "Thank you, *Señor* Jimenez."

Platters filled with grilled fish, pork, and chicken were at the center of the table. Tortilla warmers held freshly made corn tortillas and there were also tamales, empanadas, soup, frijoles, and rice. Bowls overflowed with mango, papaya, and pineapple. To the side, containers held diced avocados and *pico de gallo*, along with a variety of Diego's favorite peppers.

"Excellent." He picked up a colorful plate. Local artisans made all his dishes and serving pieces.

Soon children and adults sat at the tables, which had been laid out on the lawn. The only person missing was Alejandro, but he would be returning to Mexico soon, where he belonged. Diego would be pleased when his son arrived. It had been foolish of Alejandro to go to the U.S. to kill the federal agent himself. Diego would not allow such a thing to happen in the future and his underlings would handle such tasks as usual. Alejandro was not expendable. They were.

Diego enjoyed the laughter and chatter of his large extended family. He wished his daughter could be here to see her beautiful daughter. He missed her as only a father could.

When Diego looked at his own four brothers, he found himself wanting to frown. They worked for him and were in line to run the family business if anything should happen to Diego and Alejandro. Unlike his son and himself, two of Diego's brothers were weak men. Diego did not like the idea of the family business falling into their hands. The youngest brother reminded Diego of his own son and he would have preferred he be next in line than the three older brothers.

His throat grew tight as he thought about his mother. She had disowned Diego and her other four sons many years ago, denouncing them when she learned of the cartel they had established. She had lived in Arizona for some years now, in that troublesome town of Bisbee. Diego still loved his mother and it crushed him she had turned her back on her five sons.

But enough of that, he told himself. He focused on the here and now. *Soon Alejandro will be home.*

Life is good.

Chapter Twenty One

They passed few cars. Tori drove the rented white Camry on the rural two-lane highway with Landon in the passenger seat. She had finally stopped shaking from that morning's insanity.

The late afternoon sky was the color of the famous Bisbee blue turquoise — a beautiful blue without the greenish hue of traditional turquoise. Grass hugging the sides of the highway remained still beneath a warm sun.

George Fallon had rented a car in his name at a car rental agency after they'd wiped down the truck and parked it at a campground in the Huachuca Mountains. The truck would be found soon enough, but at a place where no one should have noticed them leaving it.

Tori glanced at Landon, whose left arm hung in a sling, as they left Bisbee's town limits. "How far is it to your ranch?"

"Twenty miles from Bisbee and twenty-five from Douglas."

She looked back to the road. "You think we'll be safe there?"

"Right now it's the safest place I can think of." He watched her while he spoke. "The phone with the tracker has been destroyed, so I think we'll be fine. How are you holding up?"

"I should be asking you that." Her stomach twisted. "You're the one who's injured."

"I'm asking you." He focused his intense gaze on her, repeating repeated his question. "How are you holding up?"

Tori's dark hair swung around her face as she shook her

head. "There are too many dead and now you're injured, just because I saw a man being murdered by the cartel." A bleak feeling settled over her. "How much more is going to happen before I testify against Alejandro Jimenez and those two men?" She stared directly in front of her at the yellow centerline flashing past on the two-lane highway. "If I live long enough to testify."

"You're going to be fine." Landon gave her a reassuring smile. "You'll be safe at my ranch. No one knows you'll be there. *No one*. Not even my superiors." He looked grim when she glanced at him. "It should be impossible for the cartel to find you at my place."

Should be echoed in her mind.

Landon added, "And as far as the cartel is concerned, we're dead from the explosion." He blew out his breath. "At least until they identify bodies and body parts, but that should take at least a day, if not longer."

Tori shuddered. *Dead.* She and Landon could have died in the explosion like O'Donnell and Danson likely had.

When they reached the turnoff to his ranch, she pulled the car off the paved road and onto a dirt road. In the distance, she saw sunlight glittering off metal. As they grew nearer, she realized the tin roof of an outbuilding had caught the light. The building stood a good distance from a nice-sized ranch-style home. Other buildings populated the ranch as well.

They reached the house and Tori parked next to a large black truck then killed the engine. Despite his injury, Landon still managed to climb out of the car with a smooth masculine ease. She liked to watch him in action, his movements so decisive and purposeful.

A windmill behind Landon's ranch house creaked as the wheel turned from the strength of the wind and the pump moved up and down. Tori looked up at the tall structure and watched it for a moment. She hadn't grown up on a ranch like Landon had, but she'd seen windmills such as this one before. They made her think of times long since past, days in the Old West when they'd been widely used to pump water for personal use and for livestock.

She walked by his side up a pathway leading to a porch. Landon had landscaped both sides of the pathway with native desert plants and red rock. When they had walked up the steps and reached the big front door, he unlocked it before turning the knob and stepping aside so she could walk past him.

His open-floor plan had a breakfast bar separating the kitchen from the living and dining rooms. The vaulted open-beam ceiling gave the house a large and airy feel.

The place looked like a bachelor's pad with mostly bare walls and not much in the way of décor, but she liked the simplicity of it all. The coffee-colored leather couches were overstuffed and bound to be comfortable and he also had a recliner and a big wooden rocker. A hat rack rested beside the door with two cowboy hats and an assortment of ball caps. A long black duster and a leather bomber jacket hung from coat hooks on the wall near the hat rack.

A messy pile of magazines lay on one end table, two stacks of books on the other. Most of the paperbacks were Westerns, but she also saw a hardcover biography of President John F. Kennedy, as well as a hardcover on World War II.

A tablet lay next to a travel mug on the coffee table. It must be his personal device since he'd used another one for work. Did Landon read news and books on the tablet too, or stick with print? A lot of people hadn't embraced the digital age, but Landon clearly worked well in both electronic and print media.

He tossed his keys into a hand-woven basket on a table near the front door and she added the car keys to the basket as well.

When he abruptly turned to face her, she almost ran into him. With his good hand, he took her by her upper arm, catching her off guard. Her heart thrummed as she looked up into his eyes. They were so green, so beautiful, she couldn't look away.

He slid his hand over her shoulder then cupped her face in his palm. "I've been wanting to kiss you all day." His words were a sexy rumble that sent a shiver of excitement through her. He lowered his head and brushed his lips over hers, back and forth in a slow, easy motion.

She breathed out her sigh of pleasure against his lips. He brought her closer to him, his arm around her waist. His kiss was slow and sensual and she never wanted it to end.

He drew away, rubbing his thumb over her cheek and smiling into her eyes. He spoke softly. "I've been looking forward to it."

She gave a wry smile. "Running for your life can sure put a damper on things."

He pressed his lips to her forehead. "I could use a beer." He nodded toward the kitchen. "How about you? I have red or white wine too."

Mind still reeling from the kiss, she followed him to the kitchen. "It's a little early for me, but after last night I do believe a glass of red would be wonderful."

Sunshine from a skylight filled the kitchen, throwing light on to the stainless-steel appliances and the dishes in the dish drainer. She couldn't call the place spotless — more like man-clean — but it seemed fine.

"I have frozen dinners." Landon looked apologetic. "I've never been one for cooking."

"Well, I am." She glanced around the kitchen, taking in what he had. "Cooking is one of my favorite things to do. I often do it just to relax." Her gaze returned to him. "Why don't I fix an early dinner?"

He leaned one hip against a counter. "I have to say it would be nice to have a decent home-cooked meal. Other than Sunday dinner at my mom's, I live on frozen dinners."

"Let's do it."

"But first a drink." He reached into a cabinet with his good arm and brought out a wine bottle and glanced at her. "For a red, I have merlot."

"Perfect." She smiled. "I can help."

He reached into a cabinet and brought out a wine glass. "How are you at using a corkscrew?"

"If I don't ruin the cork, I'll be doing well." She took the bottle from him along with the corkscrew and went to work.

She successfully removed the cork, a minor triumph since she ranked about fifty-fifty on the ability to take one out with a simple corkscrew and not get small pieces of cork in the wine. He took the bottle from her and poured wine into the glass. He grabbed a bottle of beer out of the fridge, managed to open it on his own and set the beer on the breakfast bar. He carried the glass of red wine to her before picking up his own bottle.

Tori raised her glass. "To survival."

Landon clinked his bottle against her glass. "Survival."

After a sip of wine, Tori set the glass down. "Let's see what you have as far as food goes." She pointed to a door. "The pantry?"

He gave a nod. "All yours."

Tori went to the pantry and searched it. She looked over her shoulder. "This is about as well stocked as a safe house."

He leaned against a counter again. "In other words, I need to go shopping."

"We just had spaghetti the other day and it looks like another pasta dinner from what I see in here." Tori gathered a package of ziti from the pantry, along with cheese from the fridge, pork sausage from the freezer, and a few other odds and ends. She set it all out on the counter and got to work.

Every time Landon was around Tori, he wanted to run his hands over her soft curves, slide his fingers into her hair, and get lost forever in the depths of her dark eyes. He wanted to kiss her senseless and he wanted to be inside her again.

He hadn't felt this way about any woman since Stacy. He'd expected to feel guilty for being attracted to another woman, but with Tori he didn't feel as if he betrayed Stacy's memory. He felt as if Stacy had said, "Time to move on, Landon."

Could Tori be the right woman to move on with? She was a witness and it was his job to protect her, to get her safely to and through her testimony and nothing beyond that.

Well, he'd gone way past protecting her when he'd spent the night with her. Way past.

Landon insisted on helping by making garlic toast with inch-thick slices from a loaf of Texas toast he'd had on the countertop, plus butter and garlic salt. He managed pretty well for a guy with one useful arm.

When he finished getting the garlic bread ready, he took a stack of newspapers off a stool at the breakfast bar and set them aside. He sat on the stool and studied Tori as she fixed dinner. She always moved gracefully and he remembered what she'd looked like when she'd played her clarinet. He frowned. Damn, her clarinet had been lost in the explosion.

A thought occurred to him. "Do you play guitar?"

She glanced at him. "A little. It's an instrument I've wanted to improve on for a long time. I just haven't fit it into my schedule."

"I can show you a few things on mine even though I can't play with this bum shoulder." He leaned back in his seat. "I'm not exceptional by any means, but I know my way around a guitar well enough to play a tune or two."

"I'd love it." She gave a small sad smile. "Now that the clarinet my parents gave me is gone, I'd love another distraction."

"Good." He wanted her to really smile but wondered if she could so soon after all she'd been through. "I'll get it out after dinner."

It didn't take too long to prepare dinner. For a macaroni dish, the ziti couldn't be beat and he ate three helpings. She'd also steamed a package of broccoli she'd taken out of the freezer and served, as well as the toasted garlic bread.

Tori had remained quiet during most of dinner and he

had no doubt her mind was churning through everything that had happened.

"I want to know how my parents are." She raised her gaze from her plate and met his gaze. "I want to make sure they're all right. Can't we call?"

"We can't take the chance." He leaned forward, his forearms on the breakfast bar as he focused on her. "I turned off my phone so I can't be tracked and we took care of yours at Beth's house. I don't want anyone to figure out too soon we made it out of there alive." His mind weighed every option he could think of. "And right now, I don't know who the hell to trust."

"I'm scared, Landon." She looked down and away. "How long can I keep running before they find me?"

He touched the side of her face and gently made her turn to him again. "I'm not going to let them hurt you. Trust me."

"I do trust you," she whispered. "You're the only person I trust."

Would she still feel the same way when he told her that he had killed her brother during the drug raid? Was now the right time?

No time would be a good time to talk about it. But it had to be done.

He opened his mouth to tell her about her brother, but she spoke before he could. "Where's your guitar?"

"In my bedroom." Maybe he should wait until she made it through what had become a terrifying ordeal for her. "I'll throw the dishes in the dishwasher then grab my acoustic."

"I'll help."

When they finished, he retrieved his instrument and they both sat on the couch. Once he handed it to her, she immediately held it correctly and strummed a few chords.

"Needs a little tuning." She looked thoughtful as she tuned the strings.

They spent the next hour or so with Tori playing the guitar. She played tunes she had already learned on the

197

instrument and he taught her a country song. She looked surprised but pleased as he sang along.

"You have a wonderful voice." She smiled when the song ended. "Do you sing often?"

He shook his head. "Not even in the shower."

She laughed, a light, carefree sound. For a moment she seemed to forget all that had torn her life to shreds and the danger she faced.

It only lasted a moment before the haunted look filled her eyes. She turned her attention to the guitar. "Teach me another one." She picked up everything so quickly it amazed him. She only had to be told once and she had the tune memorized. "I haven't listened to a lot of country music." She easily repeated a melody he had just taught her. "One thing I've always admired about the music is the artists are such amazing storytellers."

"I grew up with country music." His mind traveled back to his school years. "Mom plays the piano and Dad handles a guitar pretty well and they both have great voices. I've always thought my mom sings like an angel." He couldn't help a smile as he thought of those days. "They taught my sisters and me from the time we were big enough to sing and play guitar or piano."

"You clearly have vocal talent." She picked through another melody. "I'd like to hear you play sometime."

He glanced at his injured arm then back to Tori. "Give me a few days and I'll be back in fine shape."

"Dr. Fallon said it's going to take longer than that to recover." Tori set the guitar flat on her lap, exhaustion in her eyes. "But she also said you'd be hard to keep down."

"She knows me pretty well." He glanced at a digital display on the DVD player, noting the time. "It's getting late. You've had a hell of a day and not much rest last night."

Tori set the guitar on the floor and leaned it against an end table. "Sleep sounds so good."

He rose at the same time she got to her feet and he stepped toward her. He touched her face with his fingers and he realized then he wanted her more than he'd wanted anyone in his life.

Her dark eyes grew heavy-lidded as he brought her close and he sensed the force of her desire.

"What about your head?" She lightly touched his forehead with her fingertips. "Dr. Fallon said you might have a concussion."

"I feel perfectly fine." He rubbed his thumb over her cheek. "More than fine."

Chapter Twenty Two

Tori shivered beneath Landon's touch, watching arousal darken his green eyes. Her exhaustion fled and renewed energy surged through her. She craved his touch with a power that awakened the fire inside her that had burned so hot last night.

When he lowered his head, she met him halfway and his mouth covered hers. His palm warmed her cheek and the heat traveled through her body. He sucked her tongue, drawing it into his mouth, and a thrill traveled straight between her thighs, causing her to grow wetter.

Her breasts ached and her taut nipples pushed against her T-shirt. His touch and the certainty that he desired her as much as she wanted him made her even hotter for him. She wanted to feel his length and thickness inside her as he filled her once again. It had been amazing having him inside her last night and she wanted to feel that sense of completion once more, the exquisite feeling of fullness.

He slid his fingers into her hair and cupped the back of her head, holding her to him. She loved the feel of the dominant, possessive move. She leaned closer and felt his arm between them. In her haze of lust and need, she had forgotten something important.

She drew away and his fingers took possession of her hair. She breathed hard as she looked up at him. "Your arm. You're injured."

A slow and sensual smile curved the corner of his mouth. "The rest of me isn't."

Her belly fluttered and she inched her palms up his broad chest, feeling the rise and fall, and she linked her arms around his neck, ever careful of his wound. "If you think you can handle me."

He studied her from beneath his heavy-lidded eyes. "Honey, I can handle anything you dish out."

"We'll see about that." Butterflies darting around in her belly, she stepped back and captured his hand in hers. "I plan on riding you hard, cowboy."

"You're killing me." He squeezed her hand in his and led her down the hall, his strides long, as if he couldn't wait to be inside her.

Her heart thumped and a shivery sense of excitement prickled her skin. He flipped on a bedside light as he brought her into a bedroom. The soft glow of the lamp illuminated the room that had a king-size bed in the center with an old-fashioned travel trunk at its foot. A bureau, a large rocking chair, and two nightstands completed the furniture.

Landon stole her attention. In moments she could only think about him, only cared about *him*.

"I want to see your body." He skimmed his knuckles along the side of her neck, his expression filled with passion that nearly swept her away. "Show me all of you."

Could she even breathe, much less take off her clothing? He parted from her, smoothing his hand down her arm before they were separated. She stepped back a few feet and thought about how she wanted to drive him crazy and all the things she wanted to do to him and have done to her.

She grasped the bottom of her T-shirt then pulled it up in a sensual movement meant to tease and tantalize him. By his taut expression, she knew it worked. She wiggled, tugging the shirt over her head then throwing it aside.

His hungry gaze and the bulge beneath his jeans gave her a feeling of power she'd never experienced before. She watched the heat flare in his eyes as she reached behind her, unfastened her bra, and dropped it to the floor.

He took a step forward, but she held up one hand, her palm facing him. "Stay right there." She heard the huskiness in her own voice, the incredible need building and building within her.

His jaw tightened and he looked as if he had to restrain himself. "Keep teasing me, honey, and all bets are off."

"No touching. Not yet." She shook her finger at him. "I'll let you know when you're allowed to."

His eyes narrowed as if he would come undone. He kicked off one of his shoes then the other, all the time watching her.

Her gaze held his as she kicked off the cheap, new athletic shoes and moved her fingers to the button of her jeans. She unbuttoned them and drew the zipper down in a slow, tantalizing motion.

"You are driving me out of my mind." His husky voice sent tremors through her. The veins in his arm stood out as he clenched his fists.

"You haven't seen anything yet." She shimmied out of her jeans, easing them down to her bare feet. As much as she wanted him, she didn't plan to hurry this erotic dance. It was too exciting, too breathtaking, knowing he wanted her so badly he could barely hold himself back.

He groaned when she hooked her thumbs in the sides of her panties and slipped them over her hips and thighs, inch by aching inch. When they reached her feet, she stepped out of the panties and the jeans.

He took another step forward, but again she raised her hand. "I'll tell you when."

His gaze followed her hands skimming over her belly and continuing up to cup her breasts. She felt the weight of them in her hands and his breath hitched as she pinched her nipples and rolled them between her thumbs and forefingers. Her sensitive nipples begged for his mouth, but she intended to finish torturing him erotically.

He took in her every movement as she slid one hand down to her mound. She slipped her finger into her wetness and stroked her clit. Her own touch on the sensitized nub caused her to moan.

He watched her like an animal straining against its leash. It made her ache even more between her thighs and she had to assuage the need. She circled her clit before sliding her fingers lower and dipping them into her wet core.

"I'm warning you, woman." He had to clear his throat to speak. "I'm about to take you over my knee and spank you for teasing me the way you are."

"Next time, you can spank me." She gave him a smile meant to fuel the fire she saw in his eyes. "This time, you watch."

Landon knew he would lose it, and lose it big. He would come in his jeans if he didn't succeed in restraining himself, or if Tori didn't stop.

Her sensual smile and the way she touched herself made his cock swell and feel as if his jeans were strangling it. Her lips parted and her lids lowered and she watched him through the slits of her eyelids as she took him to the very edge.

She moaned at the touch of her finger slipping over her clit while she pinched her nipple with her other hand. Her finger moved faster and she gasped, looking ready to climax. He almost dropped to his knees, wanting to lick her sweet flesh and bring her to orgasm with his mouth.

But she clearly enjoyed what she did to him. Her breathing became harsher and she tipped her head back, falling into the sensations. A few more strokes and she gave a cry. Her hips bucked against her hand and her whole body seemed to shudder.

Unable to stop himself, he took the few steps between them and trailed his hand to her lower back as he brought his mouth down on hers. Her body still vibrated from her orgasm, drawn out with her fingers. He stole the rest of her breath with his kiss, needing to feel her orgasm when he held her. When her body stilled, he raised his head and looked down at her.

He put his hand over her heart, feeling the rapid beat beneath his palm. She took a deep breath, tension easing from her features, and she freed her fingers from her wet folds.

Her pupils dilated as he replaced her fingers with his and she shuddered when he touched her clit. He brought his fingers from her folds and raised them to his nose. He inhaled her scent, drawing it into him, and a rumble rose up in his chest. Her lips parted, her gaze smoky, as he slipped his fingers into his mouth and tasted her.

He slid his fingers from his mouth. "I love how you taste. "I want to make you come with my mouth and my tongue."

The flash of pure desire in her eyes almost drove him to his knees. "I have the control and I intend to take full advantage of you."

Before he could form a reply, she gave him a sensual look and slipped from his grasp to kneel on the floor in front of him.

He nearly groaned aloud. What she'd done before—he'd never been with a woman who could deep-throat him, taking all of him. Last night she hadn't even come up for air often when she'd sucked him. He didn't think he could handle another round.

She pushed up his shirt and splayed her fingers on his abs. A sigh escaped her as she slid her palms higher, touching the expanse of his chest before running her hands down to the waistband of his jeans. He swallowed when she trailed her fingers along his skin, just beneath the waistband above his erection, and his heartbeat grew louder in his ears.

"I loved having your cock in my mouth last night." She smiled, deftly releasing the button with her musician's hands. "I want it again. More than anything." She looked up and met his gaze as she pulled his zipper. "Almost anything."

She pushed his jeans and boxer briefs down just enough to release his cock and balls and he groaned. She was too much. "I'm warning you—" Words failed him as she grasped his cock and he hissed out a breath.

She circled the head of his cock with her tongue before licking the pre-cum. He clenched his fist at his side and gritted his teeth. Damn it, he refused to climax. He intended to fuck her—if he survived.

"I love the taste of your come." She sighed, her breath warm on his cock and causing him to damn near orgasm without her even taking him completely into her mouth. "I love the salt of your skin."

"Damn it, Tori." He tried to make it sound like a warning, but he could barely get it out through gritted teeth.

Her eyes never left his as she caressed her mouth along its length.

"Jesus." He grasped a handful of her hair and pushed her head all the way down. She took him willingly all the way into her throat. "I never knew musicians were so damned talented."

A smile curved her lips as she slid him from her mouth, then took him deep again. She stared up at him and sucked while fondling his balls, making little circles with one finger behind the sac. She traced the skin between his balls to the front and a shudder of pleasure traveled over him.

With her other hand, she grasped his cock as she moved her head up and down. Watching her head bob while she took him deep only made the feeling in his groin tighter and powerfully intense. Sweat broke out on his skin as he felt the strong suction of her tongue and mouth that threatened to make him come. She'd been right. When she went down on him, she had all the control.

He had to stop her from taking it too far, to the point of no return. He pulled her hair hard, tugging her head back, and his cock slipped from her mouth. She bit her lower lip as she looked up at him and he stared into her liquid-soft brown eyes.

I'm a goner.

"Hold on." He removed his belt and laid his Colt on the nightstand. He turned back to Tori, his heart beating a mile a minute.

She grasped his jeans and boxer briefs and tugged them all the way to the floor and he could tell she loved what she saw. He stepped out of his clothing and she slipped off his socks with his help.

This woman would be the death of him. Death due to being deep-throated by a gorgeous woman.

What a way to go.

When Landon stood naked from the waist down, Tori took in his rock-hard muscular body. She loved sucking his cock, loved to have the hard length of him in her mouth and down her throat. He felt so good, tasted so good.

Tori eased up from the floor, pressing her lips to his flat belly and skimming them over his ripped abs. She smoothed her palms beneath his shirt and over his muscular chest as she rose and placed her lips on his collarbone but avoided touching the other shoulder, where he'd been shot.

For a second, the memories of last night washed over her and threatened to tear her away from the moment. But she held on to her composure, determined not to let the horrible men ruin her time with Landon. Right now was for the two of them.

He bunched his fist in her hair and buried his nose in it, and she heard his audible inhale as he breathed in the scent. "You smell so damned good." He nuzzled her. "All of you."

She sighed when he slid his lips over her cheek and his mouth claimed hers. He seemed to know exactly what she wanted and what ways she loved to be kissed. He sucked her tongue into his mouth and kissed her hard.

He raised his head. "I want to take off this damned thing." He reached for the fastening on his sling. "I don't need it."

She braced her palms on his chest, her breathing ragged. "Are you sure?"

"Damned sure."

He needed her help removing the sling and she tossed it onto the rocking chair. She had to unbutton his shirt for him and she took her time, slowly undoing each button while she skimmed her fingers along his hot skin. She could tell by the slight tremors in his body he had a hard time restraining himself. When she'd taken care of the last button, she gently pushed the shirt over his shoulders and helped him slide it off.

She ran her fingers lightly along his shoulder, staying away from the injured area. Only a small spot of red dotted the dressing, so it didn't appear to be bleeding.

"I want to taste you again." His words came out in a deep rumble that sent a thrill through her. He moved his body close to hers, his cock bumping her belly, his chest rubbing her nipples. He ran his fingers down her side to her hip and back up again.

"I need you inside me." She pressed her mouth to his and whispered against his lips, "I *need* you. Lie on the bed."

Still watching her, he sat on the bed then lay back, resting his head on a pillow. His hunger for her flamed in his eyes.

She trailed her fingers up from the base of his cock to the head and back again. "Where are your condoms?"

He stroked her hip as she teased his cock. "In the nightstand drawer."

She smiled and inched closer to the nightstand. He had tucked a new box of condoms in the back of the top drawer. She opened the box, took out a foil packet, and closed the drawer.

Her fingers trembled a little, tearing open the foil and pulling out the condom. She eased onto the bed and straddled his legs.

"Come on, honey." His dark, intense expression captured her. "I want you to ride me. I want you to fuck me good and hard."

She almost dropped the condom. She nearly came unglued from the heat of his words and the wicked desire in his gaze. With her eyes focused on him, she grasped his thick cock and put the condom over the head before slowly rolling it over his erection. He groaned as she pushed it all the way down to the base.

When she raised her head, she smiled at him. "*Now* I'm going to fuck you."

She moved up his body until she straddled his waist then rose and grasped his erection and placed it at the entrance to her core. With her gaze focused on him, she lowered herself onto his cock.

Her eyes widened and her lips parted at him filling her, stretching her. It struck her again how amazing it felt having this man fit so perfectly inside her. No one else had ever satisfied her the way he did.

She threw back her head and thrust her breasts out as she began riding his cock as he thrust up to meet her. He cupped one breast with his big hand and she closed her eyes, the heat of his touch adding to the fire inside her. He pinched her nipple hard and she gasped, her eyes opening in surprise. The brief but electric pain shot a current to her belly and her clit.

"That's it, honey." He urged her on and reached for her other breast. "Fuck. Me. Hard."

Her breaths came faster as she rode him. His cock easily reached her G-spot, rubbing against it and drawing her closer to orgasm. Everything in her body felt tight, buzzing with electricity.

"Look at me. I want you to come with me."

"Yes." Her words came out in a whimper, his eyes holding hers. "Yes, please."

She rode a few more hard thrusts when he commanded her, "Come now, Tori. Come *now*."

Her orgasm exploded through her, throwing her into a world that seemed to spin uncontrollably. She could barely process the moment as her core clamped down on his cock, pulsing around him.

He shouted his release and his cock throbbed inside her as he drove in and out a few more times before his entire body seemed to relax completely.

Would her mind ever stop spinning?

When it finally did, she let his cock slip out of her and she slid onto his right arm, resting her head on his good shoulder. Her breathing came harder and faster than ever, her heart pounding in her ears.

Perspiration slicked his skin and hers and the smell of sex permeated the room. His breathing came out as hard as hers.

For a long moment they rested together, sated and relaxed. When her breathing finally slowed and her heart no longer pounded like a drum, she tipped her head up and smiled at him. He kissed her softly and she snuggled against his side.

Gradually she fell into a deep sleep, feeling safe with Landon, as though nothing bad could ever happen to her again.

Chapter Twenty Three

An early morning thunderstorm darkened the sky and the desert monsoon rain pounded down on the rooftop, a constant thrum. Distant thunder followed lighting flashes.

Landon realized something that caused him to pause in picking up a breakfast dish. He hadn't had any nightmares about Stacy since he'd met Tori.

What did it mean? He put the last of the dishes into the dishwasher. He hadn't had the desire to drink. He wasn't an alcoholic — he didn't miss it or think about it when not drinking and he didn't crave it. But he had used it to self-medicate after Stacy had died.

He realized then too that the leg that had shattered in the motorcycle accident hadn't been bothering him for some time now. He wondered if the pain had been part of what he hadn't been able to let go of.

As he straightened, he glanced at Tori who wiped down the breakfast bar with a damp sponge. She wore a blue T-shirt and jeans along with the athletic shoes George Fallon had picked up at Walmart.

He closed the dishwasher and watched her for a moment. So damned beautiful. Not just her looks, but also her spirit, personality, intelligence, and more. Much more.

After all she'd been through, how would she feel about what he had to tell her?

Out of nowhere came the words of the old woman wearing the mantilla at the church. *'You will die if you tell her the truth. If you don't tell her, she will die.'*

Hair at his nape stood on end. He rubbed the bridge of his nose and closed his eyes. He didn't believe in omens or predictions or any other bullshit like that, but he'd intended to tell her the truth regardless.

Tori rinsed out the sponge, put it away, and looked at him. "Is something wrong?" She frowned. "I don't know if I can handle any more bad news."

He moved toward her and enveloped her in a one-armed hug before kissing her on the top of the head. When she put it that way, maybe he should hold off.

She drew away, tilting her head to meet his gaze. "What's the hug for?"

"You are stronger than you think." He trailed his finger along her cheekbone. "In a matter of days, you have handled more than most people go through in a lifetime."

"Doesn't mean I'm up for more of the bad news variety." She appeared fragile in that moment and he'd never seen her look as if she might shatter. He could understand why, he just hadn't seen it in her before. "If it's not going to kill me and it doesn't involve my family, I don't want to know. At least not now."

He ran his finger along her cheekbone and down the curve of her neck. Her words mingled with the old lady's.

'If it's not going to kill me...'

'If you don't tell her, she will die.'

Damn.

No, he didn't believe in crap like that. Hell, even if he did believe in them, how did he know the old lady been talking about the fact he'd killed Tori's brother?

If the slightest chance existed of the old woman's prediction coming true, he needed to tell Tori, and he needed to do it now.

"Tori." He captured her attention and she turned her gaze to meet his.

"You have something bad to tell me, don't you." She just glanced at him as she said it as a statement. "And you're going to tell me anyway."

He nodded. "I have to. It's something I should have told you long before we...before we went to bed together."

She frowned. "How bad is it?"

He dropped his gaze, then lifted it back to her. "Your brother worked as a dealer for the Jimenez Cartel."

She looked as if she held her breath, waiting for him to tell her something bad.

God damn it.

Landon gripped his good hand into a fist then relaxed it again. "And as you said, a DHS agent killed him during a raid."

She didn't say anything, as if she knew what storm barreled her way.

"He shot at us and we returned fire." Landon studied her widening brown eyes. "Ballistics came back that my bullet killed your brother."

Tori put her hand over her mouth as if she held back a cry or a scream. He reached out to touch her arm but she backed away. She lowered her hand and shook her head. "No." A tear rolled down her cheek. "I don't want you to touch me. I need—" Her breath caught. "Oh, God."

She buried her face in her hands and her shoulders trembled with her sobs.

Landon reached out and grasped her shoulder, but before he could say anything, she straightened and shook him off. She distanced herself from his touch and headed into the living room. He followed her.

She went still. "I hear something over the storm." She hurried to the front window and peeked through the blinds. "Someone's driving up the road in an SUV." She looked over her shoulder at him, a slight edge of panic in her voice. "What if it's the cartel?"

Landon frowned as he moved toward her. "No way anyone could know we're here." He squinted, peering through the blinds. Even in his surprise, he relaxed. "It's Dylan." Landon gave Tori a glance meant to reassure her.

"I met Dylan at the DHS office." Her chest rose and fell as she took a deep breath. Then she looked a little flushed. "And he walked in on us that night."

"Yes, he certainly did." Landon strode to the front door, opened it, and stepped onto the porch as Dylan parked in front of the house. He climbed out into the rain and approached Landon, the man's expression both relieved and pissed off.

"What the hell did you mean by disappearing?" Dylan strode up the stairs to the porch where Landon waited for him. Rainwater drenched his clothing from the downpour and dripped from his Stetson. "We thought you'd been blown to hell. Your family did too." He glanced at the front door to see Tori peering outside. "And we thought the cartel had killed the witness."

"I didn't know who the hell to trust." Landon shook his head, his frustration tensing his muscles.

Dylan's scowl turned into a frown. "You're telling me that you didn't trust me?"

"I didn't want to use my damn phone." Landon moved the hand of his right arm to the nape of his neck. "I wanted everyone to think we'd died in the blast." He rubbed his neck, trying to ease the ache.

"How did the bastards find the second safe house?" Dylan asked. "An inside job?"

Landon shook his head. "I confiscated Tori's phone after she took out the battery, and both were with me. After the explosion, I found a tracker in the phone that worked independently of the phone and battery."

"Holy shit." Dylan's jaw dropped. "How did they get it on her phone?"

"We think her boyfriend put it there." Landon frowned. "They likely got the information when they tortured him."

Dylan's mouth tightened into a thin line. "Damn."

Landon lowered his hand from his nape. "I would have bought a burner phone to use to call you, but I'd passed out cold before our help went to the store for us."

Dylan looked at Landon's left arm.

He hadn't used the sling today, but he favored it, the bandages peeking from beneath his T-shirt sleeve.

"What happened to your arm?"

"One of the sonsofbitches shot me in the shoulder." Landon grimaced. "It's slowing me down."

"Well, that's fucked-up. The last thing you need." Dylan quieted. "We confirmed by dental records O'Donnell and Danson died in the explosion."

Landon pinched the bridge of his nose and squeezed his eyes shut. He'd been sure they had been killed, but the confirmation made his chest hurt and his blood boil even hotter.

When Landon looked up, Dylan nodded toward the house. "How's Tori?"

Landon peered over his shoulder to see Tori had gone back into the house. He thought about all she'd been through and on top of that he'd dropped the bomb about killing her brother. "She's pretty shaken up, but she's tough. She'll be all right."

Dylan nodded but still looked concerned for Tori.

Landon returned to the fact Dylan had just shown up. "What are you doing here? How did you figure out we'd be at my place?"

"We processed the scene and got the report back." Dylan hooked his thumbs in his front pockets. "The two pairs of footsteps clued us in. One large and one small, headed away from the safe house into the tree line of the mountains."

"How did you guess the footprints were ours?" Landon asked as lightning flashed and thunder rumbled.

"You bled all over the place, Landon." Dylan rocked back on his heels. "As soon as we got that news, Sofia sent me to your ranch to see if you'd made it and decided to hide out here."

Landon hadn't been himself after being knocked out, as well as weak from blood loss, so he hadn't even thought about the fact he might have left a bloodstain behind. It damn sure should have occurred to him. "You've found us, so now what?"

"We get you back to the office." Dylan rocked on his heels

again. "We need to double down on all the precautions we have available to make sure Tori is safe."

If the RAC figured it out so easily, then others would as well.

"When we found out you were likely alive, Sofia called the U.S. Marshals," Dylan said. "They'll be at the DHS office to take Tori into WITSEC sometime after we get there."

"Damn." The thought of Tori going into the Witness Security Program and disappearing from his life didn't sit well with Landon. He couldn't begin to imagine never seeing her again. But he had to think of the best options for her now.

"Don't mention the program to her yet." Landon kept his voice low. "She got pretty upset the night when Claire Danson told her that's what she might be looking at. We can wait until we're at the office."

"Can't say I blame Tori." Dylan raised his Stetson and scratched a spot on his head. "To give up your life as you know it, and everything and everyone in your world, would be pretty damned difficult."

Landon nodded as he started to turn. "I need a few moments with her, then I'll follow you in my truck." They could leave the rental car at the ranch for now. He felt safer in his truck with its powerful engine on a par with law enforcement vehicles, and its sturdy build, as opposed to a mid-sized car from a rental agency.

Dylan leaned back against his SUV and folded his arms across his chest. "I'll wait out here for you."

Tori stood in the living room when Landon walked into the house and closed the door behind him. She crossed her arms over her chest as if protecting herself from him. The fact he'd killed her brother had clearly affected her and he couldn't blame her.

"We're going into the office." He let her have her space at his words. "You'll be safe there while we plan our next move."

* * * *

Tori's belly clenched and she kept her arms crossed over her chest as Dylan drove his SUV behind the truck she and Landon were in. Landon, the damned macho alpha male, had insisted on driving despite his shoulder that couldn't have been close to being healed enough. His head probably still ached too after being hit from the explosion.

But she was too upset, too torn, too confused to argue. Feeling sick to her bones, she stared out of the window, raindrops rolling down the pane, the rainy landscape blurring when they passed it.

Landon had killed her brother.

Dear God. She had fallen in love with the man who'd put the bullet into her brother and taken his life.

Falling in love with? She fought back tears. How could she already have fallen for Landon? And what did it mean now that she knew the truth? Damn it, he should have told her before they'd become intimate.

Dylan had told them he would call ahead to have Tori escorted into the building. Once they reached headquarters, before they allowed her out of Landon's truck, they put a Kevlar vest on her. She walked into the DHS office, surrounded by Landon, Dylan and four other agents.

Rain soaked her clothes and her damp hair clung to her cheeks. The summer storm had grown worse as they'd driven to the DHS office.

She didn't like what churned inside her at all...the feeling of being constantly in danger and the fear someone she loved would be killed. Not to mention the two agents, O'Donnell and Danson, who had died protecting her after the house they'd been in had exploded. Thoughts of Gregory and his intern, both murdered because of what she'd seen, remained in her mind.

A shiver caused goosebumps on her skin and she rubbed her wet arms with both palms. Four people had already lost their lives and Landon and Johnson had been injured.

When they walked into the office, Landon escorted her to a room with no windows. He helped her take off the Kevlar vest and he set it aside on one of the chairs at the table. They were alone and she took a seat.

He braced his hand on the table's surface and studied her. "Do you want water or something else to drink?"

She swallowed and her dry throat ached. "Water."

He watched her as if she might get up and run screaming from the room. "How about something to eat?"

"I'm still full from breakfast." That was partially true. Mostly, she doubted she could eat anything if she tried.

"Will you be all right here alone for a while?" She heard concern in his low voice. "I can send someone in if you'd like."

"No." She shook her head. "I don't need anyone to stay with me." She paused a moment and met his gaze. "Please arrange for a call on a secure connection between my mom and me."

Landon looked thoughtful. "I'll see what I can do."

"That's not good enough." She leaned forward and spoke in a firm tone. Anger flared in her. She deserved to talk with her parents and there had to be a way to do it safely. "Make it happen, Landon."

She refused to keep running. She was tired of being afraid, tired of fearing for the lives of her loved ones, and tired of people dying. Tired of everything being out of her control. Somewhere, somehow, she had to regain some semblance of control over her own destiny and over what happened at this very moment.

He rested his hand on hers, his touch heating her. She remained motionless, not wanting his comfort at this moment. He nodded before letting his hand slide away from hers, and left the room, closing the door behind him.

She stared at the door for a long moment, trying to think all of this through. There had to be something she could do now, something to help end this nightmare. Maybe she was finally waking up.

* * * *

"Absolutely not, Sofia." Landon clenched his jaw as he stood in his RAC's office and stared at her. "We're not going to use Tori as bait."

Sofia Aguilar leaned back in her office chair behind her desk and gave Landon a hard look. "This has to end and we need to rope in Alejandro Jimenez. Our best shot right now is using Ms. Cox to lure him in. The marshals will help and between them and us we'll make sure she's safe. It'll be quick and she'll never be in any real danger."

"No." Heat burned beneath Landon's collar. "We're not doing that to her. Hell, what if we get Alejandro? His father will be right behind him." Landon shook his head. "No."

"It's not your call, Landon." Aguilar narrowed her gaze. "We'll let Ms. Cox decide for herself."

"Decide what?" Tori's voice came from behind Landon.

Frowning, he turned and faced her. "You were to stay in the room."

"You didn't say I couldn't leave." She looked from Landon to Aguilar. "What is it I need to decide for myself, Special Agent Aguilar?"

Landon angled his gaze to Aguilar, but she looked past him, directing her attention to Tori.

Aguilar spoke with quiet authority, "Ms. Cox, we would like your cooperation in setting a trap for the cartel and specifically Alejandro Jimenez."

Fear flashed in Tori's eyes, but then it vanished. She gave a slow nod. "What do I need to do?"

"Tori, it's too dangerous." Tension gripped Landon like an iron fist. "You don't need to do this."

"I do need to." She straightened and raised her chin. "We're going to get them." She fisted her hands at her sides. "Everything that happened — all the sacrifices, all the deaths — is not going to be for nothing."

Landon rubbed the bridge of his nose, his mind rejecting the thought of intentionally putting her in harm's way.

When he looked at Tori again, she focused on Aguilar.

"Just tell me what you want from me and I'll do it." Tori moved closer to the RAC's desk. "My only condition is I get to speak to my mom. However you can do it, with some kind of secure connection, that's what I want."

Aguilar nodded tersely. "We'll get you that phone call."

Landon's gut tightened. He wanted to argue they shouldn't take a chance by using her as bait. By the look in Tori's and Aguilar's eyes, he knew whatever he said wouldn't make a damned bit of difference. Tori had already made up her mind.

"Thank you for arranging the call." Tori's chest rose and fell. "What's the plan?"

Landon dragged his hand down his face. It took everything he had not to jump in yet again and insist Tori should not be used as bait. It involved too much risk. If anything happened to her, he didn't know what he'd do.

Aguilar picked up a pencil and tapped it on the desk pad, which had doodles down the left side. "Now that we know we have your cooperation, we'll take care of the rest."

Tori's throat worked. "Now about my phone call?"

The RAC turned to Landon. "Set it up."

Landon couldn't hold back the terseness in his voice. "Yes, ma'am." He met Tori's gaze and gave a nod in the direction of the door to Aguilar's office. "We'll take care of it now."

A relieved expression made Tori look more relaxed, the furthest thing from what he felt.

"You shouldn't put yourself in danger." He nearly growled the words once they were out of Aguilar's office. "Anything could happen."

Tori pursed her lips before speaking. "I can't sit on my hands and do nothing anymore. All I've been doing is running and running and running. I have to do *something* that will help end this and all the death."

Landon grasped her arm and brought her to a complete stop in the hallway, facing him. "This is beyond dangerous,

Tori." He scowled. "You could get yourself killed trying to play hero."

She jerked her arm away from him, her face flushing as though her temperature had just gone up by twenty degrees. "I'm not trying to play hero. I'm trying to do what's right and I'm trying to keep more people from getting killed."

He struggled to cool the anger burning inside him. What Aguilar discussed had been done before with other witnesses and most had gone as planned. It wasn't logical to be so concerned about Tori being used as bait. DHS agents would protect Tori and bring down Alejandro Jimenez at the same time.

Fuck logic. I'm not a god damned Vulcan.

Diego would be out for blood when the dust settled.

He opened his mouth to say something to her but she shook her head. He dropped his gaze to the floor a moment before meeting her gaze again. "All right. I'm not happy about it, but I *will* protect you. I won't let *anything* happen to you."

She looked away from him. When she met his gaze again, she said, "You took my brother's life and I'll never get him back."

Landon's gut sank.

"But…" Her words were soft and the light in her eyes told him she meant every word. "I trust you with my life."

Landon studied her beautiful features, the strong pull he always felt around her threatening to turn him inside out. "What is it about you?" He didn't mean to say the words aloud.

She cocked her head, looking puzzled. "What do you mean?"

He shook his head. "I don't know."

That wasn't entirely true. He did know. He had fallen for Tori and he had fallen hard, a bad idea on all counts.

This precious woman fought to remain alive and make it to the witness stand. After that, she could end up in WITSEC, where he couldn't follow. If he did fall for her, it might take him off his game, making him the weak link.

Instead of trying to explain himself, he turned the subject back to what they were supposed to be doing. "We'll arrange that call to your mom."

He escorted her to his office. "Stay here. This is my office. I'll be right back with a phone."

"Okay." She took a seat on the left side of the desk. "I'm not going anywhere."

He met her gaze one more time. He felt as if he should say something comforting, like she'd be okay and they'd make sure nothing would happen to her.

The agency *would* do everything in its power to keep her safe, but the Jimenez Cartel had powerful tentacles reaching across the U.S.-Mexico border. No one knew how far those tentacles went.

Considering the cartel had found Tori not once, but twice, Landon wasn't so confident they wouldn't find a way to harm her, even with every bit of protection the agency had to offer.

He should have said something, done something, but he simply turned and walked away.

Tori sat at one side of Landon's desk, staring at the doorway long after he'd left. An irrational part of her feared he wouldn't return, that she'd never see him again. Everything in her life seemed to be disappearing piece by piece. Even if for a short time, Landon had become one of those pieces in her life.

But the man she'd fallen head over heels for had killed her brother.

Her brother.

She tucked her damp hair behind her ear. Her thoughts turned to the fact she'd just agreed to be bait so the agency could get Alejandro Jimenez.

A stronger emotion took hold of her, surpassing her fear.

Anger. It burned hot and bright inside her chest, like a flaming torch.

She turned her gaze from the doorway to the blank wall directly in front of her and listened to the rain on the rooftop. She had meant what she'd said to Special Agent Aguilar. Tori would do anything she could to help take down those men who had already destroyed so many lives from drugs, human trafficking, and murder. The people they'd killed—they'd all had families and friends who would never see them again. Would never hold them in their arms again. The men and women who'd died, including Gregory and her brother, were…gone.

She swallowed. Just gone.

A deep, soul-wrenching shudder came over her. It felt as if this nightmare would never end.

"Tori?" Landon's voice had her looking back to the doorway. "Are you sure you're all right?"

She straightened in her chair. "Yes." Her gaze dropped to the phone he held in his hand and he set it on the tabletop. She met his eyes.

"Your mom is on the line." He pressed the Speaker button. "Mrs. Cox, you and Tori need to remember, no matter how secure we believe this line to be, do not give out anything that might reveal your whereabouts, or anything else in relation to this case. Understand?"

Tori nodded. "I do."

"Yes," came Josie's agreement over the speaker.

Tori's heart felt as though it jumped into her throat as she settled her forearms on the table. "Mom?"

"Mija." The relief in her mother's voice brought tears to Tori's eyes. "You are all right?"

"Yes." Tori barely got the word out, a tear rolling down her cheek. "How are you and Dad?"

Josie sighed. "Your father is slowly being weaned off the whisky, but once we're home again, I don't think it will last."

Tori sniffled, trying not to think of the possibility of any of them not being allowed to go home and heading straight into WITSEC. "But otherwise you're okay?"

She could picture her mother nodding. "Yes. Everyone is good to us." Josie hesitated. "Are you someplace safe?"

Tori met Landon's gaze and he shook his head. Another tear made its way down her cheek. "Nothing for you to worry about."

"I miss you, *mija*." Josie had tears in her voice.

Tori wiped her own tears from her eyes with the back of her hand. "I miss you too, Mom."

Landon reached for the phone. "Time's up."

"I love you," Tori got it out in a rush. "I'll talk with you soon."

"You have our love," Josie's voice cracked. "Don't wait so long to call again."

"I won't." Tori managed to get the words out right before Landon disconnected the call with a push of his finger on the End button.

Tori buried her face in her palms. Her emotions pinged all over the place, from one thing to another. People dying, Landon having killed her brother.

But mostly anger at the cartel burned hot and furious inside her. The Jimenez Cartel had done this to all of them.

When she raised her head, Landon now sat at the table, watching her. By the tightness in his expression, she had a feeling that whatever he was thinking couldn't be good.

She wiped away the rest of her tears. "What's wrong, Landon?"

He clenched the phone on the tabletop, his knuckles white. "I don't like putting you in danger."

"Have other witnesses done this before?" She knew the answer without him responding. "Of course they have. So what's so different about me?"

"Because you're special, Tori," he spoke in a quiet tone. "You're special to *me*."

Her eyes widened a bit. Of all the things he could have said, she never expected to hear those words.

She reached for his hands. His fingers felt big and strong beneath her palm. "I will be fine. Everything is going to work out."

He rested one of his hands over hers while she squeezed his other. "Yes. It will all work out," he spoke firmly, but she couldn't tell if he meant to reassure himself or her. Maybe both.

"Thank you for being here." She swallowed. "You've saved my life more than once. It's a debt I can never repay."

"It's not something you repay." He leaned closer to her. "It's my job. I protect people."

Then he cleared his throat before continuing. "But you will be going into WITSEC shortly and I can't be with you while you are in the program. You'll be taken out of hiding for only a short time to get Alejandro Jimenez, but then you'll go right back into the program."

It was happening. A cold chill traveled over her skin and she wanted to scream she didn't want to go into the program. She wanted to say she'd be safe with Landon, but he couldn't always be there for her. And as long as she stayed with him, he would be in danger too.

Even though they might—would—get Alejandro, his father would still be at the top of the ruthless organization. The head of the snake, *El Demonio*, would still be free somewhere in Mexico. So, more than likely she would end up staying in WITSEC, unless somehow Diego and Alejandro Jimenez were taken out. Dead.

The thought of being in WITSEC echoed in her mind and her chest squeezed. What if the cartel got to her family and friends once she disappeared? What if the cartel hurt Paula, Sue, and Janice while trying to find Tori?

An explosion ripped through the air.

Landon grabbed Tori, pulling her out of her chair. He landed on her back, pinning her to the floor, knocking the breath from her. She heard his muffled cry as the impact jarred his shoulder.

Debris rained down on them when the whole building rocked.

Terror filled her at the shouting and screams.

Oh, God. The cartel had found her again.

Chapter Twenty Four

A section of the ceiling slammed down on Landon's injured shoulder. He barely held back another shout of pain. His ears rang from the volume of the explosion and his head swam. The lights had gone out and darkness enveloped everything beneath the debris.

Landon's body pinned Tori and he tried to push himself up so his body weight wouldn't crush her, yet he could protect her. His heart pounded. More debris rained down on them and he gritted his teeth to keep from crying out every time something hit his shoulder.

It seemed to last forever, but mere moments had passed before everything went still. An alarm blared, all Landon could hear. He rose, feeling a little dazed, the debris on his back sliding off and falling away. Fortunately, the panels making up the ceiling were fairly light.

Emergency lighting came on, allowing him to see.

He got to his feet, unsteady from the ringing in his head and the pain in his shoulder. He looked at Tori who pushed herself to her haunches and held her head between her hands. Clearly shaken, her eyes were wide as she pressed the sides of her head. No doubt her ears rang like his.

His heart pounded like thunder in his head and his adrenaline spiked. His colleagues, his friends, were in the building. He had to get to and help whomever he could.

Jesus. How many had been hurt or killed in the explosion?

He looked at Tori. Thank God she hadn't been injured.

His mind raced through the options and he had three choices. One, he could grab another agent and get Tori outside to the truck and risk the cartel being outside waiting for them. Two, he could keep her hidden, stay with her, and protect her in here. Or three, he could have her hide while he found out whatever he could about what had happened, who might be injured, or worse, and see if members of the cartel occupied the building.

And pray the cartel didn't have yet another bomb.

His head ached and for a moment he felt dizzy. He fought to clear it. Someone had to stay with Tori to protect her, and right now that someone had to be him.

"Get under my desk." He didn't know if Tori heard him over the alarm and he pointed to the kneehole as he crouched. She scooted into the space. He took his backup weapon, a small Sig Sauer, out of the holster on his ankle and handed it to her. "Know how to shoot?"

He didn't know if she could hear him, but she seemed to understand and shook her head. He showed her how to hold the weapon then put his lips close to her ear and spoke loud enough that he hoped she heard him clearly. "It's fully loaded and the safety is off. Don't point it at someone unless you intend to shoot. Keep your hand off the trigger unless you're sure of your target. Got it?"

She nodded and kept the weapon pointed at the floor. Her hands were trembling, the gun shaking.

"You'll be fine." He squeezed her upper arm as he yelled the words. "I'll be close."

Her expression hardened and he saw the same determination in his gaze he'd witnessed earlier when she'd insisted she wanted to be bait for the cartel.

He gave her one last look before getting to his feet and drawing his Colt. He climbed over debris to the office door and peered out. He turned to his left, in the direction of the blast then to the opposite end of the hallway and back.

The ringing in his ears started to lessen, but the blare of the alarm didn't help. He saw movement and raised his weapon.

Sophia Aguilar limped into the corridor from her office across the hall. She held her weapon, but pain twisted her features as she tried to walk. Her gaze met Landon's and she hobbled to him. When she neared him, he saw blood seeped from a cut on her forehead and rolled down the side of her face.

The alarm stopped blaring but the ringing in Landon's ears seemed worse. He lowered his weapon but not his guard.

"Got thrown across my office and I think my god damned leg is broken." Aguilar gritted her teeth.

Landon narrowed his gaze. "Sonofabitch."

Aguilar's furious expression could have melted steel. "If the fucking cartel bombed us, they've declared war. We're going to come down on them so damned hard they won't know what hit them."

"Sure as hell." Landon looked up and down the corridor as he spoke.

Aguilar frowned. "How's our witness?"

"Uninjured so far as I could tell." He inclined his head toward his office doorway. "She's in my office, under the desk."

"I can protect her." Aguilar nodded in the direction the explosion had come from. "Make sure no one from the cartel is in the building and help who you can."

Landon hesitated a fraction of a second. Aguilar was more than capable of protecting Tori, yet he felt as if he had to be the one to stay by her side.

"Go." Aguilar gestured her weapon. "That's an order."

"I need to let Tori know you'll be here with her." Landon turned back into his office, stepped over the debris, and made it to his desk. He crouched near the kneehole, close to Tori's hiding place. "Tori." He didn't want to startle her but raised his voice. "It's me, so don't shoot."

"Okay." She had the Sig pointed at the floor as he peered in at her. She appeared both afraid and determined at the same time. "What's going on?"

"My RAC will stay with you." He glanced at Aguilar who limped into the office. "She'll make sure you're safe." He put his hand on Tori's and squeezed. "I'll be back as soon as I am able to."

"Go help who you can." She didn't falter. "We'll be fine."

"Whatever might happen, do not come out from under the desk."

She nodded.

He gave her hand one last squeeze then turned and walked to where Aguilar stood, just in front of his office door.

"Tori knows you're staying with her." He gripped his weapon, ever on the watch as he spoke. "She has my Sig, so don't surprise her."

"She'll be fine." Aguilar gave Landon a firm nod before he left the office.

"I'll get some paramedics here to help you," Landon said.

Aguilar shook her head. "Not until those seriously wounded are taken care of. All I have is a fucking broken leg. I'm not losing blood and I don't have any other injuries. Get the hell out of here and do your job."

Landed nodded. He held his Colt in a two-handed grip as he headed down the corridor in the direction of the blast. He stepped over debris and peered around corners before continuing. Two agents, helping injured personnel, passed him in the hallway. The men were drenched as if they'd been outside and they left dirty wet footprints in the hallway. No doubt the blast had taken out part of the building, leaving it open to the elements.

Next came Dylan, also soaked, who supported another agent named Conway, who seemed pretty banged up and dazed. "There are more injured." Dylan's wet skin had split along his cheekbone, blood mingling with water as the cut bled down the side of his face. He had small cuts all over his face and arms—it looked as though he'd been hit with shattered glass. His expression turned grim. "I think we may have lost a couple of agents and administrative staff."

Landon cursed and gripped his weapon tighter. "Where did the bomb detonate?"

"Near the holding cells." Dylan glanced up and down the corridor, as did Landon, both men continually on guard. "Graves and Perez were in there. I don't know if they're dead or if they managed to escape."

"Shit." Landon clenched his teeth.

Dylan looked past Landon. "Where's the witness?"

"In my office." Landon cocked his head in the direction he'd just come from. "With Aguilar, who's injured. She thinks her leg is broken."

"Damn. At least they're both alive." Dylan shifted to get a better hold on Conway. "I'm going to get Conway out of here then check on Tori and Aguilar."

"Thanks." Landon gave Dylan a nod before he continued down the hall.

The farther Landon went, the worse the destruction. He passed other agents and administrative personnel assisting individuals who had sustained significant injuries.

As he approached the corridor to the holding cells, he saw the door ajar and water seeping through the opening. Dirty puddles from footprints crossed the floor, leading away from the door.

A gust of wind slammed the door open and rain pelted onto the floor at the opening. He moved to the doorway and had to squint to see through the downpour.

Where once a roof and walls made up an office, a gaping hole filled with rubble had replaced it. The storm muted the light.

The parking lot was a good distance away and Landon couldn't see if anything else had been damaged.

Thank God no fire had accompanied the explosion.

Still gripping his Colt, Landon climbed over support beams, concrete, twisted pieces of metal, and glass. Sirens blared, louder now that he stood outside. He glanced in the direction of the highway and saw emergency vehicles turning onto the road leading to the DHS office. Red and blue lights flashed, reflecting off wet surfaces.

As Landon looked around him, he saw a male figure half

buried in the rubble, face turned away. Landon climbed over debris toward the figure. His stomach clenched when he saw the remains of the man's upper torso and head, the face unrecognizable.

Fury burned Landon's skin, but he continued on. He would be fooling himself to hope no others had suffered similar fates, yet prayed no one had. He hurried the best he could toward the still intact corridor where the holding cells were. The door, a twisted mess, hung on one hinge and swung in the wind. No doubt the door could go flying at any minute.

He climbed over debris to get to the door. He checked the hinge and saw only one screw held it in place. He hit the door with his good shoulder and the door broke away from the hinge and landed harmlessly on rubble. Still, the impact jarred his other shoulder and he gritted his teeth.

Rain had been pouring in through the open doorway and into the hallway and water covered the floor.

He saw the holding cells were open and strode toward them. He narrowed his gaze when he saw the cells. *Fuck.*

Graves and Perez were dead. The cartel had been there to take care of loose ends.

Moans came from farther down the hallway and Landon headed in that direction, still holding his weapon and making sure none of the cartel's men were nearby.

Tori never left Landon's thoughts as he helped the injured out of the building, through the storm and into the hands of emergency personnel who had arrived.

He knew Tori was in capable hands. Aguilar had set records as a sharpshooter when she'd trained at FLETC, so she could more than hold her own.

Dylan met up with Landon a good twenty minutes after Landon had passed him and Conway in the hallway. Dylan had stopped by Landon's office before he'd returned to the blast zone to assist. He'd told Landon that, when he'd checked, Aguilar's only serious injury was the broken leg and she refused to acknowledge any pain she might be feeling. She'd insisted she would watch over Tori and had reiterated she didn't need medical attention. Those seriously injured needed aid first.

Landon had done all he could at the moment and he intended to return to his office, where Tori and Aguilar waited. The wind and rain had never stopped buffeting the men and women working the scene.

His head seemed to ache even more from the blast and the debris that had landed on him in his office. His shoulder burned and hurt like a son of a bitch and it had started bleeding again, enough that the blood wet his T-shirt and spotted his overshirt.

A paramedic noticed Landon holding his shoulder as he trudged toward the door that would open up into the hallway.

"Hold on." The female paramedic tried to stop Landon. "Let me check your shoulder."

Landon gritted his teeth and shook his head. "I'll be fine, but the Resident Agent in Charge is inside. If everyone in serious condition is taken care of, per her instructions, she needs medical attention."

The paramedic signaled her partner and in moments they were hurrying toward Landon's office. Water ran in rivulets down his face and arms and onto the floor as he walked to the open doorway leading to the corridor. His steps quickened, heading to his office. He needed to see Tori, needed to see her safe.

He entered his office first and his heart nearly stopped.

Aguilar lay on the floor, blood soaking her shirt. Her chest rose and fell with rapid, harsh breaths. Her hand pressed a piece of bloody cloth over her abdomen.

Blood soaked almost all of the cloth, but the edges were the same color of blue as Tori's shirt.

Heart pounding hard enough to feel as if it were hitting his ribcage, Landon turned to the paramedics. "Take care of Special Agent Aguilar." His voice tightened. "I need to check on someone else."

The paramedics were on Aguilar before he'd finished speaking and Landon hurried to the desk where Tori should be hidden.

Before he had a chance to look, he saw his Sig resting on the floor. Chest squeezing with fear for Tori, Landon looked under the desk.

His heart nearly stopped.

Tori was gone.

* * * *

Tori lay curled up on the floor of a van, her hands and feet bound with duct tape and a piece of the tape covering her mouth. Cold and wet, her body prickled with icy fear as men laughed and spoke in Spanish. Thanks to her mother she spoke, read, and understood the language fluently.

Their words caused terror to clench her belly and grip her heart.

They intended to take her to Diego Jimenez's compound in Mexico. The head of the cartel had decided to make her pay in ways other than death.

God, no doubt death would be better than anything they might do to her.

Someone kicked her in the back and laughed and she gave an involuntary muffled cry as pain lanced her body, especially her chest. Her eyes watered and a tear rolled down the side of her face.

She should have stayed hidden, like Landon had ordered her to.

But she'd *had* to go to try to help the agent.

After a man had shot Special Agent Aguilar, Tori waited until certain the man had left. She'd crawled out of the kneehole, scrambled over debris and had gone to the agent to try and stop the bleeding. She hadn't seen any cloth around, so she'd torn off part of her shirt, like she'd done for Landon. She'd pressed the cloth to the agent's wound, her hands almost immediately covered in blood.

She'd been just about to take off her whole shirt to use when a man had come by the office and peered in. Tori had raised her head to ask for help when terror had blocked a scream in her throat. The man had his gun pointed at her. She didn't recognize him, but he'd clearly recognized her.

She hadn't been able to run. She'd been trapped in the office. In that instant, she had prayed for Landon to return, but he hadn't. There had been no way to save herself.

The man had yanked her by her hair, dragging her to the doorway and forcing her to her feet. He'd taken her by gunpoint from the room, the gun digging into the small of her back. They'd gone out into the storm and the chaos and no one had noticed.

No one.

Her head still ached from being dragged by her hair. The man had pressed the barrel so hard against her back he'd almost certainly bruised her skin. She had bruises on her face and body from the men kicking her and backhanding her. It hurt to breathe and she likely had a broken rib.

Far worse than the pain in her head and chest, and the bruises all over her body, was the fact she'd been kidnapped. These men intended to take her across the line, into Mexico.

If they got her out of the U.S., there would be no hope for her. The U.S. government would do nothing—she'd just be one more person who'd been abducted into Mexico like so many others.

Tears squeezed from her eyes. What if they sold her to human traffickers? Would she become a sex slave? The very real and frightening possibility tightened her chest and made her feel ill, as if she might throw up behind the duct tape. She'd drown in her own vomit.

More tears rolled from her eyes. What could she do, bound and gagged and surrounded by determined men?

Pray.

She looked at the duct tape binding her wrists in front of her. The rain hadn't washed away all of Special Agent Aguilar's blood from her hands and it remained around her fingernails as well as having stained the remnants of her shirt. She prayed too that the agent would survive. She had a lot to pray for, including Landon's safety.

Landon. Her heart squeezed. If her kidnappers got her across the line, she'd never see him again. She hadn't known him for long, but she knew one thing. She'd fallen in love with him. She had truly fallen in love with a man for the first and only time in her life. Now that she had experienced true love, she knew what she'd felt for Gregory had been infatuation while he'd treated her well. Before things had changed.

Landon had killed her brother, but it had been in the line of duty. Maybe it was screwed up, but she loved Landon with everything she had.

Her heart swelled with the emotion but ached at the fact that how she felt wouldn't matter if she ended up in the cartel's compound.

Yet, somehow it did matter, even though she may have seen Landon for the last time. The saying was true...she would rather have loved and lost than to never have loved at all.

Even though six men surrounded her, all of whom were likely hardened criminals and murderers, she still held out hope of escape before they crossed the line into Mexico.

Somehow, some way, she would make it.

Chapter Twenty Five

The morning dawned crisp and bright. Diego smiled, truly pleased for the first time since the woman had witnessed Alejandro murdering the federal agent. Yes, he'd thought she'd died in the explosion and had been furious yesterday morning to find out she'd somehow escaped.

Now that his men had her and had crossed the line into Mexico last night, he had no more concerns about Alejandro being arrested and prosecuted by the Americans. Any time now, when they arrived, he would see the woman for himself and he would determine what her destiny would be.

The bugs planted in various agents' offices had worked perfectly. Alejandro had arranged for two members of the federal office's cleaning staff to be blackmailed. If they didn't plant the bugs, their families would die.

Diego whistled as he walked through his exquisite home, morning sunshine pouring in through tall arched windows. He paused and looked outside at the preparations.

An event planner and her staff, along with his own employees, were working tirelessly to prepare for his granddaughter's party later this evening. It would take place outside where a wide stone staircase swept down to the grounds below.

A stage had been built for a live band and two enormous tents had been erected on a portion of the expansive lawn. Workers had spread a dance floor beneath one tent. The other tent stretched over table after table with many chairs. White slipcovers with large pink bows decorated the chairs. The staff had covered tables with fine linen cloths with floral arrangements at the center of each round. Lovely cut-crystal glasses glittered in the light on tabletops. His people had purchased the expensive china serving pieces and polished silver flatware, just for this special event.

Flowers in pots and vases were arranged in brilliant displays and balloons in light pink, dark pink, and white hung from every corner and the center of both tents.

Balloons and ribbons decorated an archway at the top of the stairs. Angelina would walk through the archway and with her court she would be presented to the guests.

The splendid day had been predicted in weather reports. Yes, everything would be perfect, nothing to mar Angelina's party, her night as *Quinceañera*.

As he entered the family wing and walked toward Angelina's suite of rooms, the now young woman of fifteen ran toward him like an excited child.

"Grandfather!" Her lovely smile warmed his heart. "Everything is beautiful!"

He gently grasped his angel by the shoulders and kissed her forehead before stretching his arms out and looking at her. His throat closed off, pride swelling within him at her rare beauty.

"So much like your mother, my angel." He hugged her as she wrapped her arms around him.

"Thank you, Grandfather." She drew back and beamed at him. "This will be the best party a *Quinceañera* could want and has ever been held in all of Mexico."

"No one deserves it more than you." He rested his arm around her shoulders and gave her a loving squeeze. "Only the best for my angel."

"Maria said I must bathe this afternoon in an herbal bath she is preparing." Angelina spoke in an excited tone. "Then she will fix my hair and help me dress and she will put makeup on me."

Diego frowned. "You need nothing to add to your beauty."

"Grandfather, please." She placed her hand on his arm.

"It is only a little. I am a woman now."

He studied her. "Only a little or I will make you wash your face of it."

Angelina's smile faltered. "I will tell Maria you will allow the barest amount. Does that please you?"

His frown turned into a smile. My God, but he loved this girl, this young woman. "It pleases me."

"Thank you." She gave him a quick kiss before hurrying to her bedroom suite.

Diego watched after her, pride making his chest expand once again.

When he turned to leave the wing, Jaime appeared at the entrance.

"What is it?" Diego held back a scowl. He did not wish for anything to disturb this day in any way.

"Alejandro is here." Jaime stood with his hands behind his back. "With the girl."

"Good." Diego relaxed and gave a single nod, pleased his son had arrived safely. He lowered his voice to ensure no one would overhear. "They are in the rooms below?"

"*Sí.*" As usual, Jaime's expression betrayed no emotion. "They brought the girl in through the tunnel."

"Excellent." Diego began walking toward the wing reserved for business activities, Jaime at his side.

When they reached what Diego considered to be his War Room, he strode toward a map-covered wall as Jaime closed the door behind them. The newest and best high-tech computers and screens money could buy filled the room.

Diego pressed what looked like a large map pin and a hidden door swung open. He glanced at Jaime. "I will return shortly for the last of the preparations for Angelina's party."

"Yes, *El Demonio.*" Jaime gave a slight bow at his shoulders.

Diego walked into a corridor, pressed a red button on the wall, and the hidden door swung shut behind him. He walked down the tunnel, lights automatically coming to life as he paced, illuminating his way.

He opened the door to the left and took the stairs to the cells below. The sound of his shoes on stone echoed against the rough-hewn walls as he continued. He heard male voices ahead, at the bottom of the stairs. They quieted, no doubt hearing his footsteps.

When he entered the cellblock, he saw Alejandro with two other men, waiting.

A young woman knelt on the floor, her wrists bound with duct tape behind her back. Her head lolled forward, her hair obscuring her face. Her bloodstained blue shirt hung in tatters and her filthy jeans fit her poorly. Bruises spotted her arms.

"Hello, Father." Alejandro gave Diego a deferential nod.

The other two men said nothing but dropped their gazes.

"Let me see her face." Diego watched as Alejandro grabbed the woman's hair and jerked her head back.

Duct tape covered her mouth and tear tracks streaked her dirty and bruised face. She met his gaze but showed neither fear nor anger, not even resignation. He could read nothing from her eyes, and that concerned him.

He stepped closer and realized when he saw her dilated pupils she'd been drugged.

"I gave no orders to drug the woman." Diego narrowed his eyes at his son. "I want her lucid for what I have planned for her."

Alejandro kept his gaze even with his father's. "My apologies, Father. She proved to be difficult and I felt she needed to be calmed down considerably."

Diego looked at the woman again. She had dark hair and fine features. She swayed and appeared as though she would soon collapse. Diego motioned to one of the cells. "Remove the tape and lock her up."

The two men with Alejandro cut the tape from her wrists and pulled off the strip across her mouth. She started to slump to the side, but one of the men caught her. He dragged her into a cell and he left her on the floor before leaving and slamming the cell door shut with a loud clang.

She curled onto her side and closed her eyes, a soft moan of pain escaping her lips.

Diego nodded with approval. "Tomorrow I will deal with the woman. Tonight is for celebrating." He slapped Alejandro on the upper arm. "Clean up and enjoy breakfast." They walked side by side to the stone staircase. "Angelina will be pleased her favorite uncle is here for her big party tonight."

"I am her only uncle." Amusement laced Alejandro's voice.

"That is why you are her favorite." Diego chuckled. "It is good you are here. She will only turn fifteen once."

Diego didn't look back at the cell. The woman did not concern him tonight and he would forget about her until tomorrow, once he'd rested from a night of festivities.

Yes, all was as it should be now and he no longer had anything to be concerned about. Life was good. Very good.

Chapter Twenty Six

"*Fuck.*" Head bent, arms rigid, Landon braced his hands on the desk in his home office. Every muscle in his body tensed and he ground his teeth so hard his head ached. His injured shoulder throbbed and his knuckles were white from clenching his hands into fists. His gut churned. "How the fuck did the bastard get Tori across the border?"

"We'll get her back." Dylan's voice held conviction. "No way in hell is Jimenez going to get away with this."

"The sonofabitch is going to pay." Landon raised his head, his gaze meeting Dylan's. "I'll make sure of it."

"When did Jimenez go from wanting Tori dead to kidnapping her?" Dylan frowned as he spoke.

Landon turned Dylan's question over in his mind. "It's become personal."

"I think you're right." Dylan nodded. "Maybe her surviving everything he's thrown at her has gotten under his skin."

"Something like that." Landon shook his head. Likely Diego Jimenez wasn't used to being thwarted. "We need to get to her before he does anything to hurt her." *More than he already has,* Landon thought and his body grew impossibly more tense.

According to Carl, Landon's most reliable informant, the cartel had bugged the DHS's ICE office and the whole attack had been a two-for-one. Kill the two men in the holding cells who had been present when Alejandro Jimenez had murdered Miguel and also grab Tori.

"Shit." Landon scratched the scruff of a beard on his face. "How the hell did they get those bugs into the office?"

"Could have been the nighttime janitorial team." Dylan frowned. "The cartel could have bought off any one of them. Or the cartel could have blackmailed a member of the administrative staff, threatening his or her family."

"My thoughts too." Landon dragged his hand down his face. "Jesus."

Dylan pulled his cell phone out and read a text message. "Joe's team is making preparations now and the chopper will be ready to take off around five. It's two now."

Joe Black's spec ops team, Black Sky International, specialized in locating and retrieving missing persons. BSI contracted with the government as well as taking on select cases for hire from civilians.

"Good." Landon tried to relax his body and calm his thoughts, but he failed. "The sooner we leave, the better."

"Joe doesn't usually let anyone not on his team join the party—" Dylan started to say.

"That's not happening this time," Landon's words sliced the air as he cut in, his expression dark.

Dylan smiled, but it held no humor. "Exactly what I told him. He's agreed to take you. And me."

"Hell, no." Landon narrowed his eyes. "You're not coming."

"Yeah, I am." Dylan gave Landon a hard look. "Don't argue because it's not going to get you anywhere, friend. Especially injured like you are."

With a shake of his head, Landon let out his breath. He'd known before he'd even opened his mouth he couldn't change Dylan's mind, so Landon didn't know why he bothered to try. "What's the plan?"

Dylan folded his arms across his chest. "We'll cross the border and get to the Jimenez compound just after dark. Apparently Jimenez's granddaughter's fifteenth birthday is today."

Landon's mind turned over the information. "I take it the girl's fifteenth birthday party is tonight?"

Dylan nodded. "Yep."

Landon sat in his desk chair, leaned his head back, and looked at the ceiling. "It's perfect."

* * * *

Tori groaned, her mind spinning with pain and confusion. She felt dizzy and unable to form a coherent thought.

Her whole body ached and stung and it hurt to breathe. She tried to raise her head, but pain lanced her skull and she clasped her head with her hands.

Tori lay on something hard and cold, the chill seeping through her body. She shivered and her eyes watered as yet another stabbing pain went through her chest.

She opened her eyelids and blinked until her eyes adjusted to the dimness. She lay on a concrete floor and bars filled her vision. Another shiver went through her on realizing someone had put her in a cell.

Tears threatened at the backs of her eyes. She wanted to cry from fear, from anger, from pain…and an overwhelming sense of hopelessness. But tears wouldn't do her any good at this moment. Tears would only make her head hurt more and cause her eyes to ache and grow puffy.

It surprised her at how rational her thoughts were. Or maybe she was too numb to be emotional.

She tried to think. Where was she? She remembered being taken at gunpoint, thrown into a van, and bound. Once men had secured her, they'd hit and kicked her. The men had spoken in Spanish and talked about transporting her to Mexico.

To Diego Jimenez, the head of the Jimenez Cartel.

Her throat ached and she thought she would cry despite her resolution not to. Was she in Mexico now? She must be. She vaguely remembered someone sliding a needle into her vein then nothing in the world had seemed to matter anymore. They'd drugged her.

Faint memories came back to her of men standing over her and talking, but she couldn't remember what they'd said. Had she even heard them?

The concrete floor seemed to grow harder and colder as she lay there. She needed to get up and figure out what to do next, if she could do anything at all.

One thing she did know—she refused to give up. She intended to do whatever it took to escape.

She clenched her teeth as she tried to push herself to a sitting position. Immediately, she cried out and her eyes watered from the sharp pain shooting through her chest. Her arms went weak, but she managed not to collapse back onto the floor.

Tears trickled down her cheeks after all, only these tears were from pain and not hopelessness. She pushed through the pain to struggle to sit up.

Tori finally made it to a sitting position, although her head spun for a moment. She held her head in her palms, trying to slow the spinning. She remembered how she'd torn her shirt to use the cloth to help Agent Aguilar. Tori remembered all the blood and prayed someone had found Aguilar in time.

The spinning subsided and Tori slowly raised her head to look around the cell. A toilet took up one corner. That was it. Nothing else was in the space. No cot or sink one would expect to see in a prison cell.

Not a cell. A cage.

Gradually, sensations returned to her mostly numb body. Tori felt filthy and sticky with sweat and she realized she had to go to the bathroom before her bladder burst.

She looked at the toilet. It seemed so far away from where she sat, huddled on the floor. Struggling to her feet, she then staggered to the far corner. Her legs almost gave out, but she made it to the old commode with its wide streak of rust around the inside of the bowl.

Tori finished and stood, then stumbled toward the cage door. She grabbed onto the bars and leaned against them, trying to regain strength and keep from falling. Tori closed her eyes and rested her head on the metal and clenched the bars until her fingers ached.

She blew out her breath and opened her eyes, which had become well-accustomed to the dimness. She looked through the bars at the large room. A bank of small monitors glowed in the dim interior to her left, but she couldn't read the screens from her position. Her cage took up space along one of the walls and other cages stood to her right and across the room. As far as she could tell, the others were empty.

If the others had only a toilet like this one did, these cages were not meant for long term. She'd bet the cages served as a holding cell, not for restraining individuals for any length of time.

A sense of despair overcame her and her legs weakened. She barely kept herself standing by the grip she had on the bars.

The bastards. The horrible, horrible bastards.

Anger replaced the despair in a hard, fiery rush. Her cold cheeks flushed with heat and if a person could truly see red, she did.

What the cartel did to people…the lives destroyed…all of the deaths…the pain. Every bit of anger she had washed through her in a hot wave.

With a burst of fury, she jerked against the door to rattle her cage.

The door opened.

She stumbled forward, almost falling as the door swung open a couple of feet. For a moment she stood there, stunned.

Just like that? The door opened?

She released the bars and walked out into the room surrounded by the cages on three walls. A door was to her right and another across the room. The monitors on the left flickered and she turned and headed toward them.

When she reached the station, she braced her hands on the back of one of three swivel chairs in front of the bank of nine monitors. A desk with enough room for three large men took up space below the monitors.

The monitors flashed, slowly changing from views inside hallways and rooms, including a dining room, an enormous kitchen, and living areas. More cameras displayed pathways, courtyards, gardens, and more than one swimming pool. The late-afternoon sun cast long shadows.

She narrowed her gaze when she saw grass-covered grounds with tents, balloons, tables, and bouquet after bouquet of flowers. Surprisingly, she saw a lot of pink. Lots and lots of pink. It looked as though her captor or captors had planned a party. A huge party. Going by all the pink, Tori guessed the party was for a girl or young woman.

A man's voice spoke at the edge of her consciousness and she remembered hearing him say, *'…her big party tonight.'* She also remembered hearing a girl's name. *Angelina.*

Tori swallowed. What if she managed to get out of here and crash Angelina's party? Would someone help her or would they be too afraid of the Jimenez family?

Hands trembling, Tori wiped her dirty palms on her jeans then rubbed her temples with her fingers. She'd stayed long enough. If she could get out, she needed to do it before someone came to check on her.

She looked from one door to the other. Would one of them lead her in a direction that would allow her to escape?

If she did escape, what next? She wondered if they had taken her to a town or to a place in the desert. Likely a drug lord's home would be in the desert, away from the Mexican police and military. From what she'd seen on the monitors, it looked as if this place could be referred to as an oasis. An oasis built with blood money.

Tori took a deep breath then grimaced at the pain in her side. She gritted her teeth and picked the door to the right of the monitors. When she reached the door, she grasped the handle and tried to wrench it open.

Locked.

Her heart stuttered. She looked over her shoulder at the other door. If it was also locked, she didn't know what she'd do. She didn't know how to pick a lock and she didn't know what she could use to try to escape.

She walked to the other door and paused. She winced as she took another deep breath then gripped the handle and pulled.

Locked.

She squeezed her eyes shut and felt hot tears behind her lids. *No crying, damn it.*

Maybe a set of keys rested near the monitors or in the desk drawers. She bit the inside of her cheek as she walked and tried not to think of the pain in her head and chest. She searched the drawers and found nothing. Not even paper or pens.

She stared at the keyboards in front of the monitors and wondered if one of them could serve as a computer monitor. It would be incredible if she could send an email, not that it would do a lot of good. She didn't even know who to send one to. Not to mention they held her in Mexico now — how could anyone help her?

At least she thought they'd taken her to Mexico. She didn't know for sure.

Still, she tried. No matter what she did, all she could get to were the cameras. She saw men and women going through rooms and walking around outside. Hired help, apparently. Then she saw people arriving at the front entrance, a young woman in what looked like a prom dress, and a young man in a suit. An older woman with a stern expression followed the couple and Tori wondered if the woman chaperoned them.

After searching the cages and around the desk and monitors for some kind of weapon and coming up with nothing, she looked desperately around her one last time. The only movable things were the office chairs. Her mind ran through her options, which amounted to one. She kneeled beside one of the chairs. Maybe if she could disassemble one, she could use part of it as a weapon.

With determination, she clenched her teeth and tried to

find some way to disassemble the chair. It took her a while, but finally she managed to remove the five-armed swivel base. When she held it in her hands, she wondered if she'd have the strength to swing it with enough power to hit a grown man hard enough to knock him out and make an escape.

God, she was tired of being afraid. She wiped away sweat from her forehead with the back of her hand and got to her feet. She looked down at the swivel base she gripped. She'd removed the rollers and the metal they'd been inserted into had hard, sharp edges.

She studied the five rollers on the floor and an idea came to her. She hurried to remove the rollers from the other two chairs then divided them up, putting seven in front of one door and eight in front of the other.

Just as she finished, the door on her left rattled.

Ignoring the pain in her chest, she hurried to the door and hid behind it, holding the swivel base in both hands. She found herself holding her breath then forced herself to breathe.

The mechanism clicked and the door swung open. A man stepped into the room and paused, probably baffled by the wheels on the floor and the chairs lying on their sides.

Heart pounding, Tori stepped behind the man as he walked in. He had his hand on the butt of a gun sticking out of its holster and he started to draw the weapon.

With everything she had, she swung the swivel base at the man's head.

He swung around in time to put his arm up to protect his face. The base hit his arm hard enough he dropped the handgun and it landed on her foot.

The man gave an angry shout as he stumbled to the side.

He tripped over the wheels she'd left on the floor and he fell, landing hard.

Her heart pounded faster.

Doing the best she could to ignore the pain in her chest, she fell to her knees and grabbed the gun he'd dropped on her foot.

The man scrambled to his knees and faced her. His eyes were like blue flames as he looked at her with fury.

He lunged for her. "Bitch!" he shouted in Spanish.

She raised the gun with both hands and squeezed the trigger.

He slammed her to the floor just as the gun jerked in her hands, the sound reverberating off the walls and echoing in her ears.

She screamed. It felt as if pain ripped her apart when she hit the floor, his big body on top of hers.

Tears flooded her eyes from the agony.

He raised his head and his fist at the same time. He swung his fist and it connected with the side of her head.

Stars sparked in her head and her mind spun.

He rose up, getting to his knees, and she saw his shirt drenched in blood. He opened his mouth and blood rolled over his lips.

For a moment he appeared to be confused. Then he looked at his belly and the blood soaking his shirt, the stain spreading.

He seemed as dazed as she felt. He started to collapse on her but she held up her arms. His muscular body and greater weight drove her onto the floor again.

Black swirled on the edges of her vision. An involuntary scream rose up inside her, but she could make no sound as blackness started to close in on her.

The man faced her as his head landed next to hers. She almost managed a scream this time when she saw his eyes were wide and sightless. Dead.

She had killed him.

She took rapid breaths, trying to fend off the darkness. Air, she needed air. The man's dead weight would suffocate her.

Tears of pain rolled down her cheeks as her vision started to clear. She felt weak and exhausted, but the thought of being found by the cartel's men gave her renewed strength.

That and the adrenaline pumping in her veins.

She used her knee against the man's belly and her hands on his shoulders. She counted to three and shoved with all the power she could muster.

The body rolled off hers. The dead man landed on his back, his body blocking open the door. A loud clanking sound echoed in the room when the gun hit the floor.

Bile rose in her throat and she thought she would vomit. She'd just killed a man.

He would have murdered her and she'd done the only thing she could. Yet, she barely comprehended she'd taken a life.

She couldn't think about it now. She had to get out of here and find someplace to run or hide or…she didn't know, but she'd figure it out.

Her stomach ached and she put her hand to her belly and felt slick flesh. She looked down. She'd torn her shirt to help the agent and now the dead man's blood covered her bare belly. His blood mingled with Agent Aguilar's.

She swallowed and picked up the gun she'd dropped when she'd pushed him off. She staggered to her feet and headed out of the door.

Chapter Twenty Seven

Angelina walked through the family wing, her belly quivering with excitement. Today she was the *Quinceañera.* It wouldn't be long now until Grandfather would present her as a woman to friends, family, and acquaintances. It had seemed as if the day would never come.

Carlos would be here tonight. Her skin tingled and she felt giddy, eager to see the handsome young man. He had turned sixteen two months ago, over a year older than she. Now that she had reached *quince años,* and womanhood, she hoped he would notice her and her grandfather would not object.

She had seen Carlos watching her many times, but he had never been more than polite and respectful. As intimidating as her grandfather could be, she had no wonder Carlos had barely spoken to her. But his dark, beautiful eyes framed by long, dark lashes made him so very handsome. He captivated her and watched her whenever he came near her.

The material felt slightly stiff against her fingers as she smoothed down the top layer of the ruffles on her dress. Ruffles. She hoped she didn't look like a child. She had wanted to wear something more sophisticated as the *Quinceañera* for the celebration, but she truly had known better when it came to her grandfather.

She paused to consider herself in a hall mirror, pushed her shoulders back, and stood straight and proud. She was a Jimenez and she would present herself like one. Not only would friends and family be here, but her grandfather had invited business partners too. Everyone loved an excuse to enjoy a party at a home designed for them.

Maria had curled Angelina's long hair into ringlets before sweeping it up off her neck and pinning it to the top of her head. She allowed ringlets to drop down from the upsweep in a very adult style. Like Angelina had promised her grandfather, Maria had applied light makeup. She liked the way the mascara and eyeliner enhanced her eyes and the light lipstick made her appear more mature.

She turned away from the mirror and wandered around parts of the house she didn't normally go to.

Guests would be arriving now and she needed to stay out of sight until it was time for her to be presented. She decided to go to the wing her grandfather had designated as off-limits for children. Now that she had reached womanhood, she felt comfortable and even excited to explore the wing.

The pink dress brushed her ankles as she walked down the hallway. The dim hall had a quiet, unused feel to it. Perhaps she would find nothing to explore in this place. Still she strolled along. When she reached the end of the wing, she turned to go back. A door to her right opened and her heart nearly stopped. Even though she was not a child anymore, a part of her worried her grandfather would object. She hated to see him angry and she did not want him angry with her.

But she would face whatever consequences she might have to. Besides, it was the day of her party. Surely she would be allowed some leniency.

With her chin raised, she looked at the slowly opening door, ready to face whoever might be coming out.

A woman peered out and her eyes widened when she saw Angelina.

Angelina's heart stuttered. The woman had bruises on her face and arms and blood covered her clothing. It stained her shirt, her bare belly, her jeans, and even her shoes. Her dark hair even appeared to be matted with blood.

The woman froze in the doorway. Angelina froze too, feeling as if she might not be able to walk if she tried.

"Help me," the woman spoke in a rasp. She seemed dizzy and as if she might pass out.

Angelina found the strength to move and neared the woman, yet kept a few feet between them. "Who are you?"

"My name is Tori," the woman responded in Spanish. She sounded fluent, yet she had a slight American accent. "I need help." The woman who called herself Tori sagged as she leaned against the doorframe. "Please."

"I don't understand." Angelina started to say more when she saw a weapon in Tori's hand. Her heart pounded and she wondered if she should run. "You—you have a gun."

Tori looked at her hand as if seeing the gun for the first time. "Protection." She licked her lips as she raised her head to Angelina. "I need it for protection."

"From what?" Angelina asked.

"Men who are trying to kill me." Tori straightened, looking as though she'd just remembered she should be on guard. "The Jimenez Cartel."

Angelina's lips parted and she blinked rapidly. "There's no cartel here. And certainly not a Jimenez Cartel."

"Diego Jimenez is the leader of one of the most ruthless cartels in Mexico." Tori continued speaking as Angelina's belly bottomed out. "I witnessed Alejandro murder a man and they've been trying to kill me ever since." The woman gave a laugh with no humor. "This time they decided to kidnap me. I don't know exactly what they plan to do with me."

Angelina shook her head vehemently. "My grandfather and uncle would never do such things. They are businessmen, not killers."

Tori seemed as though realization had just dawned on her. "You must be Angelina."

Surprise made Angelina nearly speechless. She managed to say, "How do you know?"

"I overheard Diego and Alejandro talking about your party tonight." Tori seemed to be less dazed as she squinted up and down the hall. "They kidnapped me from Arizona."

Angelina just stared at Tori. "You are from the United States?"

"Alejandro and his men brought me here and they beat me." Tori switched to English and spoke in a perfect American accent. "Do you speak English?"

Angelina nodded but confusion made her head spin. She replied in almost perfect English, "I do not understand why you are here and why you look as you do."

A thought entered Angelina's mind. She hadn't understood what her grandfather had said when she'd stood outside his study the day she'd tried on her party dresses, but his voice had sounded harsh in a way she'd never heard before. It had been as if he were a different person.

She shook her head to shake the thoughts out.

"Hide me, please." Tori spoke in an urgent whisper. "I hear voices coming this way."

The desperate plea in the woman's voice convinced Angelina to want to help. She pointed to a tree in a massive pot across the hall from where Tori stood. "You can hide behind there for now. Grandfather will probably send me away from here. I will think of someplace else and come back."

Tori slipped through the door and closed it behind her before hurrying across the hall. She slid down the wall behind the potted tree and huddled in the corner.

Angelina couldn't stop thoughts from whirling through her mind. The woman must be crazy. No Jimenez Cartel existed, unless another Jimenez family ran one. Her grandfather was a legitimate businessman, as was her Uncle Alejandro and her four great-uncles.

Why was the woman here? Why did she really look bloody and beaten?

Should she tell her grandfather? Even though she'd heard his voice being rough and cold, that meant nothing. He couldn't possibly be responsible for whatever had happened to Tori. Could he?

The voices came closer. For one terrible moment, Angelina did not know what to do.

She was a Jimenez. She knew how to act like a lady and remain calm. Maria and her grandfather had drilled it into her since childhood.

Once again she raised her chin and started in the direction of the voices and recognized they belonged to her uncle and grandfather. She forced a bright smile.

"I sent a man to check on her," her uncle's voice hardened. "He has not returned."

Her? Angelina thought. *Are they talking about Tori?*

"See to her." Her grandfather sounded annoyed. "Nothing is to ruin tonight."

"Hi, Grandfather, Uncle." Angelina's smile didn't falter as she walked around the curve in the hallway. "Are you ready for my party?"

Both men looked surprised but recovered. "What are you doing in this wing?" Diego frowned. "I have told you many times it is off-limits."

"You told me children are not allowed in this wing." Angelina stopped walking and stood in front of the two men. "I am no longer a child."

Grandfather had a hard light in his eyes that surprised her. He had never looked like that at her. He rested his hand on her upper arm. "Come, my angel." He gently tugged on her arm and his voice sounded as if he forced warmth into it. "It is almost time for your party." He glared at Alejandro. "Join the guests after you have checked up on the matter we discussed."

Alejandro gave a nod. "Yes, Father." He turned and headed down the curved hallway.

Her grandfather guided her out of the wing. "Yes, you are a young woman. But I must make it very clear to you no one is allowed in this wing but a few select employees and myself. Do you understand?"

Angelina lowered her eyes. "Yes, Grandfather."

He put a finger under her chin. "Smile. I do believe it is

time for you to make your entrance and I will present you to our guests."

Angelina glanced over her shoulder, wondering how she could help the woman hide like she'd promised. She did her best to smile even though her confused thoughts were on the bruised and bloody woman. "I am ready."

Chapter Twenty Eight

Tori bit down on her fist, trying to keep from making a sound as she huddled behind the planter. She listened to the voices in the hall and heard the girl speaking but couldn't make out what she said.

Would Angelina tell her grandfather and uncle where Tori was hiding? God, she hoped not.

Alejandro walked to the door of the room Tori had just left. She held her breath, her heart thundering. He closed the door behind him. A few moments later she heard Diego's and Angelina's voices fade as they walked away.

Any moment now, Alejandro would bolt out of the room and come after her. Would he think to look behind the planter?

Should she wait for Angelina, who had promised to think of something?

Tori shook her head and put her hand to her temple as a dizzy spell overcame her. No. She couldn't wait. She needed to find someplace safer.

The door across the hall banged open and through the tree leaves she saw Alejandro with a cell phone to his ear. "Find the bitch. She must be someplace around here. She couldn't have gone far and couldn't have escaped the compound." A pause. "She killed one of our men." Another pause. "Send men to the north wing. We will search for her here, first. This must be done discreetly so guests are not disturbed or aware of any problems." Alejandro shoved the phone into his pocket.

Tori shrank into the smallest ball she could, burying her face against her knees. *Please don't look here, please don't look here,* rang over and over in her head.

Alejandro's footsteps clicked against tile as he strode away, and she breathed a sigh of relief. It might be temporary, but it gave her more of an opportunity to escape.

Her battered body ached when she got to her feet. He planned to send men to this wing to search first. If she could leave it, find another place…

"Tori," Angelina's voice startled Tori. She hadn't seen the girl approach. "Come with me, now."

Tori got to her feet and stepped out from behind the plant and Angelina motioned for her to follow. The girl looked like a fairy princess in her pink gown and upswept hair with ringlets spilling down the back.

"My grandfather went to attend to something before he presents me." Angelina glanced over her shoulder. "We must hurry."

Tori didn't question the girl and followed her down the hall. The girl slipped through a back way, avoiding the main areas.

As she walked, Tori felt for the gun she'd taken from the man she'd killed. Her skin prickled with a cold chill once she realized she must have left it on the planter while she'd huddled behind the plant. *Damn.*

"This is the way the servants get around the house." Angelina held up her skirts, revealing sparkling pink flat shoes and looking like Cinderella as they hurried. "The servants are all busy with the party, so no one should see us."

Even though she felt weak, Tori managed to follow the girl. She began to lag behind and Angelina motioned to her to move faster. "Almost there."

"Where are we going?" Tori asked.

"My rooms." Angelina pushed open a door, peeked around it then motioned for Tori to follow. A few steps later and Angelina opened a door and held it open for Tori to enter.

Tori found herself in a beautiful suite of rooms as Angelina closed the door behind them. The girl gestured to the right. "They won't think to look for you in my bedroom."

The door to the bedroom opened.

Angelina gave a squeak of surprise and Tori's heart thumped when a woman stepped in front of them. The woman wore clothing a housekeeper might be expected to wear. She must have been in her late fifties.

The woman held her hand to her heart, obviously shocked by their appearance. *"Dios mio!"*

"Shhh, Maria." Angelina held her finger to her lips. "I need you to help me hide Tori. She is in danger." The girl shook her head. "Grandfather and Uncle Alejandro — she said they have hurt her." Angelina didn't look as though she truly believed it, but she helped Tori nevertheless.

Maria looked over Tori, clearly taking in her condition. "I know what to do." By the woman's expression, she had no problem believing Tori's story. Maria turned to Angelina. "Get to the party. I will take care of her."

Angelina flung her arms around Maria. "Thank you." She hurried to turn and slipped through the door and closed it behind her.

"If her grandfather finds out we have helped you." Maria made the sign of the cross. "It will not be good."

"I'm sorry." Tori gripped her hands together. "But please help me."

Maria gave a nod. "This way." She turned and headed into the room she'd just come from.

Tori followed and Maria shut the door then locked it behind them. She looked Tori up and down again. "Angelina is smaller than you, but you may be able to fit into one of the dresses we have not returned to the dressmaker. The yellow one hasn't been taken in."

"A dress?" Tori frowned at her in confusion.

"But first a bath." Maria gestured for her to follow again.

Tori felt compelled to do what the woman told her to do. "A dress and a bath?"

"Take off those clothes." Maria gestured to the bloody

mess of clothing Tori wore. She turned on the water in the tub. "You are going to a party."

* * * *

Night had settled across the Mexican desert, the earth refusing to let up its stored heat from the brutally hot day. Joe Black and two members of his team, along with Landon and Dylan, eased through the darkness as they closed in on the Jimenez compound. The stealthily silent night-black chopper carrying them into Mexico had landed far enough away it wouldn't have been seen and couldn't possibly have been heard.

The compound might as well have been lit up for Christmas, so night-vision goggles would be of no use. Joe had two snipers in place, one stationed at the front entrance and another at the back. The gates were well guarded and security cameras were in place.

Landon gripped his assault rifle as he moved and he felt the weight of his Colt .45 in his thigh holster. His black gear magnified the heat and sweat trickled down his spine. His fury over the cartel having kidnapped Tori had his temperature rising even higher. He needed to tamp it down and keep a cool head. If it got any hotter, he felt as if the camo paint on his face would melt. It wouldn't, but it sure as hell felt like it might.

Their belts were equipped with all manner of devices, from grenades to flash bangs, smoke bombs, and tear gas. They carried extra ammo on their belts and in various pockets and they wore bulletproof vests. The vests wouldn't stop a rifle round if the men patrolling the compound's perimeter managed to shoot one of them, but the vests could come in handy once they entered the compound.

Earlier, Joe had sent a high-tech surveillance drone overhead, mapping out the compound and where the party was being held. Tori could be anywhere inside the huge place.

If it weren't for the civilians at tonight's event, Landon would have wanted to go in hot. But they couldn't take the chance of injuring any innocents. They'd watched as vehicle after vehicle had approached the compound. After lists and IDs had been checked, the vehicles had been waved through into the huge area surrounding the Jimenez mansion.

Landon had seen the satellite images of the grounds and the monstrosity of a home that had two two-story wings. It had been some time since the last guest had arrived. Almost time to go in.

His gut clenched as he thought of Tori being locked away inside and he narrowed his gaze, anger heating him even more. He prayed that if God existed He would protect her and help Landon and his men get her out of there safely.

With the snipers in place, the other five men spread out, each with his part to play. Landon checked his watch. Almost time.

Landon adjusted his earpiece so he could hear better when Joe spoke over the comm. "Everyone in place?"

Affirmative responses came in from the snipers and the four other men, including Landon and Dylan.

Landon let out his breath. "I'm coming for you, honey," he murmured. "I'm coming for you."

* * * *

The bath water had turned red from blood and Maria had drained it to let Tori quickly rinse herself off with the fresh water pouring into the tub from the spout. Pain had lanced Tori's head as Maria had washed her matted hair, red with blood from a cut on her scalp. Bruises had appeared in black and blue splotches all over her body, including the area where she'd broken he rib. She ached and it hurt to breathe.

Maria had Tori rush so quickly the bath lasted just over five minutes. Exhaustion and pain caused her to care less about being naked in front of a stranger and she didn't argue as Maria toweled her off. The older woman used gentle hands, taking care not to rub too hard in bruised places.

The woman hurried out of the bathroom then returned with undergarments and a yellow chiffon dress with bared shoulders and puffy sleeves. The lovely dress was the opposite of the conservative gown Angelina had worn. Tori slipped on the panties and bra and Maria hung the dress by its hanger on a hook behind the door. Then Maria sat Tori down in front of the bathroom mirror.

"I will arrange for one of the guests to take you with them when the party is over." Maria worked quickly and efficiently as she dragged out a box filled with makeup. "This belonged to Angelina's mother. I am glad I kept it all."

Maria brought out fat pots of foundation and trays of blush and eyeshadow and dug out eyeliner and mascara. Tori's Hispanic heritage reflected in her golden skin tone, and the foundation worked well. She watched Maria put it on her. The heavy base covered the bruises.

While Maria worked, Tori wondered at how quickly the woman had come up with the scheme to rescue Tori and wondered if it would work. Prayed it would work. Would someone be willing to risk taking her away from the compound?

Maria avoided the laceration on Tori's scalp as well as the bruises on her face. The woman even applied makeup to the bruises on Tori's arms. When Maria finished applying everything and had transformed Tori's hair into a chic and elegant style, Tori looked in amazement at her reflection in the mirror. "I look like a different person."

"We are running out of time." Maria took the yellow dress off the hanger and helped Tori slip it over her head.

The dress fit, although snug around her breasts, revealing quite a bit of cleavage thanks to her woman's figure.

Maria gave her a once-over. "Your feet are larger than Angelina's." She frowned. "One of her pairs of ballet slippers would be the best."

The woman took Tori by the elbow and led her out of the room, and Maria went to a closet. She brought out a pair of white slippers a size too small. With Maria's help, Tori managed to cram her feet into them. Thank goodness the soft material stretched.

By the time Maria had prepared Tori, not much more than fifteen minutes had passed. *The woman is a miracle worker*, Tori thought, checking her reflection again, this time with the dress on. No one would recognize the bedraggled and bloody woman who had staggered into the suite with Angelina—at least she hoped not.

Maria crammed Tori's dirty and bloody clothing and shoes into a duffel bag and put it on a shelf in Angelina's closet. "I will burn them later." Maria beckoned for Tori to follow her to the bedroom door.

Tori's belly flip-flopped as they left the room. "Stand up straight and raise your head." Maria put her fingers under Tori's chin. "Act as if you belong here."

Maria glanced out of the door to the suite and nodded for Tori to follow. "Walk ahead of me." Maria ushered her ahead. "You would not walk beside hired help."

With Maria following, Tori listened to her directions, taking turns as needed. She would have become lost in the massive place without Maria's help.

When they rounded a corner, Tori almost came to a complete stop. Three men carrying weapons hurried toward them. She didn't recognize any of them, but she felt blood drain from her face. She kept walking, chin in the air.

One of the men asked Maria if she'd seen a strange woman, but Maria shook her head. "Do you mean some of the guests at the party? Many I do not know."

The man who had spoken sneered. "If you see someone who does not belong, report to Alejandro at once. You will know what I mean if you see her."

Maria bobbed her head. "*Sí.*"

The men barely spared Tori a glance, although one did

look at her cleavage before moving on.

Tori let out her breath and winced from the pain in her ribs. She felt an even greater need to get into the crowd where she could hopefully hide from Alejandro and Diego Jimenez. They couldn't possibly expect to see her among the guests, wearing an evening dress, her face made up and her hair styled.

But would they recognize her?

Maria took Tori the way guests had come through the house on the bottom floor, as Maria told her, and to an archway leading out onto the grassy grounds and to the tents. Bright lights pushed away the darkness of the night.

"I can go no farther." Maria nodded in the direction of the tents. "Remember what I told you. Act as if you belong here. Angelina or I will find you later."

"Thank you." Tori gripped the woman's hand in both of hers. "I'd hug you if it wouldn't hurt so much."

Maria smiled for the first time, showing her teeth, and motioned toward the archway. "Go now."

Tori did as instructed, keeping her posture ramrod straight, her chin up, and her steps purposeful. Her heart pounded and the fear of being discovered made her scalp prickle. She felt tense and jittery, as if all eyes were on her even though she knew they weren't. Although, she did notice a couple of young men ogling her cleavage.

When she stepped beneath the tent, an usher asked her if she had a seat and she shook her head.

He extended his hand, gesturing forward. "This way, *señorita*."

"*Gracias*." She gave a slight nod of her chin and followed the man to one of the round tables with one seat available. He seated her, put her napkin in her lap then excused himself.

All went quiet and Tori looked in the direction everyone stared.

Diego Jimenez stood on a landing at the top of a sweeping staircase above the grounds, next to Angelina. To either side of them stood her Court of Honor, seven young men and seven young women.

A sense of queasiness made Tori's stomach ache and she glanced down at the empty china plate in front of her.

Through the rushing in her ears, Tori could barely hear Diego speak as he presided over the guests. He gave some kind of speech about Angelina and how precious she had been to him as a child.

One of the young women in the court walked to Diego and Angelina, a crown on the pink velvet pillow she held. Diego took the crown off the pillow and gave a nod to the young woman, excusing her. She returned to join the others in the court.

Diego placed the sparkling crown on Angelina's dark curls and she looked even more like a princess. A short religious ceremony came next, followed by the ceremonial changing of the shoes, from flat shoes to high heels.

When all had concluded, Diego turned to face the crowd, beaming. "And now I present to you Angelina, my pride and joy, who on this day is now a young woman."

The guests broke out into applause and stood. Tori joined them, trying to edge herself behind a tall man in an attempt to avoid being seen. Diego escorted Angelina down the steps to the tent where everyone would be enjoying dinner.

Her blood ran cold as she saw Diego and Angelina were being seated at the table closest to her.

She swallowed and avoided looking in their direction as she and the other guests took their seats.

Tori couldn't remember the last time she ate. It must have been at least a day ago. She struggled to find her appetite with Diego sitting just feet from her. A server set in front of her a plate of a traditional Mexican meal of enchiladas, tamales, and tacos. She didn't want to be noticed in any way, so she forced herself to eat. She needed her strength, so best to eat something now.

It occurred to her that eating alone without talking with other guests might get her noticed too. She forced a smile and turned to the young man next to her and caught him staring at her breasts.

He gave her a leer meant to be sexy, as if he were a young Don Juan. Tori managed not to roll her eyes. Instead she engaged him in conversation, praying her Spanish held no American accent. With so many people speaking Spanish around her, she found it easier to fall into the language with the same accent. The man's gaze frequently dropped to her cleavage but she pretended not to notice.

A chill crept up her spine and the hair at her nape prickled. As if she had no control over her actions, she looked away from the young Don Juan—

And found Diego watching her.

Chapter Twenty Nine

Landon looked through the scope of his assault rifle at the front gate and the eastern perimeter. He checked his watch. Seconds left.

Joe's voice came over the earpiece. "Go time in five… four…three…two…*one.*"

Through the scope, Landon saw guards at the gate and along the perimeter drop as Joe's snipers took them down. The silenced weapons made sounds no louder than a soft *thwat, thwat.*

Landon's muscles tensed while he waited for Joe's command, when all the guards would be down.

"*Now.*"

Landon and Dylan charged toward the compound wall. From the images gathered by the drone, they knew the area they were breaching would be far enough from the party to keep civilians from getting injured, but should cause a good amount of panic.

As he approached the wall, Landon removed an explosive device from his belt. He exposed the adhesive, clicked the device once to the left, and stuck it to the wall.

He ran, joining Dylan on the ground, both of them plugging their ears.

The explosion rocked the night. Debris shot sky-high when the device blew a hole the size of a tank into the compound wall.

Screams came from within the compound.

A second deafening explosion drowned out the screams and took out more of the wall.

One more explosion breached a third location in the wall.

The bastards wouldn't know which way they were coming from or how many of them there were.

"Go, go, go!" Joe shouted into the earpiece.

Landon and Dylan ran through the dust and smoke to the wall and peered around to make sure no men with weapons waited for them.

When they looked, Landon saw what he'd expected to. Utter chaos.

People ran for cover, screaming. Others had fallen and were being trampled.

The dust and smoke started to clear as Landon and Dylan made it into the house to take cover behind an archway in front of a door. Before Diego's men charged out into the melee, assault weapons in hand, Landon and Dylan had their handguns drawn.

Guests continued to scream, running and trying to find someplace for cover or a way to get to their vehicles. People saw the men with the weapons and ran screaming from them too.

Some guests tried to come to the door behind the archway Dylan and Landon were stationed at, but anyone who reached them turned and ran the moment they saw the guns.

One of the tents went down, collapsing onto guests who struggled to get out.

They planned to locate Alejandro or Diego Jimenez, preferably both.

They would take the men hostage in exchange for Tori. Landon and the rest of the team didn't have enough intel to figure out where the bastards could have hidden her in the massive home.

If she's still alive. The unwelcome thought went through his mind.

No. Tori was alive. She had to be.

* * * *

Terror ripped through Tori as Diego dragged her from beneath the tent and onto the lawn. He had her by her neck and kept the barrel of a pistol against her side where guests wouldn't see. He had taken the gun from an inside pocket of his suit right before he'd grabbed Tori.

People were running. Screaming. Smoke and dust particles floated in the air. Gunfire cut through the night. Her ears rang from the explosion.

Could it be possible someone had arrived to rescue her? Could Landon be here?

Or had she found herself in the middle of some kind of drug war?

When Diego had looked at her in the tent, he had just stared. But she'd known he had recognized her. He clearly hadn't wanted to create a scene during the party. But the moment things had started exploding, he'd lunged for her. She'd tried to run, but her dress had tangled up around her ankles and she'd stumbled.

Then he'd had her, gripping her tight. She'd struggled, but his strength had proved too much for her.

Everything had gone insane. Explosions—first one and a second then a third. People panicking, fleeing or getting trampled. Diego and Tori had been jostled and she'd almost blacked out from pain a couple of times. She might have fallen if Diego hadn't been gripping her arm so tightly.

And now one of the most ruthless cartel leaders in all of the world held her hostage. Diego Jimenez. *El Demonio*.

"Angelina." Diego sounded almost panicked as he held on to Tori while he turned his head, searching for the girl.

"I have her." Alejandro's voice came from behind them.

Diego appeared relieved when he saw his son and granddaughter. "I will take care of our problem." He clenched Tori's upper arm tight enough to bruise it.

"Grandfather, please." Angelina was horrified. "Do not hurt Tori."

"You know her name?" Diego's expression went from relieved to angry. "Did you help her escape, *mija*?"

"Let her go, Grandfather." Tears in her eyes, the girl looked from Diego to Tori and back. "Please."

Diego's grip on Tori intensified. "Get Angelina to the house and lock her in her room. I will deal with her later."

"Grandfather?" Angelina could barely be heard over the commotion around them, but she seemed she might be sick.

"Go." Diego wrapped his arm around Tori's neck and dug the barrel of his gun into her side.

For one wild moment, Tori thought he would shoot her and be done with it.

When Alejandro didn't move, Diego shouted, "Go! Do as I tell you."

Tears rolled down Angelina's face and she sobbed. "Grandfather, no."

Alejandro grabbed Angelina by her arm and jerked her toward the house.

"Your American agents have done this." Diego growled the words. "They will die tonight, as will you."

* * * *

Landon ground his teeth and put a bullet into a man carrying a machine gun, taking him down. Landon and Dylan picked off as many of Diego's men as they could amid all the commotion.

Searching the crowd with his gaze, Landon's sights found a familiar face.

Diego Montego Jimenez. *El Demonio.*

"Diego. By the tent." Despite the pain in his shoulder, Landon kept his weapon trained on Diego. Landon narrowed his gaze as he saw the man controlling a woman in a yellow dress. "He's holding a woman hostage." Diego had his arm around her neck, his gun to her head.

When Landon saw the woman's face, his body went tense. *Tori.*

Relief at seeing Tori alive hit him for one moment before fear for her life followed.

"He has Tori." Landon's voice came out hard with fury.

"Motherfucker," Dylan snarled the words on catching sight of Diego too. "Got any ideas?"

Diego met Landon's gaze and pressed his gun barrel so hard against Tori's head her neck bowed to the side. He could read the pain in her expression, but something other than the fear he'd expected to see.

Landon saw anger in her eyes. Hot, hard anger.

Good. He could work with anger, as long as she didn't do anything that might put her in danger.

Gunfire continued to erupt across the compound. With absolutely no fear in his expression, Diego pulled Tori with him toward Landon and Dylan.

Landon never took his aim off Diego. Dylan continued to cover them, making sure none of Diego's men got close.

Diego's gaze bore into Landon's as he got within ten feet. The cartel leader spoke in perfect English. "I will put a bullet into her brain unless you lay your weapons down. Now."

Landon didn't even twitch. "If you don't let her go, I will kill you, Jimenez."

The man's cold words, as harsh as an ice storm, came out in a snarl. "Do not try my patience."

Landon remained steady. "Don't try mine."

The hard bite of the gun barrel pressed into the side of Tori's head. She winced involuntarily as it cut into her flesh when he dug it farther in. It stung and caused pain to shoot through her head but didn't compare to the pain she felt in her chest and the rest of her aching body.

She did her best not to let Diego see her injuries or show pain in her expression. She ground her teeth and tried to think of a way out of this. She was tired of being afraid and unable to defend herself—with the exception of the man she'd killed. She had to do *something* and not wait for Landon to be her knight in shining armor.

Neither Diego nor Landon appeared to blink as Diego

271

dug the gun into her head while Landon kept his weapon trained on Diego.

Alejandro came into view and Tori caught her breath. Alejandro had Angelina at gunpoint.

"What are you doing?" Diego sounded confused and furious when he saw his son with his granddaughter. "Why do you have a gun pointed at Angelina?"

Alejandro's evil smile made Tori think of devil spawn. "Tonight I will be rid of you and the spoiled little bitch."

"Mijo?" Diego's grip on the gun pressed to Tori's head faltered.

She grasped both her hands together and swung them up. The gun flew out of Diego's hand and she pushed away and ran toward Landon.

Tori glanced over her shoulder in time to see a bullet hole appear in Diego's forehead. The man slumped to the ground as Alejandro turned the gun on Angelina.

"Grandfather!" Angelina screamed.

Alejandro had just shot his father.

"Behind me," Landon shouted to Tori.

Tori darted around Landon and behind the archway.

The moment after Alejandro shot Diego, Landon immediately turned his weapon on Alejandro. Landon wanted to shoot the bastard so badly he shook with it.

Landon gripped his weapon tighter. "Let the girl go."

Angelina visibly trembled, her face streaked with tears and black trails of mascara. "Alejandro, why? You killed Grandfather."

Alejandro kept his gun to the back of Angelina's head. "It's time for me to take over the family business, infant."

"Let her go." Landon repeated the words slowly. "If you hurt her, you *will* die." Landon intended to avenge Miguel's death, but not at the expense of Tori's life.

"You are the one who will die." Alejandro shouted out in Spanish to men who were approaching. "The Americans have killed our beloved *El Demonio.*"

"Shit." Dylan's jaw looked tight as he and Landon kept their weapons trained on Alejandro while men with machine guns ran toward them.

Just as the men started getting close, they began dropping, one by one.

It took only a fraction of a moment to realize Joe's team of special operatives must be taking down the men.

Angelina sobbed. "Why are you doing this, Uncle?"

"Because I can." He smiled and petted Angelina's hair.

The young woman looked at her grandfather's body. With fury on her face, she raised her foot and brought the high heel of her shoe down hard on Alejandro's foot.

He shouted in surprise and pain.

She turned in his arms and rammed her knee into his groin.

Alejandro cried out, releasing Angelina as his face crumpled with pain. Still, he raised his gun.

Dylan dove for Angelina, driving her to the grass.

At the same time Landon pulled his trigger, something hot and fierce penetrated his body just below his bulletproof vest.

Alejandro slumped and fell forward.

The unimaginable pain in his abdomen drove Landon to his knees.

He toppled back and his head struck the archway. His vision blurred and his eyes started to roll back.

"Landon!" Tori screamed. "Oh, God." Then she kneeled beside him. "He's bleeding, but I can't tell where."

Dylan shouted for Joe's men to call in the chopper and to stand watch while Dylan attended to Landon. Dylan ripped open Landon's bulletproof vest and Tori pressed a piece of the yellow dress against his wound.

Tori is getting good at this, he thought before he slipped into darkness.

Chapter Thirty

Tori sat in the hospital waiting room at Tucson Medical Center, her chest tight as doctors operated on Landon. The doctors had said Landon might not make it and terror had a tight grip on her. She couldn't bear it if he died.

The pain in Tori's chest had nothing to do with her broken rib and everything to do with her feelings for Landon as she prayed for him. She'd fallen in love with him and she'd fallen hard.

While the doctors worked on Landon, the hospital staff had insisted on going over Tori, taking X-rays and examining her. They'd treated the laceration on her scalp, bandaged her ribs, and had taken care of other injuries she had sustained.

The whole time a nurse had patched up Tori, she had only been able to think about Landon and the need to get to him.

After Landon had been shot, the men who had come to rescue Tori had grabbed her and taken her to a helicopter on the expansive lawn. A powerful draft from the rotors had sent the second tent flying.

Dylan and another man had carried Landon while others had covered them with their weapons, taking out as many of Diego's men as they could.

Only one of Joe Black's special ops team members had sustained a bullet wound before they'd escaped by helicopter, the Jimenez Cartel's men still coming after them. Somehow Tori and the spec ops team had managed to get off the ground with no one else on the team being shot.

Tori had feared for Angelina's life so the men had snatched her and taken her with them. The girl had stayed huddled next to Tori who had kept close to Landon in the helicopter. Angelina had never left Tori's side, almost clinging to her.

At the hospital, nurses had treated the young woman for shock and had given her a mild sedative. Angelina had been dazed from all that had happened in front of her — Alejandro shooting her grandfather, the same uncle having taken her hostage, then her uncle being killed.

As soon as they had gotten into the helicopter, one of the men had taken what they'd called a sponge syringe and injected a special sponge into the bullet hole in Landon's gut to expand and stop the bleeding.

Once they had reached the hospital, the new technology had been explained to her. The FDA hadn't approved it yet, but Joe Black's company, Black Sky International, had gotten hold of the device filled with small sponges that sealed up gun wounds like Fix-a-Flat. A radiopaque X on each tiny sponge made sure the doctors could find them once they started working on the patient.

The sponge had kept Landon from bleeding out and losing his life.

And now Tori waited, not knowing if Landon would live or die.

She squeezed her eyes shut. *God, please, let him live.*

The doctor and nurses had finished patching up Tori and had left her with Angelina to clean up and dress. The nurses had provided scrubs for Tori and Angelina to put on so they didn't have to wear the torn yellow and pink dresses covered with dirt and blood. Angelina and Tori had both cleaned up and combed their hair the best they could.

Just as Tori had finished dressing in the scrubs she'd been given and Angelina had come out of the private bathroom wearing hers, a tiny elderly woman had walked into the hospital room. She'd worn all black with the exception of a white lace mantilla and had looked even older than Landon's grandmother.

An eerie sensation had washed over Tori, a feeling not unlike déjà vu.

Angelina had looked nervous and had backed up against the hospital bed and sat on the edge.

"Do I know you?" Tori had asked the elder woman.

"I would like to rest my legs," the woman had said in a strong Hispanic accent.

"Of course." Tori had pulled up one of the chairs in the hospital room for the woman. She'd thought she'd been able to hear the woman's joints creak as she'd sunk down onto the chair.

"Bring it closer." The woman had gestured to another chair in the room. "And sit."

Tori had done as the woman had instructed and sat facing her.

"I am Juanita." The elderly woman had looked at Angelina, who had still been sitting on the bed. "You have grown to be a lovely young woman, Angelina."

A surprised look had crossed Angelina's face. Before Tori had been able to ask Juanita any questions, the woman had reached out and had taken Tori's hands in hers. "We will pray for your man."

Juanita had closed her eyes, her cold, bird-like hands holding Tori's. Something about the woman had given Tori a sense of peace and she'd closed her own eyes.

For a long moment, Tori had prayed with Juanita.

After several minutes, Tori had raised her lashes. Angelina had watched with wide eyes.

"He told you the truth." Juanita had studied Tori. "Now it is up to the will of God." To Angelina, the old woman had said, "These are good people. You will be welcomed and loved here. You belong."

Tori's thoughts had spun and she'd seen Angelina look just as confused.

"What do you mean?" Angelina had asked.

"My sweet one, I am your great-grandmother. With your father's death, your custody is my responsibility." Juanita had held Angelina's gaze. "I am old and I will soon die. I want you to be with people who will love you and keep you safe." She narrowed her gaze. "Safe from your father's brothers who are as bad, if not worse, than Alejandro."

Angelina's face paled. "They would hurt me?"

Juanita gave a grave nod. "Child, now that your father, my son, is no longer here, you would have no one to protect you in Mexico."

The woman turned her gaze back to meet Tori's. "I will have my people contact you and we will arrange for you to adopt my darling great-granddaughter."

Tori's mind whirled and she couldn't quite wrap it around the idea of adopting Angelina. She would love the girl with everything she had, but it was a new thought she needed to digest.

Juanita stood and Angelina and Tori did as well. Juanita kissed Angelina on each cheek then patted one cheek with her hand.

She turned and rested her hand on Tori's arm. "Thank you."

Both Tori and Angelina remained speechless as they watched the elderly woman slowly make her way out of the room.

Angelina and Tori looked at each other, both still at a loss for words.

Everything felt as if it had come to a standstill once the woman had prayed with Tori.

Neither spoke as they'd stepped outside the hospital room and all that happened continued to pass by in a blur.

Tori and Angelina sat in the waiting room now. Tori started biting one of her nails as she waited for the doctor to return to give an update on Landon's condition.

Dylan had contacted Landon's mother and father, who'd called Landon's three sisters. One of his sisters lived close and within thirty minutes she and Landon's parents arrived in a flurry. When Dylan introduced Tori to Landon's family, Mrs. Walker gave Tori a hug, clearly seeing how distraught she was.

Mr. Walker left to get Grandma Teresa and when she

arrived, the old woman went straight to Tori and started questioning her in her no-nonsense tone. Tori didn't mind. It took her mind off the possibility of Landon actually dying.

As they waited, Tori held Angelina's hand tightly, letting her know she wasn't alone. Tori didn't know what the future held for the fifteen-year-old, but she'd do everything in her power to keep her from being sent back to her great-uncles who would now be running the family business.

Juanita's words came back to Tori. *These are good people. You will be welcomed and loved here. You belong.*

Special Agent Sofia Aguilar had been transported to Tucson Medical Center after the cartel's attack. She had graduated from ICU to a private room, her prognosis good. Some of the other agents and staff hadn't fared as well. The explosion at the DHS office had been a tragedy all the way around.

It had also been big, big news, with stations around the world televising the aftermath.

Tori had heard Dylan speaking to another agent. The feds would come down hard on every aspect of the cartel's business.

All of DHS in the southwest would be involved, with agents brought in immediately. Arrest warrants would be issued, the cartel's men tailed, and business disrupted. DHS would give the cartel's business as much grief as possible.

This was war.

Tori leaned her head back against the waiting room wall. God, when would they find out about Landon?

Angelina had fallen asleep, her head on Tori's shoulder, when the doctor finally appeared. Tori refused to think the worst, but it hovered at the back of her mind.

"We were able to resuscitate Landon after he died on the operating room table." The doctor looked tired and spoke to them as a group.

Tori's heart nearly stopped and Landon's mother sucked in her breath. Landon had died on the operating table?

"He is now in a stable condition." A huge, shuddering

breath of relief made Tori weak as the doctor spoke.

While the doctor continued talking, Tori held on to the fact that Landon remained stable. She knew the doctor was covering his ass by not giving them an absolute, "He will make it." Tori knew with all her heart that Landon *would* survive.

But dear God, Landon had *died* on the operating room table before being resuscitated.

The doctor allowed Landon to have a few visitors. His parents went in first with Grandma Teresa. When Mrs. Walker came out, her eyes were bleary as if she'd fought off crying, but she smiled. "He's going to be all right."

Tori went next, after Angelina had agreed to stay with Mrs. Walker. The girl looked fearful but let the motherly woman sit next to her. Dylan had taken Mrs. Walker aside earlier, so likely he'd told her about Angelina.

When Tori entered the room, her chest ached even more to see Landon hooked up to monitors, his tanned skin unusually pale.

He saw her and smiled. "Hi, honey."

Her heart flipped over to hear his voice. "It's good to see you."

She couldn't have been happier than to see him alive. *Thank God.*

She moved to the side of hospital bed and took his hand in hers before she sat in the chair next to the bed.

His fingers were warm when he squeezed hers. "How are you feeling, Tori?"

"The better question is how are *you* feeling?" She rested her other hand on his good shoulder. "You scared me."

"Then we're even." His expression turned serious. "When you were taken, I nearly lost my mind."

She thought about how much she loved him as his gaze held hers.

"I have something I want to tell you," she said at the same time he said, "There's something I need to say."

The looked at each other and laughed. Landon coughed

and winced, the movement clearly hurting.

His voice croaked a little from the aftereffects of the cough. "Ladies first."

"I wanted to—" She took a deep breath. She could do this. "I love you, Landon. I know it's too soon, but I just…I just needed to let you know."

A warm smile eased over his face. "Honey, that's exactly what I planned to tell you. I love you."

Her breath caught. "You do?"

He slowly stroked her hand with his thumb. "I think I've loved you from the moment I saw you running up the hill."

Tears made her sight blur and she had to blink them away. "It feels as though I've loved you forever."

He shifted on the bed, trying to scoot up and winced. "Come here."

She stood, their hands still joined. He tugged her down and she lowered her head. He released her hand and slid his fingers into her hair before drawing her in closer to him. Their lips met in a kiss that took her breath away.

He kissed her, the moment sweet and long. She'd missed his taste, she'd missed his scent. It filled her, as if he had become a part of her. She couldn't imagine ever living without the man who had captured her heart and soul.

When she drew away, he skimmed his fingers down the side of her face. "You are mine, Tori. I'm going to love you forever."

She captured his hand in hers. "Me too," she said softly. "I'm going to love you forever too."

Chapter Thirty One

The conductor cut off the symphony with his baton at the end of the last triumphant note.

Thunderous applause erupted from the audience as Jean Luc Leon, the conductor of the Tucson Symphony Orchestra, bowed to Tori, the Concert Mistress. He motioned for her to stand while the applause continued. He gestured to each of the soloists, who also stood, then to the entire symphony.

Jean Luc turned and bowed to the audience as the applause went on and on. The concert had been the highlight of the symphony's eighty-fifth season.

Tori felt the familiar thrill, a high after an amazing concert and the applause of an appreciative audience. It was a feeling like none other.

When the applause died down, the audience began to file out. Some came up to Jean Luc to express their pleasure in a concert well done.

Tori searched the crowd with her gaze and spotted Landon. He wore a broad, proud grin that made her feel warm and tingly all over. She waved to him before taking apart her clarinet and setting each piece carefully into the velvet lining of its case. When she finished, she hugged her fellow musicians before walking backstage.

She waved goodbye to some friends, hugged others then finally made it to the steps leading down from the exit into the Tucson Music Hall. She gripped the handle of her clarinet case. Her long black dress swirled around her ankles and her high heels clicked on the wooden steps.

Landon looked so delicious in a black suit that didn't hide the broadness of his shoulders and his tall, muscular physique. She was so wrapped up in looking at him she didn't see right away the bouquet of red roses he held.

She grinned as he presented them to her and brought her into the circle of his arms. She tilted her head back and he placed a kiss firmly on her lips.

Almost a year after meeting Landon, she still felt swept off her feet and madly in love.

He carried her clarinet while she held her roses in the crook of one arm. He touched the base of her spine, escorting her from the concert hall and out into the parking lot where they'd parked Tori's black Mercedes-Benz convertible.

The Mercedes had been Tori's gift to herself when she'd sold the score she'd composed for a major motion picture soundtrack. The studio would soon release the movie and Tori had been invited to the movie premiere in Los Angeles. She and Landon would attend the premiere the following Friday.

Even with her composing career taking off, Tori hadn't wanted to leave the symphony. She might have to eventually, but for now she *needed* to play and perform, for her heart and soul. It was a part of her. She'd been invited to audition for some very prestigious symphonies, but now that she lived with Landon on his ranch and she spent her time composing, she had no desire to go anywhere else.

Tori saw her parents more often now that she lived closer than she had when she'd been in Tucson. Josie had recovered from the ordeal the cartel had put her through, although she did admit to having a nightmare or three at the beginning.

Henry had vowed to cut down his drinking so that he could be there for Josie when she needed him. That hadn't lasted long and her father was once again a regular at St. Elmo's.

Angelina lived with them at Landon's ranch and she would soon celebrate her sixteenth birthday. She didn't want any kind of celebration and Tori understood — after the nightmare of her fifteenth birthday, who could blame her?

Somehow unspoiled despite her upbringing, Angelina was a sweet, intelligent girl who was a joy to have around. Tori took Angelina to a therapist regularly and it seemed to help her adjust. It would be fantasy to expect the girl to magically have a happily-ever-after with Tori and Landon, but they could help transition the way.

Angelina was a special young woman and Tori felt blessed to have her in their lives.

Not long after Angelina had come to live with them, they had learned she played the piano brilliantly and Tori had taken her under her wing musically as well.

At first, Tori thought they'd have to fight to keep her away from her uncles in Mexico. The uncles still kept the Jimenez Cartel running strong and were wanted men who managed to stay one step ahead of the law. If Angelina had been shipped back to them, she could have faced a terrible fate.

Angelina's great-grandmother Juanita had smoothed the way to Tori winning custody of the young woman who had nowhere else to go. They'd had some help from people in very high places. Next, they would work on the adoption.

Tonight Angelina had remained in the southeast part of the state with Landon's mother and father at their ranch while Landon and Tori stayed in Tucson to celebrate.

Landon had booked a room at Loews Ventana Canyon Resort, set against the foothills of the Santa Catalina Mountains in Tucson. The classic luxury resort was one of Tori's favorites. Tucson was a hundred miles from Landon's ranch and even though it was only a two-hour drive, he'd suggested a getaway for the two of them for the weekend. They had checked into the resort earlier before leaving for the concert.

When they arrived at the resort and the valet took the car to park it, Landon escorted Tori inside. She carried the bouquet of roses with her to the resort's fine restaurant and they were seated at a table for two on the patio with an amazing view of Tucson's nighttime city lights. One of the things she loved about Arizona was the ability to see for miles, whether at night like this, or in the daylight. Especially at dawn or in the evening at sunset.

"Beautiful." Tori smiled up at Landon as he pushed her seat in before taking his own. "What a lovely restaurant and the view is amazing."

He gave her a sensual smile as he let his gaze rest on her. "My view is perfect."

Her cheeks warmed and she reached out and trailed her finger down the scar on his cheek. "Mine's not so bad either."

Landon caught her hand in his and pressed his lips to her fingers, causing her to shiver with awareness. He always managed to stir desire within her with just a look, a touch, a kiss.

The server approached them with a bottle of wine and presented it to Landon. After Landon had approved, the server poured glasses for Tori and Landon before retreating.

"To the most beautiful composer and clarinet player." He raised his glass. "Whom I love with all my heart."

She smiled and clinked her glass with his. "To the sexiest cowboy lawman, my knight in shining Kevlar, who couldn't possibly love me more than I love him."

He grinned and they sipped their wine.

She let out a happy sigh. "Marvelous."

All of dinner turned out to be marvelous. She couldn't remember feeling happier than she was with Landon at that very moment.

After they'd finished dinner and the table had been cleared, Landon excused himself for a few moments before returning. He took her hand and smiled at her.

A server appeared with a dessert with two spoons, which he set on each side of the plate. "Our pine nut lava cake." The man gestured as if presenting a royal dish. "It has salted caramel raspberry ice cream, pine nut brittle, and a port reduction." He bowed. "Enjoy," he added before he retreated.

"Pine nut lava cake?" Tori raised an eyebrow. "I'm intrigued."

Another server arrived with a bottle of champagne before Tori could taste the lava cake. The server poured them each a glass of the bubbly before setting the bottle in a champagne chiller. The server bowed and left.

They clinked glasses once again.

"It's been quite the celebration." Tori sipped her champagne, enjoying the tickle of the bubbles. "Thank you for tonight."

"We have a lot to celebrate." Landon dipped his spoon into the ice cream and raised it up to her.

She started to lean forward to let him slip the dessert into her mouth when she saw something glittering on the spoon, half in and half out of the ice cream.

A large princess-cut diamond was set in between two smaller diamonds on a white-gold band.

Tori's eyes widened and her lips parted. She looked at Landon as heat rushed over her. "Landon?"

He retrieved the ring from the ice cream and set the spoon on the plate before he got out of his chair and kneeled beside her.

"I love you so damned much, Tori." His gaze, such a beautiful green, was fixed on her as he held up the ring. "Everything we have been through together only makes me appreciate the gift of loving you even more." He smiled. "Will you marry me?"

For a moment, she thought she was going to hyperventilate. She couldn't breathe. Tears bit at the backs of her eyes then she nodded. "Yes. A million times, yes."

He smiled and slipped the ring onto her finger, remnants of ice cream and all. Tori slid out of her chair, onto her knees, and flung her arms around his neck. "I love you so much."

"Honey, you make me happier than I ever thought I'd be." He brought her to her feet and held her like he would never let her go.

"That makes two of us." She reached up and kissed him, a long kiss she never wanted to stop.

Vaguely she realized people around them were applauding and cheering.

When Landon drew away, he smiled in a way that reflected everything she felt inside.

"I don't think I could eat a bite of dessert." And she didn't think she'd ever stop smiling. "Let's get out of here."

He offered her his arm. "I was hoping you'd say that."

They walked out of the restaurant and toward a life filled with possibilities and everlasting love.

More books from
Totally Bound Publishing

Book one in the Crossing Forces series

A bad boy FBI agent and a feisty widowed police detective collide pursuing a human trafficker in small-town Texas on their way to true love.

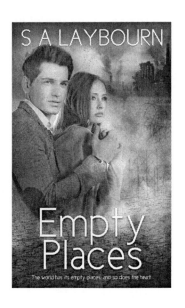

The world has its empty places, and so does the heart.

A LOVE TO
KILL FOR

HEAT

CONOR CORDEROY

Book one in the Heat series

For Murdoch, women are bad news. Trying to stay alive in war-torn Andalusia, tracking a vanishing femme fatal, hunted by The Brotherhood, the last thing he needs is love…

A cop with a mission. A woman with no memory. A killer who hunts them both.

About the Author

Cheyenne McCray

Cheyenne McCray is an award winning, *New York Times* and *USA Today* bestselling author who loves to torture characters—whether they're misbehaving or not—and kill off deserving individuals. She also totally gets off on blowing things up. All fictionally, of course. She'd rather chew glass than write sweet and sugary. Give her a hideous demon or particularly nasty villain to slay any day.

Cheyenne enjoys creating stories of love, suspense, and redemption. She loves building worlds her readers can get lost in. If you would like to find out what odd and unusual things Cheyenne is up to these days, cruise her website any time, take a look at the bizarrely normal yet strange FAQs, and even drop her a line or two.

Cheyenne McCray loves to hear from readers. You can find contact information, website details and an author profile page at https://www.totallybound.com/

TOTALLY
BOUND

Home of Erotic Romance

CPSIA information can be obtained
at www.ICGtesting.com
Printed in the USA
FFOW03n0444170117
31312FF